CELEBRATE IN GOOD HOPE

CINDY KIRK

D1715816

WAVERLY
HOUSE

CHAPTER ONE

Rosalie Carson stared at the rapidly filling tables and fought a pang of unease. This was her first day at Muddy Boots, and Roe wasn't sure she was ready for her own section.

The café, located in the center of the Good Hope business district—and, some might say, the heart of the vibrant community on the Door County peninsula—was extremely popular, especially during the holiday season.

Roe turned. "I don't know if I can handle four tables alone."

"You're ready." Helen, her trainer this morning, met her panicked gaze with a no-nonsense one. The older woman, known for her orange hair and lipstick, waved away her concerns.

She appeared to have no doubts about Roe's ability to fly solo. Roe only wished she felt as confident.

For the next two hours, Roe took orders and delivered food. Beckett Cross, the owner of Muddy Boots, had hired a high school boy to keep coffee cups full, but Roe refilled the cups for those in her section when she had time.

Peyton Lenz, a young woman in her late twenties with

burnished-copper hair and chocolate-brown eyes, returned to the window to place an order at the same time as Roe.

Peyton's job as a receptionist at a local mental health center kept her busy during the week, but she'd confided to Roe that the money she earned from tips on the weekends at Muddy Boots had made it possible for her to take a trip to Cancun with friends last year.

Roe liked the staff at Muddy Boots. She'd instantly felt welcomed and part of the team. Was that because they knew she was Dakota Slattery's friend? Or maybe they were just that friendly.

"You're doing amazing." Peyton offered an approving smile. "I dropped a whole tray of food the first time I was on my own."

Before Roe could respond, Peyton gave a little shudder. "Lettuce and salad dressing everywhere."

"And yet, they let you keep working." Roe kept her tone light and teasing. It was more a comment than a question, because Peyton was still waiting tables at the scene of the lettuce crime.

"Beck said it could happen to anyone." Peyton leaned close and lowered her voice. "Helen, well, I think she'd have sacked me right then and there if she'd been in charge."

"These orders aren't going to take themselves out." Janey Eversoll, one of the cooks on the other side of the window, spoke loudly, prompting a censuring look from Helen in Roe and Peyton's direction.

"Right away." Grabbing two plates of burgers and fries, Peyton slipped past Roe, suddenly all business.

Roe lifted two plates from the pass-through, each holding a crock of chicken pot pie.

As it was cold and snowy outside, the classic pot pies, with chicken, carrots, peas, potatoes and celery nestled in a golden crust and topped with thick chicken gravy, were extremely popular.

She'd noticed the crocks tended to slide on the plates, so Roe moved slowly as she wove her way across the dining area to the table against the wall.

Two older women, one with a swath of silver in her dark hair and another with hair the color of champagne, sat patiently waiting for their lunch.

The one with the skunk stripe had attempted to engage her in conversation when Roe arrived to take their order. Roe would have loved to stand and talk, but with Helen's steely-eyed gaze on her, the only information the two had managed to get out of her was that she was Dakota's friend and would be here through the holidays.

As she traversed the narrow space between tables, her gaze once again found the dark-haired man who'd come in alone but now sat with a young woman with a brilliant smile.

They made an attractive couple, him with his thick dark hair and stylish scruff and her with her blond prettiness.

Roe was almost to the table where the two women sat when a man at a table to her right abruptly stood and, without warning, stepped in front of her.

Stumbling backward, Roe willed herself not to fall, to stay steady and especially not to release the plates in her hands. She nearly succeeded, but then the crock on the left plate began to slide.

The chatter of voices and laughter surrounding her became distant as everything shifted into slow motion.

Watching in horror—and powerless to stop it—she watched the crock slid off the plate, do a one-eighty and drop right into the hunky man's lap.

Jason Boone had taken a slight detour on his eleven-hundred-mile trek from Denver, Colorado, to Good Hope, Wisconsin.

Along the way, he'd stopped to spend Thanksgiving in Dubuque, Iowa, with his sister and her family.

Before that, it had been nearly a year since he'd spent time with Lydia, her husband and his two nieces. They'd begged him to stay with them while he recuperated, but he'd told them he already had plans and was looking forward to spending the holidays in Good Hope.

The truth was, their house was small, and he would be in the way. Not wanting to burden those he loved was why he hadn't accepted his parents' invitation to stay with them.

They both had room, and he'd have accepted if they'd still been married. But they'd divorced years ago. Each had a new family and busy life. He'd given them the same excuse he'd given Lydia.

Thankfully, by the time they'd offered, Krew Slattery, Boone's football coach with the Colorado Grizzlies, had already offered him the use of his cabin in Good Hope through the end of January.

Boone had arrived in the community on the Door County peninsula late this afternoon. Instead of heading straight for the cabin, he'd stopped in town to get something to eat.

Krew had mentioned Muddy Boots numerous times, so Boone decided the café was as good a place as any to grab lunch.

"How long will you be staying?" The blonde across the table from him had big brown eyes and an infectious smile.

They'd exchanged names and basic information when she'd pulled out a chair and sat. She was Evie Eastman. She'd told him she could see he was new in town and wanted to welcome him to Good Hope.

"Would you like to order something?" Boone glanced around for the server, who'd taken his order for a burger and fries moments earlier.

Evie waved a dismissive hand. "I'm fine. I came in to grab a kouign amann since Blooms Bake Shop was out. Unfortunately, they were out here as well. Not that I need one. Those pastries have got to be a gazillion calories each."

Boone had no idea what a kouign amann was or even looked like, but he wasn't much for sweets. He'd always tried to eat healthy during football season.

Doesn't matter now. He'd ordered fries without a flicker of guilt.

"Do you live here year-round?"

"I do." Instead of elaborating, as he'd hoped, Evie fixed those brown eyes on him. "Where do you live?"

"Denver." Boone smiled his thanks when a young man, a boy, really, refilled his coffee.

"I like Denver." Evie leaned forward. "Are you here with your wife or girlfriend?"

Boone took a sip of coffee. He'd still been in the hospital when Celine had moved on to another player with more potential.

Their relationship had been new, so her shifting focus hadn't hurt—unlike Ella, who, after three years together, had broken it off a year ago. Those women were his past. Boone smiled at the young woman across from him. "No wife or girlfriend. How about you?"

"No wife or girlfriend for me either." Evie laughed, the bright sound reminding him of the tinkle of a bell.

Something in how she shifted her gaze told him there might be a guy. He hoped the man was good to her. While she seemed nice, he was here to recuperate, not hook up or start a relationship destined to go nowhere.

He hoped to be back in Denver and practicing with the team soon.

"What about a guy?" Boone took another sip of coffee and kept his tone casual. "Unless all the men in this town are blind, there has to be someone…"

A soft pink rode high on Evie's cheeks. "There is someone I

date occasionally. I like him, but Hunter has made it clear he's not ready to get serious."

Boone began to nod.

The slight movement had Evie quickly adding, "Neither am I. I like being able to date who I want when I want. I'm only twenty-eight. That's young. I'm nowhere near ready to be tied down to one man."

Methinks the lady doth protest too much.

It was Boone's last coherent thought before a scalding hot something landed in his lap.

Letting out a yelp, he pushed back his chair, and a piece of crockery fell to the floor.

His surgeon had warned him to avoid sudden moves, but this was an unforeseen event. That didn't lessen the pain.

The dark-haired server swooped in as he stood there, her face filled with apology. "I am so sorry. Here, let me wipe off the gravy."

She reached forward with a cotton cloth just as Evie jumped to her feet, pushing the server into him. Her fingers jammed into his incision.

If Boone thought the pain from jumping up was terrible, her fingers diving into his stitches fell into the excruciating category. The intense pain had Boone sucking in a breath and pushing both of the women away.

By now, everyone was watching, and he was ten seconds away from losing it.

Pulling two wadded-up bills from his pocket, Boone dropped them on the table.

"I'm so sorry," the server said again. "What can I do—?"

Maybe she said more.

Maybe she apologized again.

He didn't know because, like on the football field, he forced himself to ignore the pain and keep walking, past the curious glances, to the door.

By the time he jerked open his truck door, Boone could think of nothing but reaching the cabin, stripping off his clothes and assessing the damage.

Then he would pop a pain pill, take a shower and pray to God that there was something in the place to eat.

~

Tears sprang to Roe's eyes, but she refused to let them fall. She had three older brothers and a father who was a military officer. Signs of weakness, like tears, had not been tolerated in the Carson household.

If there ever was a moment where tears might be justified, this would surely be a top contender. She'd dropped a pot pie, hot from the oven and covered in gravy, onto a man's lap.

Then she'd somehow hurt him further while trying to wipe it off.

A hand on her shoulder had her jumping.

Roe whirled.

"Help Gregory clean this up." Helen gestured to the boy scooping up the ceramic shards. "Then take fifteen."

"But my customers—" Roe protested.

"Peyton and I will split your section while you're on break."

Was that a flash of sympathy in Helen's eyes? Roe hoped that was the case, but she couldn't be sure. If so, the look had come and gone with the speed of a blink.

Roe opened her mouth to protest again. She'd already messed things up big-time, and the last thing she wanted was to make things more difficult for her coworkers by sitting around feeling sorry for herself while they worked.

"You need to get steady, or you're no good to anyone." Helen's tone brooked no argument.

So, after helping Gregory clean up the mess, Roe headed for

the break room. She would sit for fifteen minutes but not one second longer.

Five minutes in, a tall man with hair the color of rich chocolate and kind brown eyes pulled out a chair. Beckett Cross, the owner and the one who had given her the job because Dakota had vouched for her, now sat across the table. Right now, he was very likely regretting his decision to hire her.

"Sounds like your afternoon turned exciting real fast." His soft Southern accent held a comforting warmth.

Her friend had told her that Beck was originally from Georgia.

Roe expelled a breath. "I'm so sorry. I—"

"It wasn't your fault."

"It was. I—"

"It wasn't your fault," he repeated, his gaze steady on hers. "Helen saw it all. A customer got up and stepped right in front of you. Didn't even look."

Roe blinked rapidly, wishing she could disappear into the floorboards. "I tried to keep my balance."

"There was nothing you could have done differently." Despite his assurance, concern furrowed Beck's brow. "I would like to speak to the man who was the beneficiary of the wayward pot pie. I fear he may have been burned. I didn't recognize him, and unfortunately, he left before I could speak with him."

"What about the woman with him? She would know where you could find him."

Beck shook his head. "Evie is a local. Seeing that he was a stranger, she stopped at his table to make him feel welcome. All she got before he bolted was that his name is Boone."

"If he's not from here, he's probably staying at one of the hotels in town."

Beck nodded. "The Bayshore and Sweet Dreams are the most popular. I'll call them to see if they have anyone named Boone registered."

"I'm sorry," Roe said again. "Once I get off shift, I'd be happy to check other hotels and B&Bs in the area."

"You let me take care of that. By the way, how do you like the cabin?" Beck's abrupt subject change told Roe he was finished discussing the pot pie fiasco. "I haven't seen it myself. Not yet."

"It's very nice. I was expecting an actual cabin. While it technically qualifies as one, I'd describe it more as a log home. It's lovely and huge."

"Doesn't surprise me." Beck's lips curved. "Krew mentioned he wanted something big enough so that their entire family could be together when he and Cass were in town."

"I'd say he picked the perfect cabin, then." Roe managed a smile. "The plan is for the bridal party to stay there the first two weeks in February until Dakota's wedding on the fourteenth."

"It's hard for me to believe Dakota is all grown up." Beck's smile turned rueful. "I still think of her as a young girl."

"She's a good friend and a wonderful person, but you already know that."

"I do." Beck inclined his head. "I don't believe you told me how you two met."

Roe suspected Beck was engaging her in conversation so she would steady. The thing was, it was working. The tension that had gripped her since the incident began to recede. "Dakota and I met in Minneapolis. We were both straight out of college."

"You worked for the same company?"

"We're not even in the same field." Roe chuckled. "Dakota secured a position with a firm specializing in crisis PR, while I had a job with a children's theater."

Beck's brows pulled together. "How did you meet up, then?"

"There's an organization in the Twin Cities called Team-Women. They bill themselves as 'a supportive community that empowers women in their professional journeys.' Dakota and I served on the professional development committee and hit it off. You know Dakota—that woman has never met a stranger."

"She's a good person." Pushing back his chair, Beck rose. "Don't let what happened today throw you. From what I've seen and from everything Helen has told me, you're doing an excellent job. We're happy to have you here."

Following his lead, Roe stood, feeling surprisingly steady. Helen had been right. These few minutes had given her the confidence to not only return to the dining room, but to pick up a chicken pot pie and take it out.

~

"You did a good job keeping your cool today."

Helen's grudging praise wove through Roe's mind on autoplay as she drove the two miles to the cabin she now called home.

The rest of her shift had been uneventful, other than remembering once she reached her car, and the couple was long gone, that she'd forgotten to bring them the ketchup they'd requested.

She winced at the memory but knew she'd done her best. Dakota had been right when she'd told her that Muddy Boots got slammed in December.

Slammed meant more tips, and what she'd earned today with four tables had been respectable. Helen would move her to a six-table section once she was confident that Roe could handle the pace.

Roe's lips lifted in a wry smile. Which, after what had happened today, would probably be never.

Not your fault, she told herself.

There had been pain in the man's eyes when he'd jumped up, and the knowledge that his pain had been the result of her actions nagged at her.

She had to put it aside. There was nothing she could do for him now. And she'd likely never see him again anyway.

CHAPTER TWO

Anticipation coursed up Roe's spine when her Subaru passed the Good Hope town limits. She couldn't wait to get home. Until she found a job in her field, she was determined to enjoy the oh-so-luxurious cabin that would be hers for the next two months.

When Dakota had offered her the use of her family's "cabin," Roe had assumed it would be comparable to the ones she and her friends stayed in when they visited Grand Marais on Lake Superior's North Shore.

That rustic cabin was not even in the same stratosphere as this place. Less than two miles from Good Hope, the Slattery log home boasted five bedrooms—each with its own bath—and a ceiling that soared nearly twenty feet over an open floor plan.

As soon as she'd stepped inside, Roe had agreed with Dakota that it would be the perfect place for her and her four bridesmaids to gather before the wedding on Valentine's Day.

Roe might have been here nearly a week, but she had yet to settle in fully. When she'd arrived, she'd checked out all the bedrooms before unpacking in one upstairs.

Though the bridal party wouldn't arrive until February first, Roe kept everything in its place. Her father, an Air Force officer, firmly believed in order, and the importance of maintaining a tidy space had been drilled into her since childhood.

She had yet to use the two-person Jacuzzi tub in the main suite, but she thought tonight might be a good time to ensure everything worked correctly.

The thought of warm jetted water caressing her bare skin while snow fell gently outside had her body quivering with anticipation.

The forested road to the cabin was dark, but the yard light was a beacon, drawing her toward her destination.

The tall and majestic house soon came into view. Light streamed into the darkness from its four oversized windows. Momentarily struck by its beauty, Roe took a second to figure out what was wrong. She swallowed hard against the tight ball suddenly lodged in her throat.

When she'd left for Muddy Boots this morning, she'd made sure all the lights in the house were out.

Her foot hit the brake, bringing the vehicle sliding to a stop at the side of the lane just outside the reach of the yard light.

Not only were the house lights on, she spotted a pickup truck in the drive. As snow mounded on both sides of the drive, she would need to pull into the cabin's yard to turn around.

And risk being seen? That wasn't happening. Neither was backing up the entire distance.

Pulling out her phone, Roe dialed 911.

When car lights came into view behind her Subaru, Roe's heart jumped.

"The sheriff sees your vehicle." The soothing voice of the 911 operator sounded in Roe's ear. "In a second, he'll be pulling up behind you. Stay in your vehicle."

"It's not a patrol car." Roe's voice shook despite her best efforts to control it. "I don't see any lights on top."

"Sheriff Rallis was not on duty but chose to take the call." The woman continued. "You did the right thing in calling and not approaching the house alone."

This was the second, or maybe the third, time the operator had reassured Roe of that fact. What else was there to talk about, though?

Roe had already answered all the questions. Yes, she'd set the alarm before she'd left that morning. No, she hadn't given anyone the code. No, she wasn't expecting anyone.

As she spoke with the operator, Roe feared whoever was in the house would leave and find her parked on the side of the road. The urge to back up the long lane and get as far away as possible was strong, but the operator kept her talking and assured her that help was coming.

The lights drew closer.

Roe tightened her fingers around the phone. "Are you sure that's the sheriff behind me?"

"Yes, Roe, those are Sheriff Rallis's headlights. He has made visual contact with your vehicle."

"Are you sure?" Roe's breath came in short puffs. "Positive that it's him?"

Now who was repeating herself?

The questions spoke to her biggest fear, that a friend or accomplice of whoever was in the cabin had come calling and made it to her bumper before the sheriff could.

"Yes. He's getting out of his vehicle now and approaching your car." The woman's voice soothed and reassured. "You can hang up now."

Roe emitted a shaky breath. "Thank you. Really. Thank you."

"It's my pleasure."

Roe had barely clicked off the call when the man, the sheriff, tapped on her window.

"Miss Carson. I'm Sheriff Rallis." He held up his badge. "Can we talk?"

The fear that had gripped her in a stranglehold for the past fifteen minutes slid from Roe's shoulders, leaving her weak and shaky.

Buck up.

Her father's voice in her head had Roe squaring her shoulders. She rolled down her window, wondering what would come next.

"May I see your driver's license?"

With hands that shook, Roe took out her license and handed it to him.

He inspected it under the glow of a tiny flashlight before handing it back to her. "Thank you."

"Are you going to go and see who's in there?"

"In a minute." The sheriff stepped back. "Would you get out of the vehicle, please?"

Roe hesitated. Though not as heavy as before, the snow continued to fall, and even from inside her vehicle, she heard the wind whistling through the trees.

Just the thought of exiting her car had her shivering.

A look of understanding crossed his face. "I'd like to speak with you in my vehicle."

"Okay." Gratitude that he wasn't taking off and leaving her alone had her stepping from the vehicle. She glanced around. The surrounding woods had never struck her as spooky, but they did now.

She wondered if whoever was inside was alone. What if he had an accomplice somewhere out here, watching her?

Roe hurried to the sheriff's vehicle. In less than a minute, Roe sat in the front seat of the SUV with him beside her in the driver's seat. She studied the laptop perched between her seat and his and watched him run her license and plates.

"Does everything check out?" It was nerves that had her

asking the ridiculous question. Of course everything checked out. She was who she said she was, and that was her Subaru.

"It does." His expression turned reassuring. "We'll get this figured out."

Roe wasn't sure what he needed to figure out. Someone was in the cabin who wasn't supposed to be there. The sheriff needed to arrest the intruder and haul him off to jail.

Sheriff Rallis angled his body toward her. "Dakota let our office know you'd be staying at the cabin."

"I got into town on Monday."

"The dispatcher said that you indicated there were no plans for anyone to join you?"

"That's correct."

Her dad would like the sheriff. Like her father, his square-cut jaw and intense gray eyes indicated he didn't tolerate fools.

Over the next few minutes, he asked the same questions as the dispatcher had and then used his phone to make a call that he put on speaker.

"Krew, this is Cade Rallis. I hate to bother you so late, but we may have some trouble at your cabin."

"It's good to hear from you." Krew's tone was hearty before turning serious. "What's up?"

"I have Rosalie Carson here with me now. Were you aware that Dakota gave her permission to stay at your cabin?"

"No." Surprise filled Krew's voice. "At least I don't think I— hold on a minute. Cass," Krew abruptly called out. "Did Dakota tell a friend she could use the cabin?"

"Yes." His wife answered immediately. "Rosalie Carson. You've met Roe. Dakota asked if it'd be okay, and I said yes. Did I forget to tell you?"

"Yes, but that's fine." Krew's focus returned to the sheriff. "We've got ourselves a problem, but it shouldn't affect you. I gave the okay for one of our players, who was recently injured, to stay there. Jason Boone should arrive in the next day or two. I'll call and tell him he needs to find somewhere else to stay."

"Too late. If I'm not mistaken, he's already here." Sheriff Rallis explained about Roe coming home from Muddy Boots and calling 911 when she saw the lights on and a pickup truck in the drive.

Krew swore. "I'm sorry to be dragging you into this mess. I should have told Cass that I'd offered the cabin to Boone. She's been busy with this wedding stuff, and things with the team have been crazy."

"It's no problem." The warmth in the sheriff's tone told Roe he liked Dakota's dad.

"Boone's a good guy, solid." Krew hesitated. "The place is big enough for two if Roe decides she's okay with him staying. I'd trust him with any of my kids. But he's a stranger to her, and if she wants to give him the boot, that works, too."

"Thanks, Krew. I'll let you know the final decision."

"Appreciate it. Give our love to Marigold and the kids."

"Same to Cass and Axl." The sheriff dropped the phone back into his pocket.

"What's the plan?"

"Once I make sure it's Jason Boone in there, you can decide."

"Decide?" A cold chill traveled up Roe's spine.

"Whether he stays or goes." Cade put the vehicle into gear, angled it around Roe's Subaru in front of him and drove the rest of the way to the house. "You heard Krew—the decision is yours."

The sound of a car engine had Boone moving to the window and parting the curtains just in time to see an SUV stop in front of the house.

Boone frowned. The way his day had gone, it figured something else would go wrong. He really didn't want to pull on his boots and go outside to see what was going on, but when he saw the tall man with broad shoulders and an almost militarylike bearing step out, he didn't see he had much choice.

When he opened the door, Boone saw not only the man but a woman standing beside him.

The sight of her had the incision just under his left ribs aching as recognition flashed.

The man flashed a badge. "I'm Sheriff Cade Rallis. You're Jason Boone?"

"Have been all my life." Boone stepped back and motioned the two inside. "Come inside where it's warm. What's this about?"

"Do you have identification on you, Mr. Boone?" It appeared the sheriff planned on doing all the talking.

The woman, about his age or maybe a couple of years younger, stayed a few steps back. With dark hair and brown eyes, she was pretty rather than gorgeous. Her quiet confidence had drawn his attention at the café. That was, until all hell had broken loose.

Pulling out his driver's license, Boone handed it to the sheriff. After a quick glance, the sheriff handed it back, apparently satisfied he was who he said.

"Mind telling me what this is all about?" Boone asked, returning the card to his wallet.

"Okay if we sit?" Cade gestured toward the overstuffed leather furniture grouped for conversation near a fire that burned cheerily in the hearth.

"Works for me." Boone glanced at the woman and stuck out his hand. "Jason Boone. Most everyone just calls me Boone."

"Rosalie Carson. Everyone calls me Roe." Her voice had a pleasing lilt, and her handshake was firm. She smiled, but her eyes remained serious. "I'm really sorry about the pot pie."

He waved a dismissive hand and tried not to wince. "Could have happened to anyone."

"Did you get burned?"

"I'm sorry about—"

"The pot pie. I get it. Done and forgotten."

"No." Roe frowned. "Sorry about the mix-up with the cabin."

"Don't give it a second thought."

"You drove a long way because Dakota's father promised you could stay here." While she'd made the relatively short trip from Minneapolis, he'd come all the way from Denver. Only to be turned away at the door.

Okay, perhaps not exactly at the door, but close enough.

"I was thinking..." Roe paused. Should she really make this offer? Once it left her lips, she would be committed.

Boone simply cocked his head and waited.

If he had pressed, she might have taken a step back...a huge step back. He didn't. Instead, he simply waited patiently for her to say her piece.

"This is a big house." She could see her mother shaking her head and her dad's expression turning thunderous. "There isn't any reason you and I can't peacefully coexist under the same roof. Krew vouched for you, so I know you're not a serial killer."

Though his expression remained serious, his lips twitched ever so slightly. If her gaze hadn't been focused so completely on him, she might have missed it.

"How do I know *you're* not a serial killer?"

Roe blinked. "Pardon?"

"Do you have someone who can vouch for you?"

"I suppose I could call Dakota, and she could—" She stopped when he grinned. "You're playing me."

"Guilty."

She found herself returning his devilish smile. "I must be more tired than I realized. I'm not usually so gullible."

"I guess I'll have to take your word for it."

"That I'm not usually gullible?" Roe found herself enjoying the banter. She arched a brow. "Or that I'm not a serial killer?"

"Both."

Boone's eyes glittered in the firelight's glow, the soft light turning his dark eyes to molten chocolate. His rumpled hair, still damp at the edges, emitted the enticing scent of lime.

As an unfamiliar longing coursed through her, Roe suspected being in close quarters with this handsome man might prove dangerous, but in a totally different way.

As soon as the thought surfaced, she brushed it aside. It was a big house. With her job and him, well, doing whatever he would be doing while in Good Hope, their contact would likely be minimal.

"What do you say?" Roe could have cheered when the question came out casual and offhand, as if it didn't matter to her one way or the other if he stayed or left.

Which it didn't. Matter, that was.

"My choices are to head out into what's turning out to be quite a snowstorm, try to find some motel or hotel with an open room, then drive back to Denver and my three roommates who love to party, or stay here with you?"

"That's right." Roe paused, then frowned as what he'd said registered. "Why do you have roommates? You had to have been in the NFL for seven or eight years?"

"Eight. How'd you know?"

"I guessed that we're about the same age. I'll be turning thirty all too soon." Roe kept her tone matter-of-fact. "If you got drafted out of college, that would mean you've played for eight seasons."

"That's a correct assumption." He flashed a smile.

Roe wished she could say she was immune to his charms, but then consoled herself with the thought that that particular smile had likely been winning him hearts since grade school. "So, why roommates instead of your own place?"

He shrugged. "I like having someone around."

She understood. Growing up, her household had been a busy one. As an adult, she'd always had a roommate. Instead of savoring the silence of the cabin, she'd found it a little too quiet. That might be another plus to having Boone around.

She met his gaze. "So, what do you say? Stay or go? Your choice."

~

After retrieving her car and parking it in the garage, Roe headed straight for her bedroom. After locking the door, she stripped off her clothes, eager to indulge in a long, hot shower. She'd reached the bathroom door when her phone rang.

Recognizing the ring, Roe quickly wrapped a towel around herself, then grabbed her phone from the charger and dropped to sit on the bed.

"Dakota, hello."

Knowing that her friend was busy with work and wedding plans, Roe hadn't expected to hear from her until after the holidays.

"How are you? Dad called and told me what happened. I'm so sorry, Roe. Are you okay?" The words tumbled out of Dakota's mouth like spilled ice from an overturned glass.

"I'm fine. I've decided to let Boone stay." The last thing Roe wanted was for her friend to worry about her. Especially when there was no reason. "It'll be nice having someone else in the house."

"Especially if that someone is Jason Boone." Dakota laughed, and Roe heard relief in the sound. "Most women would kill to trade places with you and spend the holidays with him. He is überhot."

Roe brought to mind the image of her new housemate's broad shoulders, lean hips, and chiseled features. Not to mention that heart-stopping smile. *Überhot* was an apt description.

"Whoa, down, girl," Roe teased. "Don't forget, you've got Nolan."

"Hey, I'm engaged. I'm not blind." Dakota laughed again. "What do you think?"

"Of Boone?"

Dakota made a scoffing sound. "Who else?"

"He's nice," Roe admitted. "And you're right, he is hot. But with everything I've got going on right now, I'm in no position to start a relationship."

The choked sound that burst from Dakota's lips took Roe by surprise. "What's so funny?"

"Who said anything about a relationship? I'm saying you've had a difficult few months, and the universe is giving you a gift— a sexy man for Christmas."

"You're saying I should unwrap Boone for the holidays?" Roe might have kept her tone light, but she shifted, conscious of her nakedness as a tiny shiver of lust coursed up her spine.

"That's exactly what I'm saying." Dakota's voice turned persuasive. "What's wrong with a few weeks of fun between consenting adults?"

"Nothing is wrong, but he's recovering from an injury, which I probably made even worse by dropping a scalding-hot pot pie into his lap earlier today."

"You did not!" Dakota shrieked.

"I did." Roe explained everything that had happened since she'd first seen Boone earlier today sitting in Muddy Boots. "So, you see, I don't think he's likely to consent to—"

"I've only met him a couple of times," Dakota interrupted. "But he struck me as an easygoing guy who doesn't hold grudges."

"That's how he strikes me, too," Roe agreed.

"Well, then, I have just two suggestions."

"Lay them on me."

"Don't drop any more pot pies, or really anything hot, in his lap." Barely suppressed laughter ran through Dakota's words.

"What's the other bit of wisdom?"

"Relax and have fun. Though, of course, only do what you're comfortable with."

"Like I said, I'm not looking for anything…" Roe paused, recalling how good Boone looked and how fabulous he smelled. "But I will admit the man is crazy hot."

~

Roe rolled out of bed at seven a.m. and went straight to the window. Though a stiff breeze that rattled the windowpanes had awakened her several times during the night, her sleep had otherwise been filled with vivid dreams. Dreams of being held by a man with shaggy hair and eyes so dark she could drown in them. Dreams of kissing him, of touching him…

Stop, Roe told herself as her heart rate spiked.

Darn Dakota, for putting those thoughts into her head.

She needed to forget the dreams and focus.

Looking out, Roe saw the snow had ended, and the yard and the driveway were covered in a thick blanket of white. She bet Boone was happy he'd decided to pull his truck into the garage.

Last night, she'd seen he was hurting. But when she'd offered to pull the truck into the garage for him, he'd thanked her for the offer but shrugged on his coat and boots and headed outside.

She hadn't argued. He lived in Colorado and should have known that if there was an indoor space for a vehicle, you didn't wait to put it inside when it was snowing.

Though she'd mentioned she was making soup and he was welcome to have some, he'd politely declined the offer. After pulling the pickup into the garage, he'd headed down the hall to his bedroom.

She stayed up, reading on her Kindle in front of the fire. Every so many minutes, Roe found herself glancing down the hall. She really hoped the pot pie hadn't burned his skin.

Over and done with, she told herself. If he was hurting this morning, she hoped he'd mention it. She pulled on her warmest outer gear before heading to the garage, where the massive snowblower awaited. It started quickly, and in minutes, she was clearing the driveway. Because the snow was so deep and the drive long and winding, she stuck to clearing the concrete part closest to the house.

That was where it had drifted the most anyway. The rest would be passable by his 4x4 and, hopefully, her Subaru.

Once the driveway approach was cleared, Roe moved to the sidewalk leading to the front porch. When that was done, she put away the monster machine, grabbed a broom and began sweeping the snow off the porch.

That's where she was when Boone stepped out the door, looking incredible in a black flannel-lined waxed trucker jacket over a flannel shirt. The insulated red and black cap with flaps that came down over his ears and neck might have looked ridiculous on another man.

On Boone, well, it looked incredibly sexy.

She wore a puffer coat, and did anyone look good in one of those?

His eyes widened. He gestured. "You did all this?"

Roe stopped sweeping. "Do you see anyone else?"

"When?"

"I got up early and jumped in with both feet."

When he didn't say anything but only continued to stare at her with a puzzled expression, she added, "I'm nearly done. You might as well go inside."

After one more glance around, Boone headed back inside.

He might have at least offered to finish sweeping, Roe thought, then shrugged off the irritation. She'd told him to go inside, and she *was* nearly finished.

By the time she'd cleared the porch to her satisfaction, another ten minutes had passed. She was eager to return to the warm and dry inside.

Sitting on the bench in the foyer, she removed her boots, pleased that her wool socks had remained dry.

Her coat, hat and scarf were carefully hung on the coat tree when her nose caught a whiff of something magnificent—cooking bacon.

Like a hunting dog who had caught the scent of particularly enticing prey, Roe followed her nose. It led her to the kitchen where Boone stood in front of the stove.

Bacon and eggs and sexy, oh my.

She felt like Dorothy seeing the city of Oz for the first time.

"Coffee." She breathed the word as she inhaled the rich aroma. "And bacon."

Boone turned from the stove, a spatula in one hand. The smile he offered had her blood turning to warm honey. "I thought you might be ready to eat after all your hard work. How do bacon and eggs sound?"

When he saw the direction of her gaze, he grinned. "There's also a pot of coffee. I can't drink it all myself."

"It all sounds wonderful. I'll wash my hands, then set the table." Anticipation of a hearty breakfast with lots and lots of coffee fueled her steps.

Soon, the table was ready, and a plate of food and cups of steaming coffee sat before them.

"Dig in," he told her.

She picked up her fork and gestured to the bacon and eggs. "Thank you for this."

Boone took a long drink of coffee. "Thank you for snow-blowing the drive and walkway."

"No problem." She scooped some eggs onto a piece of grainy toast. "Growing up, we lived in various cold-weather climates. My brothers and I rotated who did the snowblowing."

"While I'm here, I can take it over."

"I can do it."

His jaw lifted in what appeared to be a stubborn tilt.

She gave a careless shrug, as if it didn't matter one way or another. "I'm also okay with taking turns."

"I'm not going to sit inside while you're out there working."

"You weren't simply sitting inside this morning while I was out there working. You made breakfast," she said pointedly.

"Still—"

"No still," she interrupted. "And you better not do the whole male-female thing. I'm just as capable as you and probably even more capable of handling Beast."

He arched a brow. "Beast?"

"I like to give things names." She offered a little smile. "The snowblower will from now forward be known as Beast."

"You know there is probably someone in town who could come out with their own Beast."

"I know," she agreed, "but I'm living here rent-free. There is no reason to pay someone to do something I'm capable of doing."

"Next snowfall, Beast is mine."

"It's hydraulic, so that's a plus, but it still takes some strength to handle." She met his gaze. "Would your doctor approve? It hasn't been that long since your surgery."

"I'm three weeks out. It'll be fine. Lifting weights and contact sports are still a no-go, but as for blowing snow, your Beast would do most of the work. I'd simply be along for the fun."

"Fun." Roe tapped her lips with a finger. "I never thought of it like that."

"I don't see any reason work and fun can't coexist." Boone offered a smile that she felt all the way to the tips of her toes. "Do you?"

CHAPTER FOUR

Gladys Bertholf stood on the terrazzo floor at the back of the Good Hope Community Theater, studying the stage. At one time, the once gorgeous Art Deco building had fallen into disrepair. Then the citizens of Good Hope had stepped up and allocated money for renovations.

She'd always viewed this building as her home away from home. Gladys had starred in so many stage productions over the past seven decades that she couldn't recall the names of them all. A handful of years ago, she had exchanged her acting crown for a director's hat.

Earlier in the year, when she'd researched venues where she could celebrate her one hundredth birthday on New Year's Eve, she'd come up with several possibilities.

Hill House, the Victorian mansion where the Women's Events League held their meetings, had come to mind first.

Gladys had not only been a part of the Cherries, the civic group that planned most of the events in Good Hope, for most of her life, but she had served as the organization's treasurer until well into her eighties.

Another possibility was the Good Hope Living Center, an

independent retirement community where she had a spacious apartment. She knew the management would be more than happy if she chose to celebrate under their roof.

Ah, but this place…

Gladys let her gaze drift upward to admire the ceiling with its ornate plasterwork and gold metallic accents before dropping it back to the stage curtain of thick red velvet.

This place really did feel like home to her. To not only stage a production at her party but star in it seemed befitting the Queen of the Theater.

"*Spotlight* is going to be stupendous."

Another woman might have jumped at the unexpected voice at her side. It took more than that to startle Gladys. She turned toward her longtime friend Ruby Rakes.

"It is indeed." The years hadn't diminished Gladys's deep theatrical voice, capable of reaching any theater's back row with minimal effort.

Gladys frowned. "Where's Katherine? I thought she was picking you up from your hair appointment and coming with you."

"I'm here." Katherine's bony fingers gripped the silver acorn that adorned the top of her "walking stick." Not a cane. Her friend, younger than Gladys by a good seven years, might need a little extra stability, but she did not use a *cane*.

She'd told them she'd chosen this walking stick because the acorn symbolized strength and longevity.

Gladys turned to offer her friend a smile. "Where were you hiding out?"

"Just inspecting the facilities." The former accountant, tall and handsome with salt-and-pepper hair that was now much more salt-heavy, smiled. "I'm pleased to report they are well maintained and up to your high standards."

These two women were Gladys's oldest and dearest friends. She didn't take their presence in her life for granted. Too many friends, colleagues and even family had passed from her life. That Ruby and Katherine would be here to celebrate New Year's Eve with her was all the gift she needed.

Of course, she wouldn't let them know that. She would graciously accept if they wanted to buy her a birthday gift.

"That is excellent news." Gladys offered Katherine a wry smile. "Now, where shall we go for lunch?"

"I was thinking Muddy Boots. They have Reubens on the menu today." Ruby wrinkled her nose. "Tom at the Living Center can't make a decent Reuben to save his soul."

"You and Gladys were just there Saturday," Katherine reminded her. "Why didn't you get one then? Even though I know Dr. Passmore wouldn't like you having so much sodium."

"Pfft." Ruby waved a dismissive hand. "I'm eighty-seven. If I can't indulge every now and then, what's the point?"

"I considered the Reuben," Gladys admitted. "But Beck had the chicken pot pie on special."

"You should have been there, Katherine." Ruby's expression instantly brightened. "When that pot pie fell into that man's lap, it was like a skit from some slapstick comedy."

"Except, while entertaining, it wasn't funny. Even though he did jump up like one of those jack-in-the-box toys." Gladys motioned for them to follow her back into the gilded lobby that even now held round tables that would be used for an upcoming Christmas event. "I wish I knew who the young man was."

Gladys took a seat at one of the tables.

Katherine frowned. "Why are we sitting down?"

"Just taking a minute to soak in the ambience." No way was Gladys admitting that her legs were tired of standing. Another sign—not that she was getting old, but simply an indication that she needed to work on her core strength.

As soon as Ruby and Katherine sat, Ruby leaned forward. "I know who he is."

Gladys pinned Ruby with a sharp look. "How long have you known, and why is this the first I'm hearing of it?"

Ruby smiled. "I just discovered his identity from Evie this morning at the hair salon."

"I have news on that front, too. But I'll let Ruby go first." Katherine's smug expression set Gladys's teeth on edge.

As far as Gladys was concerned, she should be the one dispensing news, not receiving it. She consoled herself that she hadn't had time yesterday to ferret out the information. Yesterday's practice had gone long when Melvin Boggs, the sound guy, had become light-headed and needed to go home.

Then it had been time for dinner, followed by several hands of bridge.

"The client Marigold had before me had arrived a few minutes late, which meant I had to wait. Only ten minutes, but it was long enough that I could quiz Evie about the man she was having lunch with." Ruby paused.

Gladys knew Ruby was hoping she would press for information. She merely smiled.

The silence stretched and extended.

Behind her cat-eye frames, Ruby's bright blue eyes darted from Gladys to Katherine, then back to Gladys. Her friend had always reminded Gladys of a chipper little sparrow, never more so than at this moment.

"His name is Jason Boone. He plays for the Colorado Grizzlies." The words tumbled past Ruby's peach-colored lips. "He was injured because of a particularly nasty hit and had to have his liver—no, no, his spleen taken out. Or it was ruptured and repaired. I'm not sure. I do know that Krew offered him the use of his cabin to recuperate."

Krew Slattery, hometown hero and now a coach for the Colorado Grizzlies, occasionally returned to Good Hope with his family, usually for special events and to visit his wife's sister and her family.

"That sounds like the same injury that Krew had when he returned to Good Hope and ended up getting back together with Cassie," Gladys reminded the women.

"I have even more interesting news." Katherine shifted in the straight-backed chair as if trying to find a comfortable position. "Roe Carson, she's the new server at Muddy Boots, the one with the dark hair and—"

"We know who she is," Gladys cut Katherine off, eager for her to get to the point. She glanced at Ruby. "Roe was our server on Saturday."

"The one who spilled the pot pie on that nice young man," Ruby added.

One thing Gladys could say about her friends was that, like her, they loved being in the know and being the first to share information.

"Well, Roe is also staying at Krew's cabin."

Gladys's posture had always been above reproach. But her spine grew even more stiff, and her heart sped up. "How do you know this?"

Katherine's lips curved. She was obviously pleased at Gladys's reaction and apparent interest. "Eliza told me when I was over for dinner last night."

Gladys admired how Eliza Kendrick, Katherine's relative, always seemed to have her finger on the community pulse. Eliza was also a reliable narrator. If she said Roe was staying at the Slattery cabin, the young woman was there.

"Who told her that?"

Gladys could have kissed Ruby for asking the question, hovering on her tongue's tip.

Katherine's gaze grew thoughtful. "Cade told Marigold, who told Ami, who told Lindsay, who told Eliza."

The string made perfect sense, except for where it started. "How did Cade find out?"

"Roe Carson called 911." Katherine went on to relay everything she knew about what had occurred at the cabin on Saturday night, ending with Cade leaving them at the cabin, ostensibly to "work things out."

"This is most excellent news, Katherine." Gladys would give kudos where kudos were due. "You know what we need to do now."

"I do." Katherine gave a nod worthy of a Queen.

Brows furrowed in confusion, Ruby flitted her gaze back and forth between her friends. "I don't. Clue me in."

"How long has it been since we matched anyone, Ruby?" Katherine spoke with far more patience than Gladys could muster.

"It's been a while. We haven't found anyone interesting and—"

"Now we have." Gladys couldn't stop the smile even if she'd tried. "You girls have been asking what I want for my birthday."

"You said you didn't want anything," Ruby reminded her.

"I'd love for us to have another successful match. It—"

"You're talking about Jason and Roe," Katherine interrupted.

"Who else?" Gladys said, showing what she felt was remarkable restraint.

"He goes by Boone," Ruby said.

Gladys blinked. "Pardon?"

"His name is Jason Boone, but he goes by Boone." Ruby twittered. "That's what he told Evie."

"Boone and Roe." Gladys rolled the names around on her tongue and found them very much to her liking. "Yes, I like the sound of them together."

"Now we just need to find out if either is involved with anyone else."

Katherine was once again the voice of reason. Gladys wished she'd mentioned that first. But no matter, her friend had a point.

"Well, Katherine, why don't you check that out and let us know?" While it was wise to be certain, Gladys's nearly infallible intuition told her that these two were both single and unattached.

After all, who would let their loved one be alone during the holidays?

And Gladys knew, just knew, that she was going to have a whole lot of fun with this match. Her heart picked up speed at the thought of how she and her friends would make this Christmas one that Boone and Roe would always remember.

CHAPTER FIVE

"Helen." Roe kept her voice low and stepped close to her trainer. She'd worked the lunch shift every day since Tuesday. It was now Friday, and she had the distinct feeling that she was being watched. "Do you see the three ladies at the four-top by the window?"

Helen glanced at the table before returning her gaze to Roe. They'd gotten slammed over lunch, but now, at one thirty, with thirty minutes left of Roe's shift, the rush had finally ended.

"I see them." Helen's placid expression gave nothing away.

Roe wondered if Helen was feeling okay. The older woman had been going since six a.m. without stopping, and while she'd tended to her tables with the same brisk efficiency that Roe had come to associate with her, today the lines on Helen's face seemed deeper and more pronounced.

"What about them?" Helen asked.

"They come in for lunch daily and sit at that table from eleven until two."

"So?"

"Doesn't that seem odd?"

Helen shrugged. "They can sit as long as they like."

"But after they're done eating, they stay and play cards, even though there is a line out the door."

And the whole time, they watch me like three hawks eyeing a mouse.

Roe kept the last part to herself, knowing that would make her sound crazy. Still, the feeling persisted.

"Gladys, Ruby and Katherine are as close as we come to royalty in this town. Just so you know, Ruby is related in an indirect way to Beck and Ami."

Roe understood without Helen needing to say more that these three were welcome to sit in the café—and stare at her—for as long as they wanted, 24/7.

From the corner of her eye, Roe watched the woman with the silver streak in her hair raise a slender, elegant hand.

Not motioning to her, Roe thought, but to Helen, their server.

Catching the movement, Helen started in that direction but skidded to a stop when Gladys pointed.

Pointed to Roe.

Helen turned back. "She wants you."

"Me?" Roe's voice rose. "Why would she want me?"

"There's one way to find out." Helen gave her a gentle shove. "I'll take care of your last two tables."

"My people already have their checks. The most they'll need is more coffee or tea." Roe spoke quickly, wanting to get it all out before Helen got frustrated and walked her to the table.

She wouldn't put it past the woman.

Pasting on a smile, Roe wove her way through the tables to where the three ladies sat. The cards that had only moments ago been scattered across the tabletop were nowhere to be seen.

"How may I help you ladies?"

Gladys's pale blue eyes lit up as if Roe had asked precisely the right question. "You can join us. We'd love to get to know you."

Before Roe could reply, Gladys turned to her companions. "Wouldn't we, girls?"

"Absolutely." The one with the champagne hair tittered.

"We would." The other, more serious, woman gestured to the empty chair. "Please sit."

"I wish I could, but I'm on duty right now and—"

"Helen," Gladys called out. "It's okay if she sits with us for a while, right?"

"Absolutely." When Helen's direct gaze settled on her, Roe realized the best—and, it appeared, the only—way to handle the situation was to answer a few questions.

These women would quickly realize that her life was downright dull. Then Roe would be free to grab her coat from the back room and head home.

"It appears I can sit and chat for a few." Roe offered up a smile. "I'm afraid there isn't much to tell. I'm far more interested in the three of you. Helen mentioned that you're the closest thing to royalty in Good Hope. I'd—"

"I'm Gladys Bertholf. This is Katherine Spencer, and that's Ruby Rakes." Gladys gestured to the serious woman first and then the woman with champagne-colored hair. "We'll get to your questions in a minute. Let's start with you. You're the mysterious one."

Roe's laugh came quickly as she pulled out the chair and sat. "I'm hardly mysterious."

"You're a mystery to us." Ruby's voice trembled with eagerness. "We don't know anything about your dating history, if you're seeing anyone, how you like—"

Roe was unsure what Ruby was about to say, because Gladys clamped her bony fingers, covered in jewels, around Ruby's arm and gave a squeeze, silencing her.

"Where is it you come from, Roe?" Katherine's voice filled the momentary silence. "Is that your given name?"

"It's Rosalie." The question was one she'd answered many times over the years. "My mother heard the name once and loved it. She told my dad that if she ever had a girl, she would name her Rosalie. After three boys, she'd nearly given up hope of ever using the name, but then I was born."

"You have three older brothers." Gladys's glance at Katherine brought to mind an executive telling an assistant to take notes.

"I do." Roe smiled at Ruby, who had written *3 brothers* on the scoring sheet before her. "They're the ones who started calling me Roe. The nickname stuck."

"Any younger siblings?" Gladys promptly asked, as if reading from a list of questions.

"No, just me and my brothers." Anticipating the next question, Roe continued. "My father is in the Air Force. We moved a lot, so there really is no place I would call home. Since leaving college eight years ago, I've lived in three different cities, the last being Minneapolis. That's where I met Dakota."

"We love Dakota," Ruby gushed.

"I don't know anyone who doesn't." Roe smiled, thinking of her intelligent, good-natured friend. "I feel honored she chose me to be one of her bridesmaids."

"She must think highly of you. Do you also do crisis PR for Sterns & Kline?" Gladys's question told Roe that these women not only knew Dakota but knew her well.

"No. Dakota and I met through a Minneapolis organization called TeamWomen. We served on a committee together and hit it off. We've been friends ever since."

"You said you don't work for Sterns & Kline." Gladys arched a brow. "What field are you in?"

"I was working for Twin Cities Children's Theatre when Dakota and I met."

The spark of interest on Gladys's face was too real to be faked. "You're in theater?"

"I was. I started as a production assistant at a theater in Kansas City. I was there for a few years before moving to a theater in Georgia, where I was the director. Eighteen months ago, I accepted a position as a stage manager in Minneapolis."

Gladys's brows pulled together. "Going from a theater director to a stage manager would be a lateral move at best."

"You could say that," Roe agreed. "But the Twin Cities Children's Theatre was well established and an environment where I felt I could learn a lot."

"Gladys has been involved in theater since she was in her teens." Ruby smiled at her friend. "There is going to be a big production on New Ye—"

"I'd love to tell you about my career, Roe, but first, I'd like to hear more about you." Gladys offered an encouraging smile. "Are you taking a couple of months off or—?"

"I was downsized." Even though the board had assured her it wasn't personal, simply saying the words brought a fresh wave of pain. "They'd taken some major financial hits during the pandemic. While that was a while ago, it started the organization on a downward course that they couldn't recover from."

Concern blanketed Gladys's face. "Did the theater shut down completely?"

Roe believed she'd have found that easier to bear if it had. Not that she would ever wish for any theater to close its doors. "No. They looked at salaries and what positions could be combined. Mine was merged with the production assistant's duties. Since he'd been there longer… Well, they kept him and let me go."

"I'm sorry." Gladys's genuine sympathy soothed a raw spot in Roe's heart that had yet to heal. "That must have been heartbreaking."

Unexpected tears pushed at the backs of Roe's lids, but she refused to let them fall. *Focus on the bright side,* Roe told herself.

"It was difficult, but I tell myself if they'd kept me on, I wouldn't be enjoying the holidays in Good Hope."

"Do you have another job lined up?" Katherine asked. "Perhaps one scheduled to start after the first of the year?"

"No." Roe did her best to keep her tone even. "I'm finding December isn't a great month to look for a job. I've got my résumé out there, but I think it will be at least January before I get any nibbles."

"I'm sorry."

Roe started when Ruby's hand unexpectedly closed over hers. The look in the woman's warm blue eyes was as comforting as her touch.

"I'll survive."

"Of course you will." Gladys spoke brusquely, though the look in her eyes was no less kind than Ruby's. "Since you'll likely be here for New Year's, I'd love for you to help with my birthday celebration and, of course, stay to enjoy the party."

"Your birthday party?" Roe spoke slowly, not sure how this woman thought she could help.

"It's not just a party," Ruby piped up. "It's a huge bash on New Year's Eve with a stage production and everything."

"It's being held at our wonderfully renovated theater," Katherine added.

"Sounds like a big deal."

"Well, some think being on this earth for a hundred years is a big deal," Gladys admitted with faux modesty.

"You're going to be a hundred?" Roe blinked. No way was this vibrant woman that old.

"It's true, though sometimes it's difficult for me to believe. I—"

"That was an awesome shot." A loud male voice drowned out whatever Gladys had been about to say.

"I could have stopped the puck, but Micah got in the way."

"You were the one who picked him to be on your team."

Roe watched three teenage boys drop into a booth by the window. Two of them had red hair, and Roe realized they were twins. The other, about the same age, had wavy blond hair.

The puck reference told her that they were talking about hockey. Her brothers had played the sport, but more for fun than anything else.

The boys continued to talk loudly, making Roe smile at their boyish exuberance.

Gladys didn't appear to have the same reaction. "Callum. Connor. Ric. Your parents taught you better than to behave this way in public. Please use your indoor voices."

The boys turned in their seats.

One of the redheads flashed a smile that was more cheeky than apologetic. "Sorry, Gladys."

The other twin added, "We'll keep it down."

"We're just jazzed," the third boy added. "We played pond hockey against a team from Egg Harbor and kicked their butts."

The boy stopped as if realizing that might not be the correct way to describe the game to three older women and a woman they didn't know.

"Good for you." Gladys gave a decisive nod and then turned to Helen. "Their tab is on me."

"Thanks, Gladys," they said nearly in unison.

When Helen strode over to take their orders, the boys spoke in quieter tones.

"The twins are Callum and Connor Brody. Beck is their uncle. The other boy, the one with blond hair, is Ric Workman. His stepfather, Liam Gallagher, is a psychologist at Connections. Peyton, who you worked with last weekend, is a receptionist at that practice."

Roe glanced at the boys before returning her attention to the women. "My mind is officially blown by all the connections in this town."

"I'll give you one more." Ruby smiled. "My grandson Jeremy is married to Ami's sister Fin."

"Ami, as in Beck's wife?" Roe considered herself good with names, but her head now spun like an out-of-control Tilt-A-Whirl.

"Ami, as in the owner of Blooms Bake Shop and co-owner of Muddy Boots," Katherine advised, "and Beck's wife."

"Yes." Helen shifted impatiently from one foot to the other. "Take it home, Roe. Eat it before it gets cold."

Roe wasn't sure what was in the bag and didn't find out until she was back at the cabin and in the kitchen.

Boone, well, his truck hadn't been in the garage, so he was obviously off somewhere.

The sack yielded two Reuben sandwiches, a pint of coleslaw and two chocolate brownies. Roe's stomach rumbled at the sight of the Reubens.

After putting one on a plate, she scooped out a hefty dose of slaw and then placed a brownie on the plate.

She was about to set the rest in the refrigerator when she heard the garage door go up. Moments later, the door leading from the garage to a mudroom off the kitchen opened.

"I've got food if you're interested," she called out.

Boone moved to study the contents of her plate. "Looks good. How much do I owe you?"

"Nothing. Courtesy of a woman at the café."

He scooped the plate off the table. "Thanks. I skipped lunch."

Roe opened her mouth to protest that that was her plate, but she didn't bother. Instead, she pulled out the rest of the food and, after filling a glass with water, took a seat opposite him at the kitchen table.

"Who is this generous lady?" Boone asked between bites.

"Gladys Bertholf. From what I understand, she's like the town matriarch. She'll be celebrating her hundredth birthday on New Year's Eve."

He blinked. "Seriously?"

"One of her friends invited you and me to a party tomorrow."

"Bingo."

Roe pulled her brows together. "Pardon?"

He grinned. "Is it a bingo party?"

"No, it's a holiday party at…" Roe paused, then rolled her eyes before pulling the piece of paper from her pocket, "Rakes Farm.

Apparently, it's a big deal. I'm going because, well, I don't want to spend my entire December sitting at home."

She also wanted to meet Fin—formerly of LA—and see if she had any connections she might be willing to share.

"Have fun." Boone took another big bite of the sandwich.

"Don't you want to go?"

He shrugged. "Not particularly."

"Gladys said to tell you that it would reassure Krew to know you aren't sitting around the cabin brooding."

"I'm not brooding, and I'm not sitting around. I went to the Y today to check out the facilities."

"You've been cleared to work out?" Roe couldn't keep the surprise from her voice. When she'd learned that Boone had ruptured his spleen, she'd checked out what that meant on the web. It appeared to be a big deal.

"Not yet," he admitted. "But I want to be ready when I get the go-ahead. Sitting around isn't for me."

"Come with me to the party, then." If he reiterated that he wasn't interested, she wouldn't ask again. "Or not. Your choice."

CHAPTER SIX

Roe cast a sideways look at Boone as he pulled into a lot several blocks from the business district. After his hesitation over accepting her invitation to the party, when he'd asked if she wanted to go with him to the First Friday celebration tonight, she'd hesitated.

Why should she go with him tonight when he hadn't shown any interest in attending the party with her tomorrow? Then she realized how ridiculous that was.

She was as free to turn down his offer this evening as he was to turn down hers.

The fact was, she wanted to see for herself what a First Friday celebration was all about.

That was why she was here. Why Boone wanted to attend remained a mystery. "Why did you want to come to this thing?"

As soon as he shut off the engine and hopped out, Roe pushed open the truck door, not giving him a chance to round the front and open her door. Which she knew he'd have done, given the chance. The guy had manners.

The thing was, she couldn't sit in the cab of the truck one

second longer. Inhaling the intoxicating scent of his citrusy cologne had her insides quivering.

The enticing aroma might be subtle, but it was no less potent.

Once outside, Roe inhaled the fresh air laced with a hint of pine and felt herself steady.

Then Boone was at her side, and her calm shattered. She couldn't believe a man could look so, well, so appealing in jeans and flannel.

"When Krew offered me the cabin, he mentioned no place does Christmas up quite like Good Hope. You were right when you said Coach wouldn't want me sitting around the cabin brooding. He told me to take advantage of all the town has to offer." Boone's eyes took on a faraway look. "Christmas used to be my favorite holiday."

"Used to be?" Roe immediately picked up on the past tense. "What changed?"

"Life. Sports." He shrugged as he walked beside her, close but not touching. "My parents divorced when I was in high school. My sister went with my mom. I stayed with Dad. He wasn't big on celebrations. We usually went to the gym on Thanksgiving and Christmas. In college and then when I got drafted by the Grizzlies, it seemed we were always gearing up for post-season play during the holidays."

Boone abruptly stopped talking, as if realizing he'd been rambling. "What about you?"

"My parents went all out for Christmas no matter where we were stationed. When I went to college, if I didn't go home for Christmas, I celebrated with any friends who were around."

"What about after college?"

"That was hit-or-miss." Roe heaved a heavy sigh. "If I could swing it, I'd go home, but once my parents moved to Germany, going home to see them became almost impossible. I tried to tell myself Christmas was more for kids anyway, but I don't think I fully convinced myself."

"Now, here we are."

For the first time, Roe paid more attention to her surroundings rather than the man at her side.

"How did I not notice this loveliness today?" Flags with Christmas sayings hung from lampposts and fluttered in the breeze as snow lightly fell.

From where Roe stood, she could see that brightly colored lights were everywhere. They encircled the front windows of businesses and lit up the evergreens. The gazebo in the town square had gone white-light crazy, along with an abundance of greenery and red ribbons.

The enticing aroma of roasted chestnuts and fresh gingerbread filled the air, providing the perfect accompaniment to the laughter and conversation floating on the evening breeze.

Santa sat on a thronelike chair on the steps of the courthouse, listening intently to the boy on his knee while other children danced from one foot to the other, waiting for their chance to tell him their Christmas wishes.

A teenage girl dressed as an elf, wearing striped leggings, a green tunic trimmed in white fur and a tall pointy hat, handed out large candy canes as she escorted the children from Santa's lap.

Roe shifted her attention back to Boone. "What exactly is the First Friday Christmas Stroll about?"

"You're asking me?"

"You're the one who mentioned coming to this," she reminded him.

"All I know is people stroll the streets, eating and meeting up with friends."

"You and I don't have any friends here."

He laughed and surprised her by slinging an arm around her shoulders. "You're hilarious."

Roe liked the closeness a little too much. She stepped forward, slipping out from under his arm on the pretext of checking out the pastries in the window of Blooms Bake Shop.

"See something you like?"

Turning to answer, Roe found him right there—so close that she gazed directly into his rich brown eyes.

Heart hammering, she murmured, "The candy-striped one."

His lips lifted in a slow smile. "Which one?"

She cleared her throat. "One?"

Breaking the connection, he shifted toward the window and pointed, forcing Roe to refocus on the window.

Immediately, she saw what he was referring to. In addition to pretty cupcakes, there were cake pops, pinwheel peppermint cookies and striped macaroons.

She sighed. "They all look delicious."

"Agree." Pulling open the door, Boone stepped back and waited for her to enter the bakery.

The warmth and the smells spilling onto the sidewalk drew her inside. Even though she told herself she should probably resist temptation, her feet had different ideas, propelling her into the line at the counter with Boone beside her.

Perhaps if the line had been moving slowly, she would have stepped away. Or if the two women wearing shirts proclaiming "Baking Up Some Love" weren't as efficient, she might have suggested to Boone they come back later.

But she'd barely had time to glance around the shop when she and Boone reached the front of the line. She smiled at the teenage girl with blond hair standing beside a woman who had to be her mother. It was easy to see how the girl would look in twenty years.

"I'll have one of those candy-striped cake pops—" Roe began.

"Make that two." Boone pulled out his wallet.

"You got it." The girl shifted her gaze from Boone back to Roe. "Anything to drink?"

"I'd like a hot cocoa." Roe glanced at Boone.

"Make that—"

"Two." The girl flashed a smile at Boone. "Coming right up."

The mother turned to her daughter. "Once you fill their order and ring them up, you can go."

A slight nod and a bright spark in the girl's eyes were her only response before she bent over the pastry case.

"Brynn," a male voice called from behind Roe. "Are you coming or not?"

"I am. Give me two minutes."

Looking over her shoulder, Roe saw the three boys from the café, along with two girls—one blond, the other with dark hair.

When Roe swiveled back, the cake pops sat on napkins, and candy-cane stir sticks rose from the hot cocoa's whipped cream topping. Boone handed the girl a twenty and told her to keep the change.

Briefly, ever so briefly, Roe considered protesting that she could pay for her own, but she recognized that would likely only delay the girl's departure.

"Would you like lids?" Brynn asked, her gaze shifting to her friends before returning to Roe and Boone.

Not wanting to disturb the candy canes, Roe shook her head. "I'm fine."

Boone smiled at the girl. "I'm good."

With Boone at her side, Roe headed for the exit, realizing that tonight wouldn't be nearly as much fun without a friend to share it with.

Not that Boone was exactly a friend—she really didn't know him well enough to confer that designation on him—but he was a pleasant companion.

She liked that he didn't appear to fill every second with conversation. Or that, while Boone was obviously confident in his own skin, he didn't go out of his way to draw attention to himself.

His rugged good looks did that all on their own.

Though not as big and bulky as a tackle, he obviously had muscles under that winter gear. His easy, confident stride would have drawn the eye even without his handsome face.

Roe smiled and thanked an older man with silver-rimmed glasses for holding the door open for them as they left the shop. Once on the sidewalk, Roe couldn't wait a second longer to take a bite of her cake pop. The red velvet interior didn't disappoint.

Roe had a college friend who insisted she didn't like red velvet cake because she didn't like chocolate cake. Roe had never understood that. Sure, there was cocoa powder in the red velvet mix, but in her mind, it was the combination of buttermilk and vinegar that gave the cake a tart edge and pulled it out of the chocolate cake category.

Her loss, Roe thought, taking another bite and then washing it down with a sip of cocoa. "I still haven't figured out exactly how this stroll works."

Boone's gaze lingered on the couples and families sauntering down the brightly decorated streets, and then he shrugged.

Roe pointed to the town square. "Let's check out the gazebo."

During the brief time that she and Boone had been in Blooms Bake Shop, a group of singers dressed in vintage garb had arrived and were now entertaining the crowd with popular Christmas carols.

Boone's hand rested lightly on the back of her coat as she stepped closer.

There was something incredibly moving about hearing songs she had loved since childhood being sung in perfect harmony in crisp December air.

"Roe."

She turned to see Beck standing beside a pretty woman holding a toddler in her arms while a school-aged boy with his father's dark hair and eyes fidgeted at her side.

"Beck. It's good to see you." Roe offered the man a warm smile, then gestured to Boone. "Have you met Jason Boone?"

Beck's smile disappeared. Worry clouded his brown eyes. "How are you feeling? The pot pie—"

"No worries." Boone waved a dismissive hand, but curiosity filled his dark eyes. "How'd you hear about that?"

"Beck owns Muddy Boots," Roe answered before Beck could. "He's my boss."

"Look," Boone spoke quickly, "the incident wasn't Roe's fault. This guy got up right in front of her. He's the one to blame."

Beck shot Roe a reassuring smile. "She's not in any trouble."

"Good," Boone exclaimed. "That's good."

The tight set to Beck's shoulders eased. It was as if he was suddenly seeing the man at Roe's side as Jason Boone the man, not Jason Boone the pot-pie victim.

"I enjoy watching you play." As if eager to change the subject from the incident at Muddy Boots, Beck shifted focus. "You've had an impressive career. That was a bad hit you took in that game against the Ravens."

"Put me in the hospital for three days."

"I hope you're feeling better."

"I'm definitely on the mend."

Roe wasn't surprised Boone didn't speak of his frustration. She'd already discovered he wasn't the kind to whine.

"Glad to hear it." Beck smiled at the woman at his side. "This is my wife, Ami, and our two boys, JT and Anthony. Our oldest, Sarah Rose, is out strolling with friends."

"Nice to meet you, Jason." Ami turned her attention to Roe. "I'm Ami Cross."

"I'm sorry, Ami." Beck gave his wife an apologetic smile. "I thought you'd already met Roe."

"Now we have." Roe smiled. "My given name is Rosalie, but please, call me Roe. It's a pleasure to meet the woman who owns that amazing bakery."

"Hearing that makes me happy." Ami's gaze dropped to the cup in Roe's hand. "I hope you're enjoying the hot cocoa."

connected in LA and might be able to help her find a new position.

The stressed look on her face, along with the hope in her eyes, had him reconsidering.

It was clear she planned to attend the party with or without him. Even though he didn't owe her his presence, Roe had been reasonable about the mix-up with the cabin.

Which was why, tomorrow night, he'd attend the party with her at Rakes Farm.

Roe headed up to her room shortly after she and Boone arrived home from the stroll. She fell asleep nearly the instant her head hit the pillow.

She wasn't sure what woke her. It might have been the extra blanket she'd tossed on the bed that added a little too much warmth. Or the quiet. The apartment she'd shared in Minneapolis had been on a major arterial, and the sound of traffic had been her white noise.

When Roe found herself still awake ten minutes later, she decided she was thirsty. Tonight, she'd forgotten to put a cup of water at her bedside.

Tossing aside the down comforter, she slipped quietly down the stairs. The lights in the house were off, but the glow from several lighted outlets provided needed illumination.

Once she reached the main floor, she made a beeline for the kitchen. She was halfway to the sink when she skidded to a stop.

Boone stood at the counter, a dark figure staring out the window, a glass of water in a crystal tumbler on the counter beside him.

Obviously, she wasn't the only one thirsty.

But she was the only one dressed.

Naked except for a tiny towel wrapped around his waist,

Boone suddenly turned toward her. "Roe, hey. I didn't hear you come down. I was in the Jacuzzi tub relaxing and came out for a drink."

Roe's gaze dropped to the tiny towel before she forced her gaze back to his face.

"You don't have swim trunks on."

"Oh, noticed that, did you?"

"Oh, I didn't see…" Roe stammered. "I wasn't looking. I just—"

"It's a private bathtub, and since it's so late, I didn't think I needed to dress for the kitchen. I didn't think you would be up."

"You're up." Roe nearly groaned aloud as the words slipped past her lips. As heat scorched her neck, she saw the amusement in Boone's eyes. "I mean, you're awake. Like I'm awake. I came down for water."

Realizing she was on the verge of babbling, Roe clamped her mouth shut, but not before adding, "I'm thirsty."

"That makes sense if you're coming for water." Boone gestured to the refrigerator. "Help yourself."

Roe wasn't sure if it was the motion with his hand or what, but the towel slipped. She inhaled sharply but didn't avert her eyes.

At the last second, Boone grabbed hold of the towel. "I'm really sorry I startled you. In the future, I'll remember this isn't my house, and I'll be more presentable when I leave my room."

Resisting the urge to glance once again at the towel, Roe made a great show of taking a glass from the cupboard and filling it with water.

"I promise you've nothing to worry about." His voice was a husky rumble. "I'll get out of your way now. Good night, Roe."

"Good night," Roe called out without turning around.

When she did turn, it was to admire strong muscular legs, broad shoulders and an amazing backside as he strode down the hall.

Heaving a sigh, she took a long drink of water. Something told her she wasn't going to get much sleep tonight.

~

Boone shut the door to his room and dropped down on his bed.

He smiled, thinking of the look in Roe's eyes when she'd given him the once-over. If the pink on her cheeks and the brightness in her eyes were any indication, she'd liked what she saw.

Boone had liked what he'd seen, too. He was used to women being perfectly put together whenever he was with them. Roe had been anything but with her face devoid of makeup, tousled hair and sleep-creased cheek. Still, his body had reacted. Some of it was that the shirt she wore exposed long, toned legs, and beneath the thin fabric, he'd seen evidence of her luscious curves.

Roe was a pretty woman, but she was also a smart, interesting one. Right now, he liked everything he knew about her.

But she hadn't come to Good Hope planning on being under the same roof with him. She'd been kind enough to let him stay, even though she hadn't had to.

He wouldn't forget that.

Besides, he was in no shape to start a new relationship. While he'd had flings in the past, Roe didn't seem the fling type. Not to mention she was best friends with Coach Slattery's daughter.

Becoming physically involved with her would be a mistake.

One that he wasn't about to make, no matter how tempted he was.

~

Roe's shift at Muddy Boots the next morning started out well but quickly took a nose dive. This was her first time handling a full section of six tables, and the place was hopping.

By the time she walked out the door at two thirty, she wanted to cry. The new shoes she'd purchased specifically for work had rubbed blisters on both heels, and dropping a pot pie on Boone was nothing compared to having an unreasonable "Karen" scream at her for bringing the salad dressing on the salad instead of on the side.

Even though the woman hadn't specified, apparently—at least according to Karen—Roe should have asked. Offering to remake the salad hadn't satisfied the woman, who'd only continued to berate her.

Roe attempted to walk that fine line between appeasing unhappy customers without letting them walk all over her. Helen had been busy with her own tables, the other servers were college girls who appeared determined to stay out of the fray, and Beck hadn't been around.

Just when Roe was ready to lash out and tell the woman to leave, Gladys stepped forward to face Karen.

"You will stop this nonsense immediately."

The woman, her round face flushed and perspiring from her tirade, ignored Gladys.

"Are you lazy?" Karen's gaze remained on Roe, a viper snake unwilling to release its prey. "Or just plain stupid?"

Roe had watched videos of both men and women acting in such unbelievable ways, but until this moment, she had never been on the receiving end of such behavior. It wasn't funny when it was happening to you.

"Did you hear what I said, madam?" Gladys spoke again, her pale blue eyes piercing the distance between her and the Karen.

"Go away, old woman." Without bothering to glance in Gladys's direction, Karen flicked a dismissive hand.

"I most certainly will not." Gladys scanned the table of four. "It is you and your family who will leave. Right this instant. If you do not, I will not hesitate to call the sheriff and have you tossed out."

With that remark, Gladys commanded the woman's attention. The woman opened her mouth, but Gladys steamrolled over her.

"I don't know where you come from, but in this community, we don't speak to anyone like you're speaking to this sweet young woman."

"I don't have to listen to you." Karen sneered. "You don't own this café."

"As a matter of fact, I do." Gladys pulled her phone out of her handbag. "You have been ordered to leave these premises and told not to return. If you do not leave now, I will call the police, and you will be charged with trespassing."

"Mom, c'mon, let's go." The woman's teenage son looked up from his phone for the first time. "You've already made yourself look stupid."

Karen glared at him. "Don't you call me stupid."

The fact that she'd called Roe the very same thing only moments before appeared lost on her.

The husband, or the man Roe assumed was her husband, rose, a long-suffering expression on his face. "The kids and I are leaving. It's up to you whether to come with us or not."

Gladys held up her phone and tapped the screen twice with one pointed nail. "TikTok."

"Well, I never." Huffing, Karen reached down and scooped up her purse. "I will not be coming here again."

"Good." Gladys hid her smile until the family left the café.

They'd barely walked out the door when Gregory appeared tableside to clear away the dishes.

Applause filled the dining room, and Gladys took an obligatory bow and then spoke to her admirers. "The show is officially over. Back to your food."

Roe touched Gladys's arm. "Thank you for that."

"No one should be spoken to in that manner."

"I didn't realize you owned Muddy Boots. I thought Beck and Ami did."

"That's correct. But they weren't here. I was."

Roe blinked. "But you told her—"

"I'm an actress." Gladys's lips curved in a sly smile. "I excel in any role."

"You were very convincing."

"Thank you." Gladys offered a regal nod. "Now, don't let this incident rattle you. I've been watching, and you're doing an outstanding job."

∾

Roe relayed all this to Boone on the way to Rakes Farm that evening. He hadn't been there when she'd arrived home after her shift. In fact, by the time he'd walked through the door, it had been nearly six.

He hadn't said where he'd been, and she didn't ask. Just like it wasn't his business where she went or with whom, what he did wasn't hers.

Still, she was happy he would be with her tonight when she strolled into the party.

Being alone in the house this afternoon had given her time to settle after her "Karen" adventure. After making a snack, Roe had taken a long bath and soaked until every last bit of tension dissolved in the sweet-scented water. Then she'd slathered herself with creamy lotion and curled her hair. Ensconced in a soft, fluffy robe, she'd cast a critical eye over her closet choices.

It was a holiday party, which likely meant dressy. Not cocktail party dressy, but maybe close. She let her gaze linger on a simple black dress. Add a strand of pearls, and she'd be good to go.

Roe reached out her hand but pulled it back. Black was definitely always a safe choice for such events, but the color didn't ring any festive bells.

She shifted her gaze to the red wrap dress—still with tags— that she'd purchased this fall in anticipation of the office

Christmas party. On the same shopping spree, she'd picked up a pair of gold metallic heeled ankle boots that would add a stylish touch.

Roe pulled the dress from the closet just as her phone rang. Glancing at the screen, she smiled. Unlike most of her friends, who hated talking on the phone, Dakota preferred it to texting.

"Hey, you." Roe sat on the bed, careful not to get too close to the dress she'd laid on the bed. "How're the wedding plans coming? I feel bad that I'm not there to help. If there's any last-minute stuff I can do to—"

"It's all done." Relief wove through Dakota's voice. "And you helped me so much in the beginning."

"I know, but—"

"No buts. All is done, and all is well." Dakota's voice held a lilt, which told Roe all was indeed well. "Now, what's new with you?"

"You'll never believe what happened at Muddy Boots today." Roe went on to explain Gladys stepping into the role of café owner.

Dakota laughed. "That sounds just like her. I wish I could have been there to see it."

"It was pretty impressive," Roe admitted, her lips curving upward.

"So, what's on the agenda for tonight?"

"Boone and I are going to a party at Rakes Farm. I'm hoping—"

"You and Jason Boone." Dakota heaved a lusty sigh. "Visions of a holly jolly end to the evening are dancing in my head."

"Puh-leeze." Still, Roe couldn't help chuckling. "There is nothing at all romantic between—"

"I can see the after-party now," Dakota interrupted, the sudden theatrical quality to her voice reminding Roe of Gladys. "The snowy night. A roaring fire. One thing leads to another and—"

"How many times do I have to say it?" Roe interrupted, trying to sound stern but unable to keep from laughing. "Boone is here to heal. Besides, it's not like that between us."

"Maybe. But I believe it's wise to keep an open mind." Dakota paused. "Things change, and a little yuletide fun just might be in your future."

~

At 6:45, Roe strode out of her bedroom. GPS had given a fifteen-minute drive time, which meant if they left now, they'd arrive a little after seven.

Roe hoped getting to the party early would give her a chance to speak with Fin privately for a few minutes and make a connection before the other attendees arrived.

While she didn't know Fin, she'd liked Ami instantly, which hopefully meant she would likely feel the same closeness with Ami's sister.

When Roe reached the bottom of the stairs, she found Boone waiting, head down, scrolling through his phone. He'd gone with dark pants and a gray sweater, a perfect combination of casual and dressy.

"I'm ready any time you are."

Her voice had his head jerking up from the phone. His eyes widened, and a look of pure appreciation crossed his face. A low whistle escaped his lips. "You look amazing."

Roe smiled, unable to stop the rush of pleasure. "You don't look so bad yourself."

"Red is definitely your color."

"That's what my mother always said." Even during Roe's gawky preteen years, her mom had always been her staunchest supporter.

For Lisa Carson, outer beauty was secondary to what a person was like on the inside. She'd wanted her children to be good and kind and, most of all, happy.

Which was why she'd supported Roe when she'd told her mom that working in theater made her happy. Now that Roe had her career, she knew her mother hoped she would find someone special to share her life.

"Wise woman."

The words pulled Roe from her thoughts. When she refocused, she found Boone staring. At her mouth.

For a second, she couldn't look away. Her heart beat like a thousand butterfly wings in her throat. She suddenly felt lightheaded.

Recalling Dakota's question, Roe considered the budding attraction between her and Boone. Did she want to act on it? More important, was it wise to act on that desire?

With no time now to give that important decision the consideration it deserved, Roe told herself that after the party, she would give it some thought.

To steady herself, she took a breath and forced her gaze to the clock on the mantel. "It's time to go."

CHAPTER EIGHT

Twenty minutes later, Roe entered the home of Fin and Jeremy Rakes, filled with confidence that came from knowing she looked her best.

An attractive couple, who looked to be in their late thirties or early forties, stood with Ruby in the foyer, greeting the guests.

The minute she and Boone had stepped through the doorway, a young man dressed in black pants and a crisp white shirt took their coats and handed them a claim check.

Several steps later, Roe stood before the couple and the woman who'd invited her.

"Oh, Roe. I'm so happy you and Boone could make it." Ruby, looking elegant in blue silk, reached out and took Roe's hands. Still holding them, she turned to the pretty woman with the sun-streaked hair and the man sporting an impish smile and a mop of unruly blond hair. "Fin and Jeremy, I'd like you to meet Rosalie Carson and Jason Boone. Roe and Boone, my grandson Jeremy Rakes and his wife, Delphinium."

"It's a pleasure." Jeremy spoke first, his gaze shifting from Roe to the man at her side. "I watched that game against the Ravens.

Wasn't that the game where you went over ten thousand career yards on receptions?"

"Eleven thousand." Boone grinned. "But who's keeping track?"

Jeremy laughed. "I'd love to hear—"

Fin's fingers curving around his bicep stopped him. "Sweetheart, we have guests arriving."

The woman's green eyes that settled on Boone were filled with apology. "My husband loves football and could talk about it all night, but—"

"You have other guests." Boone flashed an easy smile at Fin, then turned back to Jeremy. "I'll be here all night."

Roe could only smile at Fin before the people behind them stepped forward. Judging by the hugs, these had to be people the couple knew well.

She and Boone entered the large parlor and found it as impressive as the outside of the house. As they'd driven up, the sight of the old Victorian had taken her breath away.

Standing three stories tall, the home boasted a wraparound porch with leaded glass above each window. The attention to detail elevated this house into a class of its own.

Roe wasn't sure she'd ever seen a home painted in salmon, green and yellow, but on this massive structure, it worked. The swaths of evergreen looped on the porch rail and secured with ribbon, as well as the large evergreen wreath hung on the front door, added a festive air without being gaudy.

"It's just as lovely inside as out." Roe breathed the words as she stared at the Christmas tree in the corner. Decorated with what she assumed were traditional Victorian decorations, the star on top came only inches short of brushing the ceiling.

Roe pulled her attention from the tree to the massive fireplace, where vintage stockings hung from the mantel.

"Looks like they have two bars set up." Boone's words pulled her attention back to him. The warm smile he bestowed on her, coupled with an odd look in his eyes, had her heart shifting into overdrive. "May I get you something?"

You. Naked.

The thought had heat rising up her neck. It took Roe a second to find her voice. Another second to clear it. "Ah, not right now."

She forced her attention back to the tree. The paper nets hanging from the branches were filled with something that Roe couldn't identify from where she stood. She gestured vaguely in the direction of the fir. "I thought I'd check out the tree."

"Cool. I'll catch you later." He gave her arm a squeeze.

"What? Oh—" Roe stammered when he strode off without a backward glance.

He didn't even make it halfway across the room before several men stopped him.

The loud, jovial voices and slaps on the back that quickly followed told her that, like their host, these were football aficionados.

When disappointment shot through her, Roe reminded herself that she and Boone were housemates, nothing more. She'd enjoyed having someone to walk in with. Now, she was on her own. That was fine with her. Navigating new situations by herself was familiar territory.

As she stepped to the tree, Roe thought of her childhood. How many schools had she attended before she graduated from high school? Eight? No, she was pretty sure it was nine.

She'd learned early how to make friends fast but not get too attached. You couldn't get too close to anyone, not friends or boyfriends. If you did, you paid the heartache price when it came time to leave again.

Her brothers had one another, so she supposed moving so often was easier for them. She'd grown tough and become adept at keeping her heart safe. Roe had even told her parents on more than one occasion that moving didn't bother her and that she loved seeing new places and meeting new friends.

To some extent, that was true. But she kept the yearning, the dream of finding her perfect home, a place where she would truly belong and could put down roots, to herself.

"Those are sweetmeats."

Roe whirled and found herself standing next to a woman with bright blue eyes and a mass of curly blond hair. "P-pardon?"

"The sugar-covered nuts in the nets used to be called sweetmeats." The woman smiled. "Decorating a tree with edible items was very popular in the late nineteenth century."

"How do you know that?" Roe asked, amazed.

"Fin is my sister. The first year she decided to decorate this tree in keeping with Victorian traditions, I helped with the research." The woman flashed a bright smile. "I'm Marigold Rallis."

"Roe Carson." Roe cocked her head. "Rallis, as in the sheriff?"

"Cade is my husband." Marigold gestured and, when Roe followed the direction of her hand, saw that the sheriff was one of the group of men clustered around Boone. "Looks like your housemate has quite the fan club."

Roe's lips lifted in a rueful smile. "I suppose your husband told you how I freaked and called 911 when I spotted his truck at the cabin."

Marigold's expression turned serious. "You did the right thing. You had no idea who was in there. I'd have done the same."

Hearing that made Roe feel a little better. "When your husband came out, well, I could tell he wasn't on duty. I didn't mean to interrupt his evening."

"He could have let one of his deputies take the call, but Krew and Cassie are friends. If there was a break-in, he wanted to be the one to deal with an intruder in their home."

Roe nodded. "Have you been inside? It's so much nicer than I expected when Dakota called it a cabin."

Marigold shook her head. "I haven't. Cade told me it's nice."

"'Nice' is an understatement." Roe hesitated for only a second, then plunged forward. She'd learned long ago not to wait if she wanted to build a friendship—even a short-term one. "You should come out sometime. I'll show you around."

Marigold's hesitation had Roe speaking quickly again before the woman could start making excuses. Identifying when someone wasn't interested in building a friendship or a relationship was another skill she'd honed over the years.

"I don't know what I was thinking." Roe's laugh pitched high. "This is the prime holiday season. I'm sure you're super busy."

Marigold placed a light hand on Roe's arm. "I'd love to come out and see the place. As long as you don't mind if I bring the children with me. The salon keeps me busy, and when I'm not working, I don't like to be away from my family any more than I have to."

"I love kids. You can definitely bring them. How many children do you have?"

"I have three. They're four."

Roe's jaw dropped. She shut it with a snap. "You have triplets?"

"Twins plus one." Apparently seeing the confusion in Roe's eyes, she added, "Cade and I had been trying to have a baby for the longest time. While we were in the process of adopting Caleb, I got pregnant with twins. Several months later, Faith and Hope were born."

"How wonderful."

Marigold flashed a bright smile. "We think so. I do hair on Tuesdays and Thursdays, but other than that, I am usually home. I'd love to find a time to get together. Is your phone in that purse?"

Roe lifted the tiny bag hanging on a silver chain. "I don't go anywhere without it."

"Same." Marigold pulled her phone from a similar small bag. They put the phones together to share their contact information. "Text me some possible times, and we'll make it happen."

"I will do that." Roe smiled. "For now, I'm going to check out the bar."

"The Santa's Sleigh is a crowd favorite. It contains Baileys, Kahlúa and peppermint schnapps."

"Thanks for the heads-up." On her way across the parlor, Roe noticed Gladys and Katherine now standing with Ruby.

Gladys's eyes lit up when she spotted her, and the older woman motioned her over.

"Are you enjoying the party?" Ruby asked, bobbling the slushy drink in her hand before tightening her grip on the stem.

"I haven't been here long, but so far, yes." She smiled at Ruby. "It's a lovely party and a gorgeous home. Thank you for inviting me."

"Your date appears to have deserted you."

Roe caught a hint of disapproval in Gladys's easy tone.

"Boone isn't my date." Roe kept her tone light. Boone had done her a favor by coming tonight. She wasn't about to let Gladys or anyone else think he was dissing her. "We arrived together, but we're not together, if you know what I mean."

Katherine nodded sagely. "It's early days."

"No need to rush into anything," Ruby added.

"What? No," Roe sputtered.

She might have said more, but Gladys was waving Boone over, along with Fin. Excitement coursed up Roe's spine. She might finally have a chance to speak with the woman about her contacts in Los Angeles.

"What are you three up to now?" A tiny smile hovered at the corners of Fin's red lips as she rested her gaze on Gladys.

Gladys widened her eyes and brought a hand to her throat in a theatrical gesture. "I don't know about these other two. I simply want to ensure you're properly aware of your guest's talents."

"I'd have to be living in a box not to know of Boone's exploits on the field." Fin spoke in a dry tone. "I swear, Jeremy is his biggest fan."

"I wasn't speaking of Mr. Boone." Gladys turned briefly to him. "No offense intended."

Boone sipped his drink, his lips curving, and amusement dancing in his eyes. "None taken."

Gladys placed a hand glittering with a thousand rings on Roe's shoulder. "This woman has a background in theater management. She will be assisting with my birthday bash. I was thinking she might also be of assistance to you."

Confusion furrowed Fin's brows. "As an understudy? It's a little late for that, I think."

Now it was Roe's turn to be confused. "Are you in the production?"

Gladys placed a hand on Fin's shoulder. "Delphinium is playing the adult me. This woman has it all—the voice, the acting chops and, of course, the beauty. I couldn't imagine anyone more perfectly suited to play the role."

"That's wonderful." Roe still wasn't clear on how Gladys thought she might help Fin. "I'm not an actor."

"Delphinium also handles public relations for Good Hope. She's in charge of bolstering tourism for the area." Gladys smiled at Roe. "Being in *Spotlight* has taken much time away from her other duties." Gladys turned from Roe back to Fin. "I thought Roe could assist you with the Valentine's Day plans."

Interest sparked in the green eyes that Fin fixed on Roe. "I thought you were going to be in Good Hope only temporarily."

"I—"

Roe didn't have a chance to confirm that Fin was correct, because Gladys spoke first.

"Do any of us really know what the future holds?" Gladys smiled at Fin. "I recall when you first came home, you planned to return to LA."

Fin glanced across the room, her gaze settling on her husband. A soft look filled her eyes before her focus returned to Gladys. "Meant to be."

There was a story there, though Roe doubted she'd be around long enough to find out. "If there is anything I can do to help while I'm here, just ask."

Fin studied her for a long moment. "The V-Day committee is concerned that Dakota's wedding on Valentine's Day may overshadow other events the town is planning around that holiday."

"What kinds of events?" Though Dakota had mentioned that every holiday in Good Hope was celebrated, she hadn't given Roe any specifics.

Fin opened her mouth and then shut it. "I'll contact you. We'll schedule a time to discuss this. I want you to enjoy the party, and I need to make sure everything is running smoothly."

Gladys offered a benevolent nod. "Sounds like an excellent plan."

When Fin hurried off, Gladys settled her gaze first on Roe and then on Boone. "There is dancing in the second parlor. It's time for you two to embrace the spirit of the season."

"Embrace." Ruby twittered. "That's a good one, Gladys."

Gladys shot Ruby a cool gaze, and the twittering stopped.

"Enjoy." Gladys gave Boone a little shove.

"Embrace the moment and each other," Ruby called, then giggled before she was once again shushed.

CHAPTER NINE

When Boone paused beside Roe in the archway, he saw that there was indeed dancing in the second parlor. Numerous couples held each other close and swayed to romantic music emanating from a Victrola in a room where Christmas was everywhere.

This scene was a far cry from the Denver clubs' loud music and gyrating bodies. Then again, this was a holiday party at a married couple's home, not a noisy nightclub filled with singles.

Since Roe appeared to be soaking in the scene spread out before them, Boone did the same. There was a tree in this room, too, though not nearly as large and grand as the one in the other room. Draped in beautiful ribbons with a large velvet bow at the top, it sported small envelopes tied to the branches with twine, instead of bulbs.

While he watched, several women and even a couple of men strode up to the tree and removed an envelope.

"I wonder what's in those envelopes," Roe murmured.

"Each guest is supposed to take one." Ami spoke from behind them.

"The wording inside varies," Beck added, "but Gladys insists that you'll pick the envelope with the message that's meant for you."

Roe glanced at Boone. "Sounds interesting."

Not to Boone, but he kept his mouth shut.

"I'm glad to see you're going to dance." Ami smiled approvingly. "It's my favorite part of the party."

"What are we waiting for?" Beck asked, taking his wife's hand and leading her to the dance floor.

Roe looked up at Boone and smiled. "Do you want to dance?"

"Do I have a choice?"

He'd meant it to come out teasing, but when her smile faded, it was as if the football had slipped through his fingers and landed on the ground with a thud.

She took a step back. "You don't have to—"

"I'd love to dance with you." When the suspicion in her eyes remained, he didn't let his gaze waver. "Seriously."

"Okay."

They reached the dance floor, and when he took her hand, Boone realized this was the first time he'd touched her. At the house, he'd been careful to keep his hands to himself. It had been a difficult undertaking.

His family was demonstrative. He'd had to break himself of the habit of touching a hand, an arm or a shoulder, knowing that even the most innocent gesture could be misconstrued.

But dancing, well, that demanded that he hold her in his arms, one hand on her waist, the other holding her hand.

"You smell good." The words just popped out. He'd noticed the enticing scent of vanilla on the drive over but hadn't said anything. Now, being so close, he noticed it again.

"Thanks." She looked up at him. "You smell pretty terrific yourself."

Boone loved seeing her hazel eyes, rimmed with thick lashes, warm with a smile.

"Now that we have that out of the way." He studied her

thoughtfully, realizing that the red on her full lips perfectly matched her dress. Her mouth reminded him of a plump strawberry. If he kissed her, would she taste as sweet? Not happening, he told himself. "How has your evening been so far?"

"Not painful."

"Hardly a ringing endorsement." While talking football with the guys, he'd kept one eye on her, awed by her beauty and amazed at how she charmed everyone around her. She appeared to be having a great time.

"Seriously, it's been fine." She told him about her conversation with the sheriff's wife and that they had three children.

"Jeremy mentioned that he and Fin have three boys." Boone shook his head. "It's like everyone at this party is married with kids. This is new territory for me. I'm used to spending time with guys who are more into hooking up with women than settling down with them."

She nodded. "I had one married friend back in Minneapolis, and now Dakota is getting married, but, like you, most of the women I socialized with were single and more into their careers than marriage."

"My sister is married with two kids," he told her, though he wasn't sure how that was relevant.

"All of my brothers are married," she said. Then she added, "With kids."

"Then there's us," he said with a wry smile. "We're the outliers."

"It feels that way." Roe chuckled. "I miss my parents, but sometimes I'm glad they're in Germany. If they were here, I know I'd be feeling the pressure from them to settle down."

"My parents are divorced," Boone said. "They're the opposite."

"What do you mean?"

"They're constantly telling me to not rush into anything, to be careful."

"Careful how?"

The feel of her body pressed against him and the soft music filling the room made it feel like it was just her and him.

"When you're in the NFL, there are always women who want to be with you. Not necessarily because they like you, but for all the perks."

When she said nothing, he continued.

"The parties, the spotlight." He gave a halfhearted chuckle. "I'd barely been placed on medical leave when my last girlfriend moved on to a player who's not injured."

Roe's head jerked up, nearly catching him in the jaw. "That's horrible."

"It's reality." Boone thought of his career, and a bleakness washed over him. "Nothing lasts forever."

Nothing lasts forever.

The words circled in Roe's head on the drive home and once she and Boone were back at the house.

She understood the sentiment. Hadn't it been her mantra for as long as she could remember? Making new friends and getting involved in a community were things that would be instantly taken away when another assignment came through for her dad, and they were ordered to pack up and move again.

It had been like that with her job at the theater, too. She'd worked hard, but in the end, all those extra hours and effort hadn't mattered.

While she didn't have the problems Boone had with a partner who'd wanted to be with him only for the spotlight, whenever she found herself falling for someone, she started preparing herself for the time she would eventually leave. In her world, that was a given.

Enough melancholy. It had been a lovely evening, and now that she was home, she would fully relax.

Roe took off her shoes the instant her feet hit the tile floor leading into the great room.

Behind her, Boone chuckled. "Go ahead. Take it all off. I don't mind."

"Har-har." Roe rubbed her instep. "These boots might look comfortable, but they were killing my feet."

Boone was at her side now, studying the heeled boots dangling from one hand. He shook his head. "They don't look comfortable. Not to me, anyway."

Once she reached the great room, she plopped down on the sofa and exhaled a heavy sigh.

"That's a pretty heavy sigh. Was the party that bad?"

"Not at all. I enjoyed it." She watched him move to stand before the hearth. "Are you thinking of starting a fire this late?"

"I'm not ready to head to bed. My apartment in Denver is probably one of the few that doesn't have a fireplace, so I figure I'm going to enjoy this one while I can."

"You're right," she agreed. "We might as well enjoy this beautiful place while we have it."

Roe watched him bend to place two small logs on top of the kindling. He really did have a fabulous backside.

Once he had the fire started, he straightened, and she resisted the urge to sigh. When she found herself wondering what it would be like to kiss him, she knew she shouldn't have had that second drink.

While she wasn't drunk—not on two drinks spread out over the course of an evening interspersed with delicious appetizers— she did have a little buzz, and her defenses were definitely down.

"Can I get you anything to drink?" he asked.

"I've had enough alcohol." She couldn't have stopped the smile even if she'd wanted to. "The Santa's Sleigh was incredibly yummy."

She chuckled. Had she really just said *Santa's Sleigh* and *yummy* in the same sentence?

Boone sat on the sofa beside her. Not right next to her, but close enough that she could smell his yummy cologne.

There was that word again. *Yummy.*

Roe smiled.

"What was in Santa's Sleigh?"

She blinked.

"The drink?" he prompted.

Oh. The drink. Yes, of course." For a second, she'd thought he'd meant, well, never mind.

Roe waved an airy hand. "Baileys, schnapps and something else. What did you have?"

"A glass of wine."

"That's it? Only one?"

"I was driving." He shrugged. "I'm not a big drinker."

"Wow."

"Wow?"

"I thought all sports guys were big drinkers."

"I thought all theater people were dramatic."

"I can be dramatic," she told him.

"Good to know."

With the fire crackling in the hearth, Roe placed her feet on the hassock and leaned back against the soft cushions of the overstuffed sofa.

The light from the fireplace cast shadows on his handsome face. Although she didn't know Jason Boone well, she believed him to be a good guy. "I like having you around."

A startled look crossed his face. Then he smiled. "I like having you around."

She wasn't sure what to think when he patted his lap. "Give me your feet."

Roe blinked. "Pardon?"

"Your feet. In my lap. I'll rub them for you."

Startled, she didn't ask why he would do that for her. She simply accepted the offer and shifted.

When he started to massage her instep, she couldn't stop the moan of pleasure.

"Tell me about your evening." Placing his palms on either side of her right foot, he gently pulled the right side forward while pushing the left side back. He repeated the twisting motion, working from her ankle to her toes.

The pleasure made thought difficult, but Roe forced herself to focus. "Fin will contact me about helping with her planning committee."

He moved his hands to her other foot. "What would you be planning?"

Roe closed her eyes briefly when those strong fingers began massaging her instep. "I don't know. Something related to Valentine's Day."

"Is that something you're interested in?"

"I like to keep busy," she admitted, feeling herself totally relax. "You know, Fin used to live in LA. She might have contacts that could be helpful."

"Helpful?" Boone rubbed her arch from the heel to the ball of her foot. "In what way?"

"The big job search." Roe expelled a breath of pure bliss. "I need to find another position. Thanks to living here rent-free, I can make it through until Dakota's wedding, no problem. But I really need to have some solid prospects by February fourteenth."

He stopped his ministrations, and concern filled his brown eyes. "Will you return to Minneapolis?"

"If there's a job there, sure. I'd be happy to stay there, but I don't think I'll find another job I want in that area." Roe wanted to be realistic and needed to be smart about this. "Most of my experience is in theater management. There are opportunities, but to pull in a big fish, I have to cast a wide net."

Like *yummy*, the analogy made her smile. Or maybe it was that he moved on to toe bends.

"What about your place in Minneapolis?"

Though his fingers continued to massage, he was giving her his full attention, and Roe found it to be a heady experience. "My lease was up December first. I hadn't renewed, as I was looking for something closer to the theater. If I do go back to the Twin Cities, I'd need to find a new place anyway."

She cocked her head. This conversation shouldn't be all about her. "What about you?"

"What do you mean?"

"What happens if, for some reason, you can't return to the team?" She stretched, the warmth from the fire making her sleepy. "Will you stay in Denver?"

His fingers stilled. "I am returning."

But what if you can't?

The question pushed against her lips, but Roe swallowed the words before they could spill out. She reminded herself that he'd lived in Denver for eight years and had played for the Grizzlies since college. The mere thought of losing all that had to be traumatic.

"Of course you will." Her words had the tense set to his jaw relaxing. Had he really thought she'd press the point? Especially when she didn't understand how any of the football stuff worked?

"Everyone at the party seemed friendly." Safer, she thought, to return to discussing the party.

"They did. A couple of the guys invited me to play on their pond hockey team. Apparently, they've got a big game with their rival coming up."

"Is pond hockey like regular hockey?"

"Similar." Boone's dark brows pulled together in thought. "The environment is different, of course, with the ice outside being uneven, and the area is smaller."

"What else is different?" She vowed to keep the focus off football.

His fingers returned to her foot, and he began pressing on the pressure points on her instep.

"Usually fewer players." Boone's gaze turned thoughtful. "While the pond hockey structure is usually more relaxed, it sounds like this rivalry is intense."

"Are you able to play?"

Boone shook his head. "I'd like to, but my doctor and the coaches would have my head on a stick if I did. I have strict orders to avoid all contact sports. There can be a lot of contact in hockey." A wistful look filled his eyes.

"When is the game? We could go watch." The second the words left Roe's lips, she wished she could pull them back. They weren't a couple.

"Next Saturday. At Rakes Farm. Two o'clock." He studied her. "Do you work on Saturdays?"

The hope that had begun to build inside Roe deflated like a popped balloon. "I work eleven to two."

"I could pick you up when you get off. We could head straight over there."

"You'd be late."

"I don't need to be there for the whole thing," he told her. "Besides, it would be more fun having you with me."

Her gaze met his. Electricity sizzled in the space between them. Roe couldn't have looked away even if she'd wanted to.

Without taking his eyes off her, Boone slipped her feet from his lap and swung them to the floor.

For a second, she swore he was going to kiss her. And she was going to kiss him back.

Her lips tingled, imagining the taste of—

"I enjoyed spending the evening with you." He stood and, before she could respond, disappeared down the hall.

~

Roe woke the next morning to the deep rumble of a snowblower motor. She hopped out of bed and had her clothes pulled on in record time. Boone better not be out there with the Beast.

Though if not him, then who would it be?

Pausing only once she reached the mudroom leading to the garage to pull on her boots, she stepped into the garage just in time to see Boone parking the Beast.

"Good morning. Perfect timing. I just finished." The pride in his voice and the healthy flush in his cheeks stopped any reproach.

Losing his spot on the team, even temporarily due to a medical reason, had to be a blow to his ego. He was an active guy, used to working hard and playing just as hard. Now, he'd been asked to curtail all that energy.

Roe walked to the opening of the garage and stared out over the drive and walkway. "I was going to see if there was anything I could do to help. I see I'm not needed."

"I wouldn't say that." He chuckled, his husky voice deep and sensual.

The intense connection she'd experienced last night wrapped around her like a tight glove. She cleared her throat. "On second glance, I see something that is desperately needed."

Stepping to a spot beside her, he studied the yard for several seconds, his brows pulled together in puzzlement. "What?"

"A snowman."

A smile lifted the corners of his lips. "I can't recall the last time I built one."

"It's been a long time for me, too." Roe hesitated as another thought struck her. "Do you think that would be too strenuous? I don't want to—"

"Let's do it."

The passion in his eyes had her heart stumbling—until Roe reminded herself that it was all about the snow and his desire to stay physically active. That passion had nothing to do with the thought of having sex with her.

CHAPTER TEN

"We did a magnificent job." Roe stood back and surveyed their masterpiece. "If I do say so myself."

The snowman, standing six feet tall, had a solid round base, a smaller midsection and a slightly elongated head.

Boone gave an approving nod. "Using the rocks for the eyes was a smart move."

"The quarters were a good idea, but they didn't stand out enough."

"Agreed." Boone's gaze dropped to the nose. "I'm glad we had carrots. A carrot nose is a classic."

"It's slightly bent—"

"Doesn't matter," Boone interrupted. "It's a carrot."

"I can't believe you had red licorice." They'd been strategizing on what to use for the mouth when Boone had suddenly remembered a package of red licorice in the cupboard.

"What can I say?" He shot her a wink. "I'm a kid at heart."

They'd certainly frolicked like two kids as they'd rolled the snow into balls. Roe had accepted his assistance in putting the second ball on top of the base but had insisted it be a team effort.

Now, it was done. "It makes me kind of sad that—"

Something hit her in the middle of the back. Though she'd never been slow on the uptake, it took Roe a few seconds to figure out he'd thrown a snowball at her.

She whirled and saw Boone already forming a second snowball. This time, she was ready. She feigned left just before he let it fly, and it flew past her and hit a blue spruce. Growing up with three older brothers had taught her many skills, including how to hold her own in a snowball fight.

Staying mobile was the key. Moving made her harder to hit. As the snowballs came fast and furious, Roe zigged, then zagged, and tried to move in unpredictable ways.

She wished she had a stash of snowballs. The attack had been unprovoked, leaving her no time to build an arsenal. Scooping up a handful of wet snow, she quickly formed the mass into a ball and took aim.

Because of his injury, she avoided his abdomen and went for the head. When the snowball hit him, she did a little happy dance.

Big mistake.

His next snowball hit her in the belly.

Under heavy attack, she pretended to retreat behind the tree, luring Boone into an ambush when he came after her.

The skirmish ended with them both laughing and out of breath. Or rather, with her out of breath.

"This was fun." It was the truth. Roe couldn't recall the last time she'd played in the snow, or really, the last time she'd played at all.

He slung an arm companionably around her shoulders. "I wasn't hungry before, but I am now."

She looked up at him. "You made breakfast the last time. Why don't you relax, and I'll do the honors?"

Before she knew what was happening, he leaned over and kissed her gently on the lips. "Sounds like a plan."

The smile remained on her lips. "What was that for?"

Boone's dark eyes turned watchful. "I'm sorry. I should have asked before I did that. I've wanted to kiss you since last night. I got the feeling you wanted that, too, but still, I should have made sure. Did I misread?"

"No." Raising up on tiptoes, she pressed her mouth against his cool, smooth lips and let it linger for several heartbeats. "You read the signals perfectly."

To Roe's dismay, there was no more kissing the rest of the day. Some might have said it wasn't smart for there to be *any* kissing. After all, their situation was a very temporary one. Still, Roe wasn't worried about getting attached. She'd been down this road many times before.

She knew there could be nothing substantial between them. Either she or he would be gone before anything could develop. That didn't mean she couldn't enjoy the time they had. And if that meant a few kisses, or maybe more, well, she would enjoy this time while it lasted.

On Monday, she showed up for a three-hour shift at Muddy Boots. The tables in her section were never empty. Once one set of customers got up, the table was quickly bussed, and more customers were seated.

Roe had found her rhythm. She enjoyed the busy pace and the tips. During December, servers wore Santa hats and red T-shirts with the Muddy Boots logo, which was a young girl wearing a raincoat and boots kicking up water. According to Helen, the wording on the shirts varied from year to year.

This holiday season, it was "Kicking up a Merry Christmas."

Just wearing the shirt and Santa hat made Roe feel more festive. On the drive home that afternoon, she found herself humming Christmas carols while wondering how Boone's day had gone.

He was a physical guy, used to working out and being

constantly on the move. Sitting around and taking it easy didn't come naturally to him.

His truck was in the garage when she pulled in, so that was a good thing—as was that no more snow had fallen.

If they'd gotten more of the white stuff, she would have worried all day about him taking the Beast out while she was working.

As she headed inside, she hoped he'd spent the day playing video games or doing laundry or something else equally easy on the body.

She found him in the kitchen, staring out the window. For a second, Roe thought he was watching the bird feeder that hung from the branch of a nearby tree directly in front of the window.

When Roe had first arrived, she'd taken it upon herself to buy a big sack of seeds to keep the birds fed.

Right now, a large dove sat perched on the feeder.

"I love doves." Roe slipped into the spot at his side. "Or is that a pigeon? Is there a difference?"

"Huh?" Boone turned toward her as if realizing for the first time that she was home.

"Pigeon?" She gestured with one hand toward the window. "Or dove?"

"I don't know," was all he said as he refocused his attention out the window.

Was there something she was missing out there? Had she been so intrigued at seeing a dove that she'd failed to see something far more important?

Redirecting her gaze to the wider area beyond the feeder, Roe searched for whatever it was that so clearly had Boone's attention.

Acres of snow-blanketed wilderness surrounded the cabin, and this view toward the back was no different. Evergreen trees with green spires reached for the sky, their snow-covered boughs a haven for birds and squirrels.

What am I missing? Roe cast a sideways glance at him.

His continued silence, solemn expression and pulled-together brows told Roe something was wrong.

Scanning the area again and still coming up empty had her asking, "What do you see?"

Once again, he turned to her. "I don't see anything."

"Then what's wrong?"

"I chopped firewood while you were gone." He winced. "My wound, ribs, whatever, are giving me some trouble."

"You chopped wood?" She stared at him wide-eyed. "Are you serious?"

"We were running low."

"I could have swung by the market and bought some."

He made a face. "Not necessary."

"It is when you're not supposed to do any heavy work, and I have no desire to swing an ax." She took a step closer. "Let me see."

"See what?"

"Your wound." Roe adopted the take-charge attitude that such carelessness demanded. "Pull up your shirt."

When he hesitated, she put her hands on her hips. "There's nothing you can show me that I haven't seen before."

His lips twitched.

"I meant that I have brothers. I've seen male chests before."

"I know what you meant."

"Just lift your shirt." A thought struck her. "I assume you've already checked your incision."

"I did." He pulled the sea-green sweater up over his head, showing the gray T-shirt underneath.

Instead of removing that shirt, he grabbed the hem and raised it.

Roe wasn't sure what she'd expected, but the eight-inch scar in the upper left part of his abdomen, just under the ribcage, didn't cause her worry meter to spike.

She reached out to trace the skin beneath it, then thought better of it and pulled her hand back.

Roe lifted her gaze to find Boone intently studying her.

"It looks okay." She offered a tentative smile. "So when you say the area is giving you trouble, do you mean it hurts?"

"A bit."

Roe guessed it probably hurt a lot for this man to admit any pain at all. "I'm sure there's a doctor or two in town. We should get you checked out."

"We?"

"You don't think I'd let you drive yourself when you're in pain, do you?"

"I'm fine."

"When I was around ten, my brother Ben—he was twelve at the time—mentioned he had this pain in his lower right abdomen. He said it was probably something he ate."

"I'm guessing since you're telling me this story that it wasn't something he ate."

"You catch on quick." Roe flashed a smile. "It was his appendix. If my parents hadn't ignored his protests and taken him in to be checked, he could have died. It was ready to burst."

"This isn't my appendix." His lips lifted in a half smile before he winced again. "And my spleen already ruptured."

"Well, then, that's one thing the doctor can rule out."

"How do you know there is even a doctor in this town?"

"Every town has at least one." Roe slipped the phone from her pocket. "It's easy enough to find out where she or he is."

Roe discovered she could drive down Wrigley Road on the outskirts of Good Hope and see nothing for a mile or so until, suddenly, businesses appeared on both sides of the street. It was as if she'd been slogging through a desert of sand and come upon an oasis.

A 3-D image of a tall shelf filled with brightly colored books topped with a cup of steaming coffee decorated the front of a business called Book & Cup. On the front of Echoes of Yesterday antique store, steps had been painted, the kind you might see on an old brownstone. As if tossed carelessly on the steps, a discarded rag doll and an old-fashioned top had been painted.

Roe recalled an afternoon she and Dakota had spent exploring the Northeast Minneapolis Arts District. Some of the art they'd admired was similar to what Roe saw now.

Dakota had mentioned that an artist in her hometown painted 3-D murals. She'd called it anamorphic art. Since one of Dakota's brothers was an artist, Dakota was well-versed in the lingo.

The building housing the doctor's office was impossible to miss, as a stethoscope and thermometer loomed out from the building.

"I don't know that I've ever seen anything quite like this art," Boone murmured, his gaze focused on the Ding-A-Ling bar with its 3-D beer mug.

"It's amazing, isn't it?" Roe pulled into a parking spot directly in front of Good Hope Family Practice. A search for the peninsula's best doctors had led her here. "Apparently, it was done by a local artist."

"Well, whoever did it has talent."

When Roe pushed open her door, Boone held up a hand.

"Roe. Stop. I don't need to go in. I—"

Without thinking, Roe reached over and grasped his hand.

"Please." Her eyes met his. "Just get checked out."

"I suppose." He gave a reluctant nod. "Since we're here and all, might as well go in."

The bells over the door jingled as they pushed it open and stepped inside. Though Roe had to admit that the interior had a soothing vibe with its light blue walls and gray chairs, when compared to the outside, it was nothing special.

There was no one at the reception window, but a man soon appeared, wearing a white lab coat. One hand rested on the shoulder of one of the rowdy redheaded teen boys Roe recognized from Muddy Boots on her first day. A woman who must be his mother followed behind.

The doctor cast a quick, assessing glance in Roe and Boone's direction, then apparently seeing nothing that required his immediate attention, shot them a smile. "I'll be with you in a minute."

He then turned back to the woman. "You know the drill, Prim. Rest, ice, compression and elevation for the rest of the week. Ibuprofen for pain. Since Callum's wrist isn't broken or sprained, I expect it to return to normal in a week."

"Max and I will make sure he doesn't abuse it," Prim promised, casting a stern look at the boy.

"The Chill Billies' starting and reserve players are battling it out tomorrow. The game with Sturgeon is on Saturday," Callum reminded her.

"You may have to skip it, Callum." His mother's tone brooked no argument. "Actions have consequences."

"Mooooom," Callum protested.

Prim shook her head. "I can't imagine what possessed you to go down that railing in a parking garage."

"I told you. It's too cold to take my skateboard outside. The garage is perfect." Pride filled his voice.

"Perfect for injuring yourself," she shot back.

"I nailed that move."

Prim's freckles shone like newly minted copper pennies against her pale cheeks. "If you nailed it, you wouldn't have fallen."

"I nailed it the first time." Callum's smile turned rueful. "Slipped out on a 5-0 grind and slammed hard on the repeat."

Her lips tightened. "You've got to stop these reckless behaviors, Callum."

"I wasn't being reckless," he protested before turning back to the doctor. "If I skip the practice, can I play in the game on Saturday?"

"If I tape your wrist before the game and you promise to wear a wrist guard, I'm good with it." The doctor shifted his gaze to Prim. "As long as it's okay with your parents."

Before Callum could say anything more, Prim pinned him with a steely gaze. "We'll discuss this tonight."

"It doesn't even hurt that much," Callum muttered as he headed for the door.

Prim shot Roe and Boone a quick smile as she hurried after her son.

The door had barely shut behind them when the doctor stepped to them. "Sorry for the wait. My assistant is home sick, so it's just me holding down the fort today. I'm Dr. Theo Holbrook."

The doctor was a little over six feet tall, with thick brown hair the color of rich walnut. He was as lean and muscular as Boone, with broad shoulders and narrow hips. The hazel eyes he fixed on them held a smile. "How can I help?"

Roe opened her mouth, her nerves pushing her to jump in and insert herself into this visit. But then she shut her mouth, reminding herself that this was Boone's deal, not hers.

That didn't mean she wasn't worried. She hoped everything was okay with him. When he'd told her he'd been swinging an ax and then mentioned the pain, she'd wanted to shake some sense into him and hug him all in the same breath. The intensity of her concern had surprised her.

Even though she knew it was best not to get attached and that anything between them would be light and casual holiday fun, she worried she was developing feelings for Jason Boone.

From the corner of her eye, Roe saw Boone study the doctor

with an intense look he likely reserved for opposing players on the other side of the line of scrimmage.

"Do we know each other?" Boone asked.

Theo studied him. "Maybe. I'm not sure from where."

"Did you play ball for U of M?" Boone asked.

A slow smile lifted Dr. Holbrook's lips. "Jason Boone. Ohio State."

"I thought you'd go pro, then you dropped out of sight."

"I injured some tendons in my kneecap the last regular game of my senior year." Theo shrugged. "Instead of turning pro, I went to med school."

"I went the pro route."

Awareness flashed in Theo's hazel depths. "That's right. You're with the Grizzlies."

"I'm on medical leave at the moment." Boone's tone remained casual. "Took a bad hit. My spleen ruptured, and I'm out for the rest of the season."

"I'm sorry to hear that." Theo's expression suddenly turned all business. "Are you having issues?"

Boone hesitated for so long that Roe was once again oh-so-tempted to jump in. She bit her tongue.

"I'm recuperating at a cabin here in Good Hope owned by Krew Slattery."

"I know Krew and Cass. They're good people."

"They are. Well, there is a fireplace, and wood was getting low, so I decided to chop some and then bring it inside." Boone continued as if simply stating he'd gone out to lunch. "Right after I did, I started feeling some pain in the area of my incision. There's no redness or swelling like the doctors told me to watch for, just the pain."

"On a scale of one to ten, what would you rate it?" Theo's entire attention remained firmly focused on Boone.

It was, Roe thought, as if she didn't exist.

"Eight."

Eight? Roe blinked. Eight was, well, far worse than she'd imagined. How could he have, for one second, considered not being checked out?

"I'd like to see the incision, maybe press around a little bit. Get a feel for what might be going on. Why don't you come with me?" Without waiting to see if Boone would follow, Theo turned and walked down the hall.

Roe hung back. Her plan was to sit in one of the lovely gray chairs and wait.

Boone stopped and turned back to her. "Come with me?"

"Are you sure you want me to?"

"Absolutely." Boone winced, then forced a smile. "That way, you can hear for yourself that this is nothing to worry about."

CHAPTER ELEVEN

Once the visit concluded, Boone suggested they grab lunch at the Ding-A-Ling bar down the street. A banner tied between two posts advertised whitefish tacos for ninety-nine cents.

Boone admitted he'd felt relieved when Theo had told him that the pain likely came from the ribs and wasn't an issue with the splenectomy not healing correctly.

"I didn't know you also broke a couple of ribs." Roe sat across from him in the booth. She sipped the hot buttered rum, the drink special of the day.

Choosing to go the healthy route, Boone stuck with water. "Rib fractures usually go hand in hand with any hit hard enough to rupture your spleen."

"I'm glad the doctor thinks you didn't do any real damage."

"I knew I hadn't." Not entirely true. He hadn't *thought* he had, but knowing all was good made the difference. Boone could now let out the breath he hadn't realized he'd been holding.

"I can't believe you knew Dr. Holbrook."

"That was a surprise." As was discovering that the man he'd once lined up against was a husband and father.

"I have three brothers," Roe confided. "I understand."

"Your boy is a good player." Boone's gaze returned to the action. "Not only does he have excellent skating skills, he has situational awareness."

Roe wasn't sure what situational awareness was, but Chelsea appeared to know.

"His first love is lacrosse," Chelsea advised.

"The skills he learned in lacrosse likely help him on the ice."

"Do you skate?" Chelsea asked Boone.

"I do, but I had surgery several weeks ago, so I'm sidelined for the season."

"I'm sorry to hear that." Chelsea made a face. "That has to be hard."

"No fun at all," he agreed but didn't elaborate.

"Is your son in high school?" Roe asked. "Or home from college?"

"Age-wise, he should be a junior in high school, but he and his sister are on track to graduate in May." At Roe's curious glance, Chelsea added, "Ric and Emily are twins. They can't wait to go off to college. Me, I can't help wishing they'd be at home just a little while longer."

Roe glanced down at Zeke. "You'll still have one in the house."

"We will." Chelsea put a hand on Zeke's shoulder. "Thank goodness."

The flash of envy that sliced through Roe took her by surprise. She'd never thought much about having children. She was fairly sure she wanted them, just not now. Especially since, in her mind, love came first, then marriage, then children. She realized she was a bit of a traditionalist in that regard, but she couldn't help how she felt.

A whistle sounded. Immediately, cheering, whistles and clapping filled the air.

Chelsea turned to Roe. "It was nice meeting you. I hope our paths cross again."

Then she was gone, keeping her son's hand gripped tightly in hers while weaving her way through the crowd.

As she and Boone walked to their car, the blond girl they'd seen behind the counter at Blooms Bake Shop handed them a flyer.

Roe studied it as she continued to walk.

"What is it?" Boone asked.

"It's advertising a Christmas tree lot that is giving twenty percent of its sales today to the Giving Tree."

"What's a giving tree?" Boone must have spoken louder than he'd intended, or maybe the older woman standing beside him, sporting a braid coiled like a snake on the top of her head, had eagle ears.

"The Giving Tree started out as a Christmas gift project sponsored by the Rotary," the woman explained. "I'm Etta, by the way. Etta Hawley."

"It's nice to meet you, Etta." Roe would have introduced herself, but the woman continued without taking a breath.

"Over the years, the Giving Tree expanded into a year-round neighbor-helping-neighbor fund. It's a way of extending a hand to those in the community who may have fallen on hard times."

"That's a wonderful idea." Roe couldn't recall any of the communities where she'd lived having such a program.

"All that to say, if you need a Christmas tree or wreath," Etta pointed to the flyer, "do it today and help a neighbor out."

CHAPTER TWELVE

Roe stood in the great room and stared at a space before the window. Her conversation at the pond with Etta had gotten her Christmas wheels spinning. "I've never gone a year without a tree."

Boone stopped himself on his way into the kitchen. "I can't recall the last time I had one."

"My trees since college haven't been big or anything elaborate," she admitted, "but I always put one up. It helps get me into the Christmas spirit. I guess that streak ends this year."

"It doesn't have to," Boone told her. "Christmas is still a couple of weeks away. There's no reason we can't put up a tree. This room certainly has space for one."

Roe tapped two fingers against her lips. "We could get a tree, but there is the issue of ornaments. I mean, this isn't our place. What we choose might not be what Krew and Cassie want. What would we do with them when we leave?"

"Toss them in the trash?"

Roe stared at him wide-eyed.

"Just kidding." Boone laughed. "Donating them is an option."

"That would work. We could take your truck and get a tree now," Roe suggested.

"Or we could do it tomorrow."

"If we get it today, twenty percent will go to the Giving Tree."

It didn't take them long to reach the lot and agree on a tree, a five-foot Scotch pine that looked as good as it smelled.

They stopped at a store to pick up a tree stand, lights and two economy-sized containers filled with enough ornaments to decorate a tree twice this size.

On the way home, they swung by Bayside Pizza to pick some dinner.

Boone now sat at the table with a pizza slice before him and a table filled with ornaments. "This has been the strangest day."

He gazed at the tree. While not particularly tall—he had wanted to go bigger until Roe reminded him of the no-heavy-lifting rule—it was perfectly shaped and looked good in the spot Roe had chosen, directly in front of the picture window in the great room.

According to Roe, the lights went on first. A background of clear lights had been strung, followed by colored lights that wrapped around the outer part of the tree.

Had they done that at home all those years earlier, before his mom and sister had left? It was so long ago, Boone couldn't recall.

Roe bit into a slice of pizza and studied the ornaments they'd carefully removed from the plastic containers and spread across the large table.

They probably could have gotten by with just one package, but Roe liked traditional ornaments with classic Christmas motifs, such as Santa Claus, angels and reindeer. Boone was drawn to the more abstract, modern designs with sleek, polished finishes.

They'd compromised by each getting a pack of ornaments.

"This one." Roe lifted a ceramic silver reindeer.

Taking a long drink of beer, Boone picked up a geometric-shaped ornament sporting a design that reminded him of van Gogh's *Starry Night* painting. He put it with her reindeer. "Your turn."

Boone had no clue what their tree would look like, but could a Christmas tree ever be ugly?

He and was considering his next pick when his phone buzzed. Glancing down, his heart jumped when he saw the name on the screen. Krew Slattery.

Roe looked up, clearly curious, as he pushed back his chair and stood.

"This should just take a minute," he told her as he strode from the room, the phone pressed against his ear. "Coach. It's good to hear from you."

Boone liked the Grizzlies' receivers coach. Krew had once played the position, and that experience translated into an ability to provide valuable insights to his players. The man also had great analytical skills. His skill at breaking down game film to identify the strengths and weaknesses of individual players and opponents was well known.

Krew was also a nice guy who built strong relationships with players based on mutual respect and trust.

"How are you feeling?"

"Better every day." Boone wished he could say that he was ready to be on the field again, but even if he could get a doctor to sign off, he knew he was nowhere near ready to play at the high level required.

To play at less than that level wouldn't be fair to himself or his teammates.

"The cabin thing with you and Roe, it's working out?"

Boone turned slightly and watched Roe bite her lip, her face a study in concentration as she picked up one ornament and then set it down. "It's working well. The cabin is big. We're both good at compromise, so I guess you could say we're peacefully coexisting."

"I'm glad to hear that." Some of the tension left Krew's voice. "Roe has said as much to Dakota, but it's good to know you both feel that way."

"I appreciate you letting me stay here. I want you to know that we're taking good care of the place."

"I did not doubt that." Krew said something to someone in the room with him, then returned to his conversation with Boone. "If there are any issues, text."

"Will do."

"And, Boone."

"Yes, Coach."

"I realize this enforced rest isn't what you wanted. But I hope you take this opportunity to relax and enjoy yourself. I can tell you from personal experience that there isn't a better place to spend Christmas than Good Hope."

After ending the call, Boone strode back into the great room and sat at the table.

"That was Krew," he told Roe, though she hadn't asked. "Checking in."

After gesturing to a metal snowflake she'd added to the chosen pile in his absence, Roe smiled. "Dakota checks in with me every few days. She's crazy busy with work and with her wedding now only two months away, but she makes the time. She's thoughtful that way."

Boone didn't know Krew's daughter well, although he'd seen and spoken with her briefly a couple of times. He still found it difficult to believe that Krew had a daughter who was old enough to get married. "What's her fiancé like?"

"Nolan is wonderful." A smile lifted Roe's lips. "He's quiet and more of an introvert, which surprise me initially because Dakota is so outgoing. Once you get to know him, though, he opens up and is a lot of fun."

"Does he work with her?" Boone wasn't sure why he was asking all the questions. It wasn't as if it mattered. It was just that there was something nice about having a casual conversation with Roe while a fire blazed in the hearth and snow fell gently outside the windows.

While Boone would give anything to be outside on a snowmobile right now or traversing a wide expanse of white in snowshoes or a pair of cross-country skis, for now, he was stuck inside, picking ornaments for a tree he hadn't known he wanted.

Shifting his gaze to the twinkling lights on the tree, he realized he couldn't wait to see what the Scotch pine looked like covered in ornaments.

"Nolan is a forensic accountant. The firm he works for is in the same building as the PR firm where Dakota works." Roe gestured toward the ornaments. "Your turn."

"Forensic accounting?" Boone chewed on the words. "Sounds like an interesting career."

"He's a CPA with some kind of certification in fraud and financial forensics." Roe gave a little laugh. "Don't hold me to that. It's something like that, anyway."

"I'm surprised Dakota didn't try to match you up with one of his friends."

Roe smiled. "Who said she didn't?"

He inclined his head.

"She tried several times, in fact."

"Forensic accountants are not your type?"

"Those guys weren't." Her smile came easily. "You know how it is. You click with some but not with others. I think I had… It's not important."

She motioned again for him to pick an ornament.

Boone ignored the gesture.

"Don't leave me hanging," he teased. "You had what?"

Two bright swaths of pink colored her cheeks. "I had a premonition I'd soon be leaving Minneapolis. Nothing had been said at the theater. I mean, I knew that the decreased revenue was a concern, but really, when isn't it in community theater? So many things can affect both the costs and the revenue. I just had this feeling I would be relocating, so I chose not to get attached."

"Do you think it's as simple as saying to yourself that you don't want to get attached?" Boone took another bite of pizza, his eyes settling for a moment on a glass—or rather, a plastic—lighted reindeer with a surprisingly cheeky grin. He could definitely see this bad boy at the top of the tree. "I mean, if you'd really hit it off with one of these guys and felt you had a strong connection, are you telling me you'd have just walked away?"

Roe carefully considered Boone's question. "I know where you're going with this, but really, what choice would I have? I support myself. If my job no longer existed, and there was nothing in the Twin Cities available—which there isn't—I'd have to move."

"So you'd leave behind someone you liked a lot, maybe even loved?"

After studying him for a long moment, Roe finally spoke. "Let's reverse things. You find a woman you like in Denver, but the team trades you to Philadelphia. What choice do you have but to pack up and leave?"

"You make a good point."

His easy acquiescence threw Roe off her stride and had her taking a step back. "I'm not saying if there was something between me and someone else that I wouldn't be willing to try a long-distance relationship, but I haven't seen too many LDRs go the distance."

"Yeah, I hear you."

"It's nice that neither of us is involved with anyone." She chuckled. "Can you imagine how our partners would feel about us living here together?"

"Thankfully, we don't have that worry."

"A true blessing," Roe decreed.

She just wasn't sure why it didn't feel like a blessing. Instead, the knowledge that she was just as alone now at twenty-nine as she had been over ten years earlier when she left home for college filled her with sadness.

It wasn't that she needed to be involved with a man to be happy. There were plenty of people she knew who had significant others and plenty without. Some were happy in their relationships. Others would have been happier single.

A partner wasn't the only thing she lacked—she longed for friends. Dakota was a close friend, but she would soon be married and living in a totally different city. Possibly—probably—in an entirely different state.

Over time, their friendship would likely be relegated to texts only at Christmas and on their birthdays.

The thought brought a tightness to her chest and an aching for all she'd lost. Roe remembered all too well the friends who had come in and out of her life with each move. Most were now out of her life entirely, and likely for good.

Would it be that way with her and Dakota? She wanted to say no, but experience had her blinking rapidly as a lump formed in her throat. She cleared it.

She started when a hand reached past her, brushing against hers.

Roe looked up to find Boone studying her.

Something in his eyes told her he saw beyond her bright façade.

"Let's put the ornaments we've chosen on the tree, then take a break," he said.

"But we just got started." Despite her words, Roe followed Boone's lead and pushed back her chair. "What do you have in mind?"

"We should take a walk." Boone's voice remained casual as he hung an ornament that reminded her of *Starry Night* on a branch. "It's a beautiful evening. It seems a shame not to take advantage of it."

Roe, who'd just picked up the snowflake ornament, paused. "Shouldn't you be resting?"

"I'm tired of sitting around and doing nothing."

"But—"

"You worry about you. I'll worry about me." Stepping close, he put his hands on her shoulders, the simple touch sending heat coursing through her body. His dark eyes met hers. "Deal?"

He'd made his feelings clear.

"Deal." Roe shoved down her worry. A walk down the lane did sound lovely.

"Great."

She returned his smile, suddenly warm all over.

Roe realized that losing her job had proven to have unexpected benefits. She couldn't even recall the last time she'd taken a vacation.

She hadn't stayed in her previous positions long enough to accrue many days off, and the days she'd had had been used for family events.

Once she started her new position, wherever it ended up being, it would be the same. While this time in Good Hope wasn't exactly a gift, that's what it was beginning to feel like.

When Boone held out a hand to her as they stepped outside, her heart gave a leap. Yes, that's what this was beginning to feel like—the gift of time to relax and enjoy a sexy man for Christmas.

The walk down the lane might have proved treacherous since the yard light's glow extended only to the immediate area around the house, but millions of stars glittered brightly tonight, and a large moon hung like a golden orb lighting their path.

Still, the snow-packed lane was icy in parts, but Boone had offered his arm once they started walking.

"It's so quiet." Roe wasn't sure why she spoke softly when no one was around to hear her. No one but Boone. And an owl hooting softly in the distance.

"I like the quiet."

She liked it that when she slipped, he tightened his hold and shot her a wink. "If we go down, we go down together."

Roe couldn't help but laugh. "That's a happy thought."

His smile flashed as bright as the moon. "I'm a happy guy."

Roe realized that at this specific moment in time, she was a happy gal. Or at least a content one. "I'm looking forward to helping out at the Community Playhouse on Wednesday."

"What exactly will you be doing?" Once again, his hand tightened protectively around her arm as they negotiated around a dip in their path.

"Likely backstage stuff. You know, working on sets, that sort of thing." Roe lifted her face, reveling in the cool, crisp breeze against her cheeks. "I'm hoping that Gladys will let me do more once she sees I wasn't kidding about my experience. I'd love to direct a few rehearsals."

"If she doesn't know that by now…" He paused. "Forget it."

"No." She stopped and turned to face him. "What were you going to say?"

"Anyone who talks to you for more than five minutes can tell you're not someone who would lie." He brushed a strand of hair that had pulled loose from her stocking hat. "You're also smart and organized and—"

Roe laughed. "Stop. All this praise will go to my head."

"It's not praise." He spoke in a matter-of-fact tone. "It's the truth."

"Well, thank you." She rose up and brushed his cold lips with hers. "Kind words are always appreciated."

His gaze traveled slowly over her, and his eyes seemed to glitter as brightly as the stars overhead. Then his arms stole around her, pulling her to him as his mouth closed over hers.

Boone kissed her with a slow thoroughness that left her weak, trembling and longing for more.

His sudden release had her stumbling back. She might have fallen, but Boone grabbed her arms and steadied her.

His gaze searched her face. "I'm sorry if I overstepped."

Roe couldn't have stopped the smile that blossomed on her lips even if she wanted to. "You didn't overstep. I kissed you first. In fact, I want to kiss you again."

She didn't say more. His arms encircled her as his mouth once again closed over hers.

CHAPTER THIRTEEN

Wednesday afternoon, Gladys tapped a bright red nail against the clipboard. Roe had promised to help with the set-building today and had promised to bring Boone with her. She'd said she'd be here at two fifteen. It was now nearly two thirty, and there was no sign of either of them.

She really should have gotten her number so she could—

The door to the theater flew open. Gladys's irritation disappeared when she saw the two enter the theater.

Roe hurried to Gladys. "I'm so sorry. We had a crisis at the café and—"

"Thankfully, nothing involving a pot pie." Boone shot Gladys a wink.

"The cash register decided to go on strike." Roe sighed. "Fortunately, it returned to life after Helen got frustrated and gave it a solid whack. By then, we had customers lined up, wanting to check out. I couldn't walk out right then."

Gladys offered an understanding nod before shifting her attention to Boone.

"I'm so glad to see you today, Mr. Boone." Gladys allowed only the tiniest bit of pleasure to creep into her voice. She didn't want to scare him off by showing her cards too quickly. "We could really use your help."

"It's just Boone," he reminded her. "I'm happy to do what I can to help. If you need an extra set of inexperienced hands, that is."

"I'd love any assistance." Gladys suddenly remembered his injury. She pointed a finger at him, pausing to admire how the jewels on her hand caught the light. "Nothing too strenuous. Understand?"

"You got it." He glanced around. "Where do you need me?"

"We have painting that needs to be done. Callum." Gladys waved a hand and motioned to the boy in cargo shorts and a graphic tee who'd just entered the lobby. "After you get Roe and Boone started painting the flats, I want you and Brynn to run lines with Sarah Rose and Ava."

"Brynn is still pissed at me about coming in late today."

"I wasn't happy about that either." Gladys spoke matter-of-factly. "I forgave you. She will, as well."

Callum shrugged. "Maybe."

The boy turned and crossed the stage.

"Sounds like he and Brynn don't get along," Roe commented.

"Oh, they get along." Gladys shot Roe a wink. "Fighting today, loving tomorrow."

Callum was nearly out of sight when he skidded to a stop, apparently realizing he was alone. He turned and gestured to Roe and Boone. "Come on. Follow me."

"You two go." Gladys made a sweeping motion with her hand. "Enjoy."

Roe hurried to catch up to Callum.

Boone didn't have to hurry, his long strides quickly closing the distance, until he was side by side with the boy.

"How's the wrist?" Boone asked as if he and the boy were buddies. His easy familiarity and ability to make conversation with anyone was a talent that Roe admired.

For a second, Callum looked blank, then he grinned. "Good as new. I get to play in the game on Saturday."

"That's great news." Boone studied the boy curiously. "Are you the man in charge of this behind-the-scenes stuff?"

Callum laughed. "Naw, I'm more of a gofer."

"How'd you get involved with backstage?" Roe asked.

"Just lucky. Or, more accurately, unlucky." Callum's droll tone had both her and Boone hiding smiles. "My brother and I took a class in technical theater at school last semester. Gladys got wind of it and talked to our parents, and they volunteered Connor and me."

"How did Gladys know about the class?" Roe asked.

Callum shifted his attention to Roe and grinned. "You haven't been around long. Once you have, you'll understand and accept that Gladys knows everything. If she's hazy on a few details, Ruby and Katherine fill in the blanks."

"Are you interested in theater?" Roe inclined her head. "Is that why you took the class?"

Callum answered immediately, apparently not even needing to think about his response. "Hardly. It was simply an elective that fit with my schedule."

"I don't think I know what a technical theater class includes." Boone's gaze shifted from Callum to Roe, then back to the boy again.

That was one more thing Roe liked about Boone. The man didn't act like he had all the answers.

Before Roe could explain, Callum responded. "Think behind-the-scenes—set design and construction, lighting and sound, stuff like that."

Though Roe could have added a lot more, the boy did a credible job explaining.

"If theater isn't your passion, what do you want to do?" Roe studied the boy. "I assume you're graduating this May."

He could also be a college freshman home on break, but high school senior appeared more likely.

"I'm planning on attending Appalachian State University in North Carolina."

"Why there?" Though Boone's expression gave nothing away, Roe knew he was likely as surprised as she was by the choice.

"They have this cool Outdoor Experiential Education program. Most of the students in the program get certified in swift water rescue and become a wilderness first responder."

Roe smiled her approval. "You like helping people."

"I do, sure, but mainly, the program and region have everything I like—climbing, skiing, snowboarding, white water boating, all the fun stuff."

"Maybe even a skateboard park or two?" Roe suggested with a smile.

Callum's lips curved upward. "Absolutely."

"What about your brother?" Roe asked.

"Connor wants to stay close. He's thinking he might want to do something with math." Callum's tone made it clear what he thought of that option. "He'd like to attend a school in the area."

"But not you?" Roe wasn't sure why she pressed, perhaps because she found the differences between the identical twins fascinating.

"If I'm close, Mom and Dad will be on my back about staying safe." His blue eyes held a sardonic gleam. "The way I see it, what they don't know can't worry them."

More questions hovered on the edge of Roe's tongue, they but remained unspoken as they'd reached their destination.

"Here we are." Callum pointed to sheets of wood positioned on sawhorses. "Apply the primer, which is right there."

Following the direction of his gaze, Roe spotted the primer and the brushes. "Thanks, Callum."

"Sure." Shoving a mop of red curls out of his eyes, he turned to go.

"Stay safe," Roe called.

He turned back, a gleam in his eyes. "Where's the fun in that?"

〜

Eighteen-year-old Brynn Chapin believed herself to be a sensible young woman. She got excellent grades, participated in numerous extracurricular activities and worked part time at both Blooms Bake Shop and at the Good Tea tearoom owned by her mother.

The first step toward her career goal of becoming a clinical psychologist was to get her bachelor's degree in psychology from a top-rated school. She was well on her way to making that happen. Just this week, she'd received her Restrictive Early Action acceptance to Stanford.

Brynn was sensible in all areas of her life except for Callum Brody. The connection between her and Callum had started in childhood.

He'd been a terror even back then, but he had a kind heart, one he didn't let many see. Like when they'd played tag by her grandmother's pool, and she'd slipped and hit her head, landing facedown in the water.

His quick action of immediately going for help had saved her life that day. But Callum had still felt responsible and insisted on gifting her his prized possession—Rafael, a Teenage Mutant Ninja Turtle, as a reward for her bravery.

He'd been as sweet as he was bold and brash.

Though they never dated, they hung out when Callum was between girlfriends. Which wasn't often. Over the years, Brynn watched him ping-pong between girls. He had a type—the popular cheerleader type.

None of those girls knew him the way that she did or were as good a friend to him as she was. Especially his latest. Celia was the dance squad captain. She was nice enough and did well in her AP classes. But she was definitely a high-maintenance girlfriend.

Once school had started and it was clear Callum was crushing on her, CeCe had played hard to get for a while and then reeled him in.

The Dancin' Queen had quickly discovered that Callum Brody wasn't as easily "handled" as her former boyfriends. The two argued all the time. Callum hadn't been with her at the stroll. Brynn had heard the two were on the outs, but she had yet to confirm that bit of gossip.

Now that Callum would be working on Gladys's birthday party, Brynn was excited to get the scoop. Callum deserved better than CeCe. He deserved someone who understood him— someone like *her*.

Her attraction to Callum was something she'd never voiced aloud, not to Zoe or Emily or any of her other friends. As far as everyone was concerned, including Callum, she was simply his buddy.

Brynn returned to the workshop with an armful of freshly laundered rags to see Callum directing two volunteers to paint a flat.

When he saw her, Callum crossed the room to where she stood and lifted the pile of rags from her arms. "Let me take these."

"You don't need to—"

"I want to help." Glancing at the couple, Callum kept his voice low. "I'm sorry about being late. My car was out of gas, and Connor had to take me to get some."

She opened her mouth and lifted a hand.

Whatever she was about to say was forgotten when he grasped her hand. For the briefest of moments, the simple touch made breathing, much less speaking, impossible.

"No excuses." Those incredible blue eyes met hers. "I should have gotten gas last night so I'd be prepared. I won't make that mistake again."

Across the room, Roe watched the teens' interaction. "I wonder what's going on between those two."

After studying them, Boone smiled. "I think they're on the verge of kissing and making up."

Roe gave a low chuckle. "Young love. Even when they don't know what it is, it's still pretty special."

Leaning over, Roe scooped up two paintbrushes, handing one to Boone and keeping one for herself.

"I bet you were a heartbreaker when you were their age."

Boone's comment had a laugh rising up inside Roe and spilling out. "Hardly."

"I don't believe it." He dipped his brush in the paint tray.

"Well, it's true." Roe's thoughts drifted back to those high school years, a time that now seemed a lifetime ago. "I didn't live anywhere long enough to break anyone's heart."

Boone studied her. "What was the longest you were in the same school?"

Roe flipped the still-dry paintbrush over and over in her hand and considered. "Eighteen months."

"More than enough time." Boone surprised her by leaning forward and brushing a kiss across her lips. "We've known each other for far less time, and I can already see that you could break my heart."

He didn't even glance at the teenagers across the room, and she didn't either. It was as if she and Boone were alone, bound together by an invisible web of attraction.

Roe wasn't certain if it was the words or the serious look in his eyes that had her heart stuttering. Still, he had to be joking, right?

The strange thing was, in the short time they'd been together, Roe had grown very—okay, *extremely* fond of him. She already knew that when their time together in the cabin was up, she would miss him.

Would she break his heart? Would he break hers?

She didn't want to consider either possibility. Not right now.

As she couldn't think of a better way to respond, she settled for a smile and gestured to the paint. "What do you say we get to work?"

CHAPTER FOURTEEN

Marigold arrived at the cabin on Friday with her three children. With Boone busy at the Y, Roe decided the timing of the visit couldn't have worked out better.

Yesterday, Boone's doctor had given him the okay to start a list of specific strengthening and cardio exercises. Boone wasted no time in setting up a session with a trainer. He'd left the house in high spirits that morning.

Of course, it didn't really matter that he wasn't there. Even if he had been home, there would have been plenty of space for him to escape any noise.

"You're right," Marigold said after Roe finished the tour. "This place is unlike any cabin I've seen. Thanks for showing me around."

"Mommy, what can we do?" Dressed all in pink, Faith looked like a petite fairy princess with her mass of blond curly hair and elfin features.

Hope reminded Roe of Cade with her silky dark hair, dove-gray eyes and penetrating gaze.

Before seeing the girls, Roe had wondered if the twins were identical, but one look answered that question.

Caleb, the only boy in the threesome, had golden-brown hair and happy eyes. Unlike Faith, who chattered constantly, and Hope, who watched and analyzed, Caleb fell somewhere in between.

Marigold glanced pointedly at the half-finished puzzle the children had been putting together while Roe showed her the cabin. "Start by finishing the puzzle. Then you can look in the bag I brought and decide what to play with next. Sound good?"

The threesome nodded and immediately reached for puzzle pieces.

"I can't imagine how difficult it was for you to move back to Good Hope and start over." Roe took a seat across from Marigold at the table. "You'd built such a successful career in Chicago."

Roe understood, or at least thought she did. She'd begun building a reputation for herself in Minneapolis, only to have to leave her friends and colleagues and start over somewhere new.

"It was hard leaving my clients. Initially, I wasn't sure where I'd land. I came to Good Hope to regroup and ended up staying." Marigold's blue eyes grew soft with memories. "I started my salon, which was supposed to be only temporary, until I could get on my feet and decide where to settle. Cade and I got together, and the rest is history."

During the house tour, Marigold had mentioned that the owner of the high-end salon where she'd worked in Chicago, someone whom she'd considered a mentor and a friend, had been dealing with some issues in his personal life. Those troubles had spilled over into his interactions with clients, and his clients had begun to request Marigold. That had led to him accusing Marigold of poaching his clients, and then he'd fired her.

"I'm happy it worked out for you." Roe hoped one day she'd be able to look back and say that being downsized had led to a happy ending she couldn't have foreseen at the time. "It's nice that you and your sisters are together in the same community."

"At one time, just Ami was here. Then Prim moved back.

Then me." Marigold smile. "Fin was the last holdout. When she returned to stay, my dad was over the moon having all of us here."

"She lived in LA, right?" Roe kept her tone casual and offhand.

"Yes, and for a number of years, she loved it."

"Was she an actress there? Did she do any movies?"

Marigold blinked, then laughed. "No. Whatever gave you that idea?"

"The fact that she's playing Gladys in *Spotlight*. I figured Gladys wouldn't give the starring role to just anyone. When I heard Fin had lived in LA, I thought maybe she had professional experience."

"Fin acted in a number of stage productions while we were growing up, but no, nothing professional. Gladys has always hoped my sister would step into her shoes once she retires."

"What would that mean exactly?"

"Perform in most productions put on by the community theater."

"Sounds to me like that would be a lot. Would she have time? I mean, between handling the PR for the town and raising three boys, it seems like she already has a pretty full plate."

"One of her current responsibilities would have to go," Marigold agreed. "I'll give you a hint—it wouldn't be the family."

That brought up all sorts of questions, but Marigold spoke again before Roe had a chance to ask.

"I've rattled on so much that I haven't given you a chance to tell me about you." Marigold took a sip of hot apple cider and smiled expectantly.

"There isn't much to tell. With my dad in the Air Force, we moved constantly. Now, with my brothers scattered across the country and my parents in Germany, there really is no place I'd call home."

"Was there any town where you lived that you liked more than the others?"

Roe thought for a moment, then shook her head. "As much as I enjoyed something about everywhere we lived, none of those towns felt like home."

"Maybe you'll find what you're looking for here," Marigold suggested.

Roe smiled noncommittally. "Maybe. What I do know is that I'm going to enjoy every minute of my time here. Christmas is my favorite time of the year."

From the corner of her eye, Roe saw Caleb snap the last puzzle piece into place. She wasn't sure what to think when the threesome smiled and shook hands with one another, saying, "Good job."

It was obviously something their parents had taught them to do when finishing a project that they'd worked on together.

Faith swiveled in her seat to face her mother. "What can we do now?"

The other two stared expectantly.

Marigold hefted the bag sitting at her feet onto the table and looked inside. As she rattled off the items in the bag the size of Texas, Roe saw by the fatigue etched on the kids' faces that even Santa Claus would be a hard sell at this point in the afternoon.

Marigold had mentioned that the children, who no longer took naps, had chosen this morning to get up at the crack of dawn, for some unknown reason.

It would take something pretty special to keep their spirits high.

"There's a pop-up tent in the garage." Roe had stumbled across the tent just that morning. "We could set it up and make stars and a moon to hang from the ceiling."

The children looked at one another.

"Yes." Faith began doing a happy dance.

Hope offered a shy smile.

"I like camping," Caleb told her. "I've never camped in the snow."

Roe realized she should have been clearer. "We'll set it up in the great room. That will be fun, too, right?"

Caleb thought for a moment, then nodded.

"Are you sure you want to go to all the work of dragging it out?" Marigold spoke in a low tone, for Roe's ears only.

"It won't take much. We'll move a few pieces of furniture out of the way and pop it up." Roe thought of the art supplies she'd bought when she and Boone had picked up the tree ornaments. Though she wasn't sure when she'd have time to work on an art project, these items had been marked down seventy-five percent, and she'd been unable to resist adding them to the cart. "I have poster board, glow-in-the-dark paint for the moon and stars, and I think I saw some fishing line in the garage."

"Well, then, what are we waiting for?" Marigold turned to her children. "Ms. Carson and I will get the tent from the garage. I need you to clear off the table. Put the puzzle pieces carefully in the box. Make sure you get them all. We don't want to leave any pieces behind."

Marigold's gaze swept the threesome. "We won't start painting until the table is clear."

The table was clear by the time they brought in the tent. Setup, as Roe had anticipated, was a breeze. With three older brothers and a father in love with the great outdoors, camping had been as much a part of her childhood as moving.

She discovered that, thankfully, just like riding a bike, there were some skills you never forgot.

After spreading papers to protect the tabletop, Roe and Marigold cut out a moon and six stars to paint. When each child called dibs on the moon, Roe made an executive decision.

"Your mom and I will each paint one moon. You will each get to paint two stars. How does that sound?"

Faith's brows pulled together. "But there is only one moon."

"I've only seen one," Caleb agreed.

Hope nodded.

"Well, in our tent, there will be two moons," Roe spoke matter-of-factly as she handed Marigold the utility knife and a leftover piece of poster board.

Roe's red, silver and blue paints appeared to offer enough variety for the children.

"Red seems to be the color of choice for the stars," Marigold commented in a low tone several minutes later. "I don't know that I've ever seen a red star."

Roe pointed to the blue moon Marigold was painting. "The same could be said for your blue moon."

Marigold chuckled. "Thank you for making this so fun for them. I'm sure they'll be talking about this for weeks."

"I love being around children," Roe admitted. "And yours are absolutely adorable."

"Thank you. I have to say the tent idea was ingenious," Marigold commented, sipping the cider that had grown cold and been reheated. "Cade and I will have to try it at home."

"Just don't forget the moons and stars," Roe teased.

"I don't think they'll let me forget them." Marigold laughed. "We were late putting up a tree this year, and they asked every day when we were going to get one."

Roe shifted her gaze to her tree. "Boone and I had fun decorating our tree. We made an evening of it, eating pizza and drinking beer."

Roe knew the memory of that evening would stay with her long after she'd left Good Hope. Not only the fun, but the kiss they'd shared would go with her wherever she ended up.

Bringing fingers to her tingling lips, Roe wondered how something that had lasted only a few seconds could hold such power. Imagine if they had made love…

"I love your ornaments."

Jerking back her attention to the here and now, Roe saw Marigold's gaze was on Boone's *Starry Night* ornament.

Marigold grinned. "Then again, I'm a sucker for anything van Gogh."

"We have different tastes, as you can see, but I think the variety works."

"That star at the top has both an old-fashioned and a modern feel."

Roe smiled at the multicolored faux stained-glass star sitting atop the tree. "It was a compromise."

"Really?" Interest sparked in Marigold's blue depths. "Tell me more."

"I don't know how interesting this story is." Roe chuckled. "I wanted an angel. Boone wanted this ugly, light-up reindeer. When we came across this star in the Christmas stuff we'd purchased, we both agreed it would be perfect. The star and reindeer were forgotten."

Marigold clasped her hands together. "I do so love a happy ending."

Roe considered. "If I decorate a tree next year, I may try the homemade route."

"Have you made ornaments before?"

"No, but seeing your sister's tree got me thinking." Roe took a sip of cider. "I loved the sweetmeat nets and the other with the little envelopes."

"Fin will be so happy to hear that her trees inspired you." After casting a quick glance at her children still intently painting their stars, Marigold refocused on Roe. "I'm curious. What message did you get? The ones we get every year are always right on target."

Roe thought back. "Boone and I each took an envelope off the tree right before we left. Gladys and Ruby were right there and insisted."

"What did your notes say?"

"I don't know." Roe gave an embarrassed laugh. "Boone

handed me his, and I slipped both envelopes into my purse. Until this moment, I'd forgotten all about them."

The sound of children's laughter spilled from Marigold's phone. Looking down, Marigold silenced it with one flick of her finger.

Roe chuckled. "What is that?"

Marigold expelled a heavy breath and rose. "A reminder that this pleasant interlude is about to come to an end."

"I wish you could stay longer." Roe also rose. "This has been fun."

"It really has. I hate leaving so soon, but my dad and Lynn are having everyone over this evening for dinner." Marigold smiled at her children. "C'mon, troops. We're going to Nana and Papa's house tonight. Daddy is probably home right now, waiting for us."

"I want to hang my stars first." Hope's chin jutted out in a stubborn tilt, the boldness of the refusal surprising both Roe and her mother.

"The paint will take at least an hour to dry." Roe offered the girl an apologetic smile.

"We could wait." Caleb's hopeful look tugged at Roe's heartstrings.

"I'm afraid not, bud." Marigold began gathering up their things. "We need to get home."

Sporting a mutinous expression, Faith opened her mouth, but Marigold gently pulled the child close. "I know you're disappointed. I wanted to see my moon hanging in the tent, too."

"I have a solution."

Every eye turned to Roe. "What if I hang the moons and stars once they're dry and take pictures? I'll send the pics to your mommy. That way, you can show your daddy and your grandparents tonight. Then, when I see your mommy next, I'll give her the stars and the moon so you can hang them in your house wherever you want."

"I want mine in my room," Faith told her mother.

"Me, too," Hope said.

"Me, three," Caleb echoed.

"Thank you," Marigold whispered, giving Roe a quick hug when they reached the door. "For everything."

"Look for those pics in the next hour or so."

In less than two hours, Roe had the art supplies put away, the stars and moons hung and photographs sent to Marigold. She supposed she could have taken down the tent after she'd taken pics, but she liked looking at it. Besides, what was the hurry?

She'd just settled down with a glass of wine and a book when she heard the garage door open.

Moments later, Boone strolled into the room, coming to an abrupt halt at the sight of the tent. "What's that?"

"A tent."

"Okay." Appearing inordinately cheerful, Boone gestured to her glass. "Got any more of that?"

She smiled and pointed to the bottle sitting on the counter.

Crossing the room, Boone grabbed a glass, splashed in some red and then returned to sit by Roe.

Roe shifted her body toward him. "How was your training session?"

"It was good." He took a long drink. "Trent, the guy I'll be dealing with, is all over the entire fitness program. He's great. I gave him the doctor's parameters, and he set me up with a program."

Roe pointed her wineglass at him. "You went through a workout today."

He grinned. "How can you tell?"

"You seem happy."

"It felt good." Setting down his glass, he leaned toward her, his dark eyes snapping with excitement. "I missed working out. I didn't realize how much."

"It's like reclaiming your life."

"You understand."

"Did you think I wouldn't?" She took another sip of wine. "It's how I feel simply being back in a theater. Even if it is just as a volunteer."

"We're both lucky."

She arched a brow. "How do you figure?"

"We won't be kept down. You and I, we fight for the lives we want."

"I like your attitude, Mr. Boone." When her eyes locked with his, Roe couldn't look away. "Did I tell you Marigold and her kids came over today?"

"Is that why there's a tent in our living room?"

"You're firing on all cylinders."

He laughed at the old-fashioned saying. "Seriously, what's with the tent?"

"When I saw it in the garage, I thought it'd be fun for the kids to play in."

"Did they enjoy it?"

"They really didn't get the chance to play in it." Roe wished they'd had more time. But the children had gotten the chance to paint, so that was something. "They were too busy."

"Doing what?"

"It'll be easier if I show you, but first, I have a suggestion." She smiled, hoping what she was about to say wouldn't sound too lame. "I thought you and I might have some fun with the tent."

Interest sparked in his dark depths. "What kind of fun?"

"First, have you eaten dinner?"

He shook his head.

Roe forced a light tone. "Interested in a picnic?"

"Ah, I hate to tell you, but it's snowing outside." He grinned. "And it's cold."

"I was thinking of an indoor picnic. You know, spread a blanket and eat in the tent. Then, for dessert, toast s'mores over the fire."

He remained silent for so long that heat crept up Roe's neck. Her plan had sounded even more lame when spoken aloud.

"Forget it." She waved an airy hand. "I—"

Further dismissal of her suggestion stopped short when his warm hand captured hers.

"I don't want to forget it." Those dreamy dark eyes never left her face. "It sounds like the perfect end to what is turning out to be a perfect day."

He stood then and reached for her, pulling her to her feet when she gave him her hand. "Just tell me we have food already in the house for our picnic. I don't want to go back out tonight."

For the first time, she noticed he wasn't moving as quickly as he had that morning. "The workout kicked your butt."

"It'll take work to get back in shape."

"Just take it easy." Worry filled Roe's voice. "Promise me you won't push too fast and backslide."

His steady gaze shot tingles down her spine. "I promise."

Once they were in the kitchen, Roe opened the refrigerator. Standing side by side, they studied the shelves. Though the large unit could hold a considerable amount of food, the fridge was barely a quarter full.

"There's salami and cheese." She turned and found him so close that her lips nearly brushed his cheek. Their gazes locked for several long seconds before she returned her gaze to the inside of the fridge. "I can also cut up a couple of apples."

"Sounds good." His sexy, husky rumble had her stomach doing flip-flops. "I believe there are crackers in the cupboard. They'll go well with the meat and cheese."

"Is that enough food for you? I mean, you probably burned a lot of calories today."

"It's enough food," he assured her. "I need to leave room for s'mores."

CHAPTER FIFTEEN

Roe and Boone settled inside the tent on a plaid blanket Boone had confiscated from a steamer trunk in his room.

Roe paused, eager to see his reaction when he stepped inside. He didn't keep her waiting.

"Moons and stars?" He turned back to her, his face a study in delight. "What's this all about?"

Roe explained about the kids painting the stars but needing to leave before the paint had dried and ended with her showing him the pics she'd sent to Marigold.

Boone fingered one of the fishing lines that attached a star to the ceiling. He looked back at Roe. "This is amazing."

Roe experienced a flood of pleasure. "Thank you."

"How did you think to do it?"

"Let's eat first, and then I'll tell you all about it."

They finished the bottle of wine and then ate tiny slices of salami and cheese between Ritz crackers. While munching on crisp apples dipped in Greek yogurt sweetened with honey, she quizzed him about his time at the Y.

"After telling Trent about my injury, he and I discussed my doctor's recommendations." Boone dipped another slice of apple into the yogurt on his plate. "I tried to tell him the doc is way too conservative. He didn't buy it."

Good, Roe thought, as relief flooded her. "What kind of exercises did he have you doing?"

"Stationary cycling and the elliptical machine at low resistance." Boone's lips quirked into a rueful smile. "I fit right into the Fit for Life class of older people who were working out."

"You have to start somewhere." Roe downed the last of the wine in her glass.

"True," he agreed, appearing suddenly serious.

"It's a good start."

"It's a start, anyway." He studied her and then glanced up at the moons and stars dangling overhead. Boone gestured with one hand. "Tell me how this came about."

"Remember the poster board and paints I purchased when we got the ornaments?"

"They were in that markdown area." He smiled. "You couldn't resist."

"That's right." Roe hadn't been certain how she'd use the items, but she'd had this image in her head of working on an art project with snow falling outside and a fire burning in the hearth.

"Moon and stars?" he prompted.

That's right, she hadn't answered his question. "When I was their age, or maybe a little older, I wanted to make a moon and stars and hang them in our family tent when we went camping. It sounds silly now."

When she chuckled, Boone didn't join in. Instead, he continued to gaze expectantly at her, telling her the ball remained in her court.

"My dad and brothers loved camping. Me, not so much. Then, one day, I came up with an idea on how to make it more fun. I would cut the stars and moon out of cardboard and paint them so they'd glow in the dark." Her lips curved as she recalled how excited she'd been for the next camping trip. "I brought them with me, along with a spool of fishing line. The plan was that once the tent was up, I'd hang the moon and stars from the tent ceiling with the fishing line. That way, we could all look up and pretend we were gazing at the sky."

"Do you feel anxious in closed-in spaces?"

The sudden concern in his eyes warmed her heart.

She shook her head. "I just thought it'd be cool, and making the stars and moon was fun."

He offered an encouraging smile.

"I thought everyone would like them," she repeated. Now, simply recalling the look on her father's face and the hoots of laughter from her brothers had Roe swiping her cheeks as if brushing back the tears that had once slid down them in a steady stream.

When she didn't say anything for a long moment, Boone didn't press. He dipped another apple slice in the yogurt and waited.

"I should have known better." Roe shook her head, disgust directed at herself in her voice. "My brothers were the rough-and-tumble sort. They'd sooner dance naked in the front yard than sleep in a tent that had its own moon and stars. My father was a boy dad, if you know what I mean. He loved me, but I was a foreign creature to him. The military officer in him was horrified by the thought of stars-and-moon décor in a camping tent."

She gave a humorless laugh. "I tried to keep it together, but I cried when the boys laughed. That made my dad angry."

Sympathy blanketed Boone's face. "He was upset with them because they were disrespecting you."

"Not at them, at me—because of the tears. He considers tears a sign of weakness."

Boone frowned. "Where was your mom when all this was going down?"

"At home. She hated camping. Mom always said the closest she wanted to get to camping was a Motel 6." Roe smiled at the memory. A smile that quickly faded. "But my father insisted his kids, all of his kids, would have the full nature experience."

Roe shut her eyes momentarily as the disappointment of that time washed over her. She opened them to find Boone's gaze on her, his eyes soft and filled with concern.

"I'm sorry that happened to you."

The warmth in his voice touched her heart.

"It's no biggie." She gave a careless shrug. "It was a long time ago. I'm surprised I remembered it."

"Did you ever sleep under the glow-in-the-dark moon and stars?"

"No." She paused, then realized that wasn't entirely accurate. "I threw the ones I'd made into the campfire. But sometimes, I'd visualize them hanging from the tent ceiling. I never mentioned that to my brothers or my dad."

"Probably wise."

Roe nodded, then spoke quickly, wanting to make sure he understood. "I don't want you to think my dad or brothers are bad people. The boys were just kids, and my dad's strength was in dealing with men, not little girls."

Boone only nodded. "How is he now?"

"If you're asking if we have a good relationship, I'd say yes. Though he still has high expectations." Of all the people she'd hated to tell she'd lost her job, her father had ranked at the very top of the list. She couldn't entirely suppress the sigh. "Since that day, I've never cried in front of him, or anyone."

Boone surprised her when he reached over and took her hand, his fingers wrapping around hers. "You can cry all you want in front of me."

"You say that now." She kept her tone light. "You may live to rue that offer."

"I don't think so." Boone squeezed her hand and then released it. He gazed at the ceiling and smiled. "Your brothers don't know what they missed."

He turned to her suddenly. "We should sleep in here tonight. Under the moons and stars."

She glanced upward, sorely tempted. "The floor is hard, and you're still recovering—"

"Hey, one night on the floor isn't going to kill me."

"I suppose we could." Roe couldn't stop the smile. "If you insist."

"I do."

Roe smiled, grateful for his understanding and kindness. Jason Boone was a nice guy. The kind of guy she wouldn't mind dating if the circumstances were different.

The thought brought her up short. Date, actually *date*, Boone?

Though she quickly dismissed the idea, the thought circled in her brain like a fly that wouldn't quit buzzing.

Would dating Boone be so bad? There were cons, of course. As their time together in Good Hope was limited, what would be the point in becoming involved in a relationship destined to go nowhere?

Except, she reminded herself, they weren't kids. They were adults who knew relationships seldom led to a happily ever after. Was there really any downside to simply seizing the moment and enjoying their time in Good Hope together?

Going in at the beginning knowing they had no future might actually make dating easier. They wouldn't need to consider if the other had all the attributes they were looking for in the long term.

They wouldn't need to worry if things were moving too fast or slow. In the end, the speed wouldn't matter.

"All of a sudden, you're looking awfully serious." Boone studied her face, his dark eyes looking even darker and more mysterious in the dim light.

Not ready to embrace a dating discussion, Roe said the first thing that came to her mind.

"Marigold brought up the fortune cookie sayings." Seeing the puzzlement in his eyes, she elaborated. "They were in the tiny envelopes on the tree in the second parlor at the party the other night."

"That's what you were thinking about?" The skeptical look in his eye said he wasn't convinced.

"I'm sure ours are still in my bag, the one I took that evening." Without any warning, Roe sat up and slipped out of the tent. "I'll get them. We can see what they say before we make s'mores."

"Or after," Boone called after her. He might have said more but likely realized she was already too far away to hear.

Boone lifted a brow when Roe returned several minutes later and dropped down beside him, two tiny envelopes clutched in her hand.

"Looks like you found them." He didn't care about the sayings. He only cared that as soon as they were out of the way, he and Roe could move on to the sweet treat part of the evening.

S'mores followed by kissing sounded like a stellar end to what had turned out to be a pleasurable evening.

Boone's gaze lingered on her mouth, on the full lips that were now curved up in a smile. Forget the s'mores. He resisted the urge to reach out and tug her to him.

"They were right where I thought, or rather where I hoped they'd be." Holding a small envelope in each hand, she held them out to him. "Pick one."

Resigned but hoping to get this over with quickly, Boone pointed to the left. "That one."

She handed it to him, her eyes sparkling. "Open it."

Whatever had caused her to frown before she'd left to get the envelopes must not have been important, because he saw no signs of any remaining distress, only curiosity.

"I picked first," Boone reminded her. "You open first."

"Okay. Sure." Still, she hesitated for several heartbeats. "Gladys said that each person will end up with the envelope or box with the saying that is meant to be theirs. But I don't recall which envelope I picked from the tree versus the one you picked."

"We picked just now," Boone reminded her. "You asked which I wanted, and I picked this one."

He held up the tiny envelope that looked even smaller in his big hand. "The other was meant to be yours."

"I guess." Chewing on her lip, she looked so serious that he nearly chuckled. "Regardless of what Gladys or anyone else says, it's a fortune cookie saying, nothing more."

"You're right. Of course you're right. I'll read mine. You'll read yours and then—"

"We move to the next phase of the evening." Boone couldn't stop the smile.

"Yes," she agreed. "Then we make s'mores."

The tiny piece of paper she slipped from the inside of the envelope resembled the thin strips of paper hidden in fortune cookies.

"What does it say?" he prompted when she frowned.

"'Move in the direction of your dreams.'"

"That fits your situation perfectly."

She looked up from the paper.

"Think about it," he continued. "You left Minneapolis to follow your dream of working in the theater."

"I'm in Good Hope." Her lips twisted in a wry smile. "Unemployed."

"Temporarily. Besides, you're working with Gladys while you're here, and you plan to speak with Fin about her contacts in LA. These are all ways of moving in the direction of your dreams."

"When you put it that way…" Her brows pulled together, and

her expression turned thoughtful. "It does fit. Let's see what yours says."

He dropped his gaze to the envelope.

"Go ahead. Open it."

Instead of carefully opening the envelope the way Roe had done with hers, Boone tore off the top and pulled out the paper, quickly reading the message.

He gave a strangled laugh. "I can't believe this was meant for me."

"What does it say?"

Boone cleared his throat and read, "'True love is not something that comes every day. Follow your heart—it knows the right answer.'"

CHAPTER SIXTEEN

"I shouldn't have eaten that last s'more." Roe moaned as she dropped an armful of blankets on the floor of the tent.

"I warned you," Boone teased.

"I've never been good at taking advice." She chuckled. "All I can say is the second one sure tasted good."

Boone straightened the blankets, pushing aside the mound of pillows he'd brought from his bedroom.

"I can't recall the last time I slept in a tent," he said.

"It's been a while for me, too." Roe glanced down at the unfashionable yoga pants, wool socks and sweatshirt she'd donned once they'd finished the s'mores.

She sighed. Frumpy but comfortable.

Boone, on the other hand, looked delectable in his fleece joggers and a long-sleeved tee.

Having the fireplace blazing had kept the furnace from kicking on. Now, with the fire nearly out, a chill had crept into the air. "Do you think we'll be warm enough?"

"We'll be fine." Boone patted the blankets next to him. "Time to lie down and look at the stars."

He didn't have to ask twice.

Roe joined Boone in gazing upward as they lay in the darkness, their heads on pillows as they studied the glowing stars and the two moons. She couldn't stop smiling. The fluorescent paint really did work.

Instead of calling it a night, with the fire simmering in the hearth and darkness engulfing them, they talked. She told him about her brothers, their wives and kids.

Boone reciprocated by telling her about his sister, Lydia, her husband and his two nieces.

"I spent Thanksgiving with them on my way to Good Hope." His lips curved up. "The girls are getting so big. Aubrey loves all sports, while Amelia is an artist. She did a charcoal sketch of me that is amazing."

"I imagine it's difficult for you to see them as much as you'd like."

"During the season, it's nearly impossible," he admitted. "I need to make getting to Dubuque more of a priority in the off-season."

"What's going to happen when you go back to Denver?"

"What do you mean?"

Roe chose her next words carefully. "The season will be over when you go back. I don't know how any of the contract stuff works. Are you guaranteed a spot on the team since you were injured in a game?"

She deliberately didn't ask what would happen if he physically couldn't go back. She knew that was something he would deal with if it happened, not before.

"It's a bit complicated. I'll try to keep it simple."

Roe smiled. "I'd appreciate that."

There was something about the closeness of the tent, the crackle of the fire across the room and the dim light that appeared to make confidence come easily.

"Each team can have up to fifty-three players on its active roster. They start training camp with ninety players, then cut during the summer. I'm on IR, which is the reserve/injured list." He glanced at her.

She nodded. "I'm still with you."

"When I'm cleared to practice, it activates a twenty-one-day window during which I must be activated to the fifty-three-man roster. If I'm not, I would be released."

"You're saying when the doctor says you're good to play, after three weeks, the team decides whether to keep you or let you go."

"There's a little more to it than that, but basically, yes. Because I've played four or more seasons, I'm considered a vested veteran." He continued without waiting for her to say she understood or ask any questions. "Which means if they release me, my contract is terminated effective immediately, and I'm free to sign with any team I want."

"Or to walk away from football."

For a long moment, Boone said nothing. Then he slowly nodded. "But I've been an asset to the team, and they know I'm a hard worker. That bodes well for them keeping me. But for now, I'm here and determined to make the most of my time in Good Hope."

It was incredible, Roe thought, all the factors that had conspired to bring the two of them together at this point in time.

If she hadn't lost her job…

If he hadn't been injured…

If Dakota hadn't offered her the use of the cabin…

If Krew hadn't offered Boone a place to stay…

They never would have met. It was a sobering thought. She was glad she'd met Boone. Happy she was getting to know him.

She liked Boone. Liked him a lot, in fact. Not just because he was handsome and sexy, but because of the man he was deep down.

Casting a glance in his direction, she found him staring—not at the stars or the two moons shining overhead—but at her.

Her pulse skittered as the air between them began to pulse.

"Roe."

Just one word. She heard the question and didn't even need to think about her answer.

She wrapped her arms around his neck and slid her fingers into his silky dark hair. Roe loved how he smelled, a woodsy mixture of cologne, soap and maleness that brought a tingle to her lips and had heat percolating low in her belly.

Even before his mouth brushed hers, she remembered the feel of his lips—the softness, warmth and gentleness. Only this time, the kiss didn't end quickly, and it didn't stay sweet.

Shock waves of sensation coursed all the way to her toes as he deepened the kiss. And when his hand flattened against her lower back, drawing her up against the length of his body, Roe heard herself groan, a low sound of want and need that astonished her with its intensity.

She wanted him.

By the heat in his eyes, he wanted her just as badly.

"Clothes off." He pulled off the long-sleeved tee in a single fluid movement.

"I'm on the pill," she managed to utter as she struggled to remove her sweatshirt with fingers that visibly trembled.

"I'm clean," he said, helping her when her hands refused to cooperate. "Let me."

Soon, the clothes were tossed aside. His mouth was back on hers, and his hands were everywhere, touching, teasing, caressing.

A smoldering heat flared through Roe, a sensation she didn't bother to fight. She longed to run her hands over his body like he was doing now to hers, to feel the coiled strength of skin and muscle sliding under her fingers.

"Are you sure this is what you want?" The words seemed to come from far away.

Had he asked? Or was that her own conscience?

It didn't matter. She couldn't stop. Didn't want to stop. Being in Boone's arms felt so right.

In answer, she wound her arms around his neck and gave him a ferocious kiss.

~

When Roe entered the house the following afternoon, she found the tent down and Boone dressed for the Y, holding a gym bag.

When his gaze landed on her, his expression was unreadable. "You were up and out of the house by the time I woke up."

Giving in to impulse, Roe stepped to him and kissed him lightly. "I forgot to mention last night that I was going in early to cover the breakfast shift for Helen."

"That wasn't what I meant."

The slight worry in his voice had her moving closer.

"Last night was amazing. We'll have to do it again sometime."

Before she could say more, he gave her a crooked, boyish smile that sent her stomach into flips and melted her heart. Then he gently touched her face before kissing her.

When her hands rose to wrap around his neck, Boone stepped back, regret shining in his eyes. "I really have to leave now, or I'll be late for my training session."

Heaving a dramatic sigh that made him smile, Roe dropped her hands to her sides.

But when he turned to go, she remembered she needed to ask him something.

"Hey, quick question for you." Roe spoke fast, knowing Boone took the time with his trainer seriously and wouldn't want to be late. "A customer gave me two tickets to this evening's performance of *A Christmas Carol*. Would you like to go with me?"

"Sure. Let's do it," was all he said before he left.

She hadn't told him when the performance was, but he

returned in plenty of time for them to be in their seats when the curtain rose at seven.

Roe could barely contain her excitement when she saw their seats were next to Fin and Jeremy and their three boys. Seeing them made her smile and think of her brothers.

"You're just the person I hoped to see." Fin leaned in front of her husband to speak to Roe.

"I can switch seats," Jeremy offered, "if you two need to talk."

"Not necessary. The performance will be starting any minute." Fin shifted her focus back to Roe. "These next couple of weeks are crazy. I want you to know I'm still interested in having you on the V-Day committee."

"Whatever time works for you will work for me," Roe said. "Maybe we could talk sometime after rehearsal."

"Let me check with the others on the committee." Fin entered a reminder on her phone. "I'll be in touch."

"I'm excited to speak with you…" Roe's voice trailed off when the houselights dimmed and Fin sat back.

Despite not having the chance to say more, Roe felt her excitement surge. Hopefully, there would be time, either before or after the committee meeting, for her to speak with Fin regarding her contacts in LA.

Settling back in her seat, Roe smiled at Boone. Though they had no specific plans for after the play, before they'd left home, Boone had suggested checking out what was open in the downtown area if the weather cooperated. Roe wore her low-heeled boots just in case.

Though the town maintenance department did a great job of clearing the sidewalks and streets, it had been snowing again when they'd left home.

Home.

How was it that that cabin felt more like home than any apartment she'd lived in since college? Of course, it was also the nicest place she'd ever stayed.

"Ebenezer Scrooge," a voice rang out, pulling Roe's attention back to the stage.

Roe loved this play. No matter how many times she saw it performed, its wonderful message never failed to make her vow to be a better woman and do better in her own life.

When Boone reached over and took her hand halfway through the performance, Roe sighed in contentment.

By the time the play ended with a standing ovation, Roe was definitely in the Christmas spirit.

Her plan to speak with Fin after the performance was dashed when the Rakes family exited the row to meet some friends across the theater.

Glancing around, Roe was surprised not to see anyone she knew. She turned to Boone. "Should we check out the downtown?"

His gaze flicked over her cashmere coat and bare head. "Are you sure you'll be warm enough?"

"I was a Minnesotan." She lifted her arm and flexed. "We're tough."

"In that case…" He offered her his arm. "Let's walk."

It didn't take long to realize that they weren't the only ones who wanted to savor the Christmas spirit for a little longer this evening.

When they walked past Muddy Boots, the line of waiting customers reached the door.

"Makes me glad we ate beforehand," she told Boone.

Roe had grown used to the Christmas music that played from speakers positioned along Main Street, but the jarring hard rock coming from the direction of the bay had her cocking her head.

"Do you hear that?" she asked Boone.

He nodded. "It's coming from the Flying Crane."

Seeing her puzzled expression, he added, "The Crane is a popular bar by the waterfront."

It surprised Roe that he knew that, considering he hadn't been in town any longer than she had. "Have you been there?"

He shook his head. "Trent goes there all the time. We should check it out sometime."

Roe nodded but didn't suggest they walk that way. The play had put her firmly in a Christmas mood. She had a feeling rock music and a crowded bar would pull her out faster than a Santa in a clown mask.

Instead, she tightened her hold on his arm and continued to walk until the jarring music faded, and the sweet sounds of Christmas carols were all that could be heard in the night air.

CHAPTER SEVENTEEN

Voices raised in song grew louder the farther Roe strolled beside Boone down the snow-dusted sidewalk. She found herself humming along to a familiar tune.

"What is this?" Boone turned to her as if expecting her to know why the street and sidewalks ahead were crowded with singing people.

"I've never seen anything like it. Other than…"

He inclined his head. "Other than?"

"I was at a mall in Minneapolis once where there was a pop-up concert." She smiled at the memory. "We were all just going about our business when suddenly someone at the food court began to sing. Others joined in until there was this whole group singing."

"It was planned?"

"There seemed to be a core group that started things, but other people joined in. It was incredible."

"I wonder who got this one started."

Roe noticed that there appeared to be a lot of high school-aged students. She thought she recognized Brynn Chapin as one of the students in the heart of things. "I'm betting that someone on the Christmas planning committee recruited students from the music or choral classes at the local high school to get things started."

Boone's lips curved upward. "When my sister and I were kids, our mother made us go caroling with her and her friends."

"Then I'd say tonight is your chance to revisit those roots, only on a grander scale."

"I don't think—"

His lukewarm protest was brushed aside as Roe grabbed his hand, weaving her way deeper into the crowd. Once they were surrounded, she smiled at Boone. "Let me hear that singing voice."

The melody shifted from a rousing rendition of "Santa Claus Is Coming to Town" to the more soul-stirring "Silent Night." The audience followed the teenagers' lead by turning on their phones' flashlights and lifting them high, making it look like the still night air was filled with dozens of candles.

"All is calm. All is bright…"

Roe's rich alto and Boone's surprisingly pleasant baritone blended with the other voices.

As they continued to sing, Roe felt tears sting her eyes as the spirit of Christmas wrapped around her heart.

When the last note ended, a watchful waiting occurred for a minute until someone called out, "That's it for tonight. Merry Christmas."

All around her and Boone, people called out the greeting to one another.

"Merry Christmas," Roe said to an older woman who stood beside her, wearing a bright red cape coat.

"Merry Christmas to you, my dear." The woman shifted her gaze from Roe to Boone. "And to you, as well."

At that moment, Roe recognized her. "You're Etta Hawley. We met at the pond."

The woman smiled. "I am so happy to see you and your young man taking advantage of all this town offers."

Roe thought about clarifying that Boone wasn't technically her "young man," though, after last night, he was more than a housemate. Since he didn't say anything, she didn't either.

"We were just at the playhouse—" Roe began.

Etta clasped her hands together. "Don't they do a fine job with *A Christmas Carol*? No matter how often I've seen it performed, it always causes me to reflect."

"I feel the same. Each time I see it, I vow to be more kind and giving to others."

"The story does bring out the best in us. Well, you two have a lovely evening." When Etta turned to leave, Roe stopped her with a hand on her arm.

"I have a quick question."

Etta smiled. "What can I help you with?"

"Do you know if this," Roe gestured with one hand to the dispersing crowd, "was a spontaneous or a planned event?"

"Planned," Etta said immediately. "I'm a retired teacher. A former colleague at the high school gave me the heads-up. Loretta told me this was planned, but it was meant to look spontaneous."

Roe pulled her brows together. "I wonder why they didn't announce it was happening ahead of time so everyone could be here to participate."

"From what I was told, the intent was to see how well this was received before planning another."

"Looks like a hit to me," Boone said, speaking for the first time.

"I agree." Etta favored him with a smile. "When they do another, which I assume will happen, it will be advertised not only in the Open Door but in storefronts and lodging places."

"The Open Door is an online newsletter that gives visitors the inside scoop on what's happening in the community," Roe told

Boone, recalling what Dakota had said. "There's even a gossip column."

"It wouldn't surprise me to see the two of you mentioned in that column." Etta's eyes sparkled with good humor.

At that moment, Etta reminded Roe of Mrs. Claus. She'd have to ask Dakota if the former schoolteacher had ever played that role on the stage.

"Why would we be mentioned?" Boone asked, appearing puzzled. "We're not from here."

"NFL star and Dakota's bridesmaid, living together in Krew Slattery's new million-dollar cabin." Etta chuckled. "It sure beats hearing about who spent seven nights sitting on a barstool at the Ding-A-Ling flirting with the bartender."

Boone chuckled, a pleasant rumbling sound. "I see your point."

"Now, I must tootle." Raising her hand in a little wave, Etta hurried off.

"Toodle?" Roe turned to Boone and arched a brow.

Grinning, Boone lifted both hands. "I don't even want to speculate on what that means."

Roe looped her arm around his. "I'm glad we came upon this when we did."

"I am, too." Boone's expression turned serious. "The play and then the caroling... It's starting to feel like Christmas."

"You know what would really make it feel like Christmas?" Roe spotted the coffee cart on the street corner.

Boone followed her gaze, and a smile lifted his lips. "Hot cocoa?"

"I was thinking gingerbread latte. Although that may be too much to expect."

"You don't ask, you don't get." He took her hand. "C'mon, let's check it out."

They stood in line for several minutes. Apparently, they

weren't the only ones who thought something hot to drink sounded good on this cold winter night.

When they reached the front of the line, Roe didn't recognize the man serving drinks with quick, efficient movements, but the girl handling the orders and the money was familiar.

"Happy Holidays." The slender, blond girl flashed a smile. "What can I get you?"

"You're Brynn's friend," Roe observed. "You were with her during the Christmas Stroll."

Confusion filled the girl's blue eyes. "Did we meet?"

"Oh, you don't know me. I'm helping Gladys out at the playhouse. That's how I got to know Brynn."

The look in the girl's eyes said she wondered where this was headed. "I'm Zoe Goodhue. And yes, Brynn Chapin and I are friends."

The man in line behind Roe shifted from foot to foot and muttered something under his breath.

"We'd like one hot cocoa and one gingerbread latte," Boone ordered, as if it was a given that the cart could supply both.

"That will be—" Zoe began.

"I've got it." Boone had a twenty in his hand but paused when he noticed a large glass jar that said Giving Tree Donations on the front. "You can put the change in there."

"Thank you." The girl turned to the man. "Did you get their order, Dad?"

"I did, and I have it ready." With his dark hair and dark eyes, the man couldn't have looked more different than his daughter, Roe thought.

Then again, like Roe, Zoe probably took after her mother.

"Thank you," Roe told the man, who was already working on the following order, and then turned to the girl. "Merry Christmas."

Zoe pressed two cookies wrapped in cellophane into her hand.

"What is this?" Roe asked. She hadn't heard Boone order any cookies.

"Merry Christmas from the Daily Grind."

"Thank—" But Roe didn't have a chance to finish as the girl had already turned to the next customer.

Roe slipped the sugar cookies into her coat pocket.

She and Boone were several feet away when Roe's lips lifted in a rueful smile. "I'm sure they, and everyone around me, were thinking, 'Who's the crazy lady, and why doesn't she just shut up?'"

Boone took a sip of his cocoa and chuckled. "I'm sure no one thought that."

"Then you didn't hear the guy behind us." Roe sipped the latte and sighed. "This is so good."

She glanced around. Everywhere she looked, there were people in warm winter coats and gloves and many wearing hats. Yet, no one rushed to get out of the cold. Instead, they seemed to enjoy the lights and being out with others.

While there were plenty of Christmas events in Minneapolis, the holidays couldn't compare to here. Roe liked the atmosphere in Good Hope and understood why tourists arrived in December every year to savor the magic.

"What would you be doing now if you were still in Minneapolis?"

Boone's question jolted Roe's attention back to him.

She thought for a moment. "I usually went out on the weekends. You know, to cocktail parties with friends or to a club to dance. Occasionally, I'd take in a theater production. What about you?"

"The same, except I didn't attend too many theater productions." His smile quickly faded. "The guys on the team, especially the younger ones, are crazy for the club scene."

"I used to love it," Roe admitted. "But the last few years, it, well, it wasn't as much fun."

"I hear you." He chuckled. "I feel like some old guy saying this, but it seemed just like more of the same."

"You had a girlfriend. You wanted to spend time with her."

"Actually, Celine loved to party. She especially liked being seen at the clubs with a Grizzlies player."

"Not with just any player—with you."

"I think, for Celine, we were interchangeable as long as we were first string." His tone was matter-of-fact, and his expression gave nothing away.

"I don't think any woman who truly knows you, Jason Boone, could ever consider you interchangeable with another man."

"That was it, then." His hold tightened on her arm when they hit an icy patch of sidewalk.

"What was?"

"She didn't know me. I certainly didn't know her, not really. It was the same with Ella, and we'd dated for three years. In many ways, we were still strangers." Boone took in a breath and let it out. "I suppose that sounds bad."

"I'm not one to judge." Roe's lips lifted in a rueful smile. "I can't recall the last time I had a relationship that dipped below the superficial. After all those years of not letting anyone get too close because I knew I'd eventually be moving on, keeping my distance became second nature."

Boone chuckled. "We make quite the pair."

She laughed, but when her gaze settled on his, blood slid through her veins like honey, spreading warmth throughout her body.

"I have an idea." Boone took her hand and pulled her along, stopping at the curb's edge.

A gorgeous carriage sat there, its body the color of ripe cherries and its runners a burnished gold. Other than a spot for the driver, a man wearing a long flowing coat and a top hat, this was a smaller sleigh with room for only two passengers.

Undoubtedly, that was why this one had no one waiting, while the other two larger sleighs down the street had lines.

"Merry Christmas," the driver said with a pleasant smile. "Would you like to go for a sleigh ride?"

"How long a ride will it be?" Boone asked, making Roe wonder if he was in a hurry to get home.

"That's up to you." The man smiled. "And the demand."

The man gestured with his head toward the other sleighs. "They'll likely only do twenty-minute rides. I can do as long or as short as you like."

"Let's do an hour." Boone glanced sideways at Roe as if to make sure that time frame was okay with her.

"I've never been on a sleigh ride," Roe admitted.

Taking that for a yes, Boone reached over, opened the door and held out his hand to help her step inside.

Instead, she handed him her drink. "You can help me more by holding this."

A second later, she reached down to take back her drink, and Boone joined her in the sleigh. The driver, a handsome older gentleman with silver hair and a bushy mustache, introduced himself as Len Swarts before handing them a buffalo plaid sherpa blanket to place over their laps for extra warmth.

Roe had wondered if excluding Len from any conversation would be awkward, but that question was answered when a Christmas medley began playing from his iPhone.

As the sleigh lurched forward, the colorful holiday harness worn by the white horse and covered with bells jingled. It added a festive touch, especially with the Christmas music wafting from Len's phone.

Roe pulled the blanket close. The combination of the cushioned seat and the blanket's warmth relaxed her completely.

She took a sip of her gingerbread latte and sighed in contentment. "I'm glad you saw this. Taking this ride is the perfect end to the day."

"When my sister and I were kids, my mom always dragged us to one holiday event or another." His lips lifted, and she heard the fondness in his voice. "But we never did a sleigh ride. When I saw the horse and carriage, I thought of your moon and stars."

Roe inclined her head.

"Just because we didn't get to do it as kids doesn't mean we can't do it now. I agree that this is a good way to cap off the night. Not quite as good as last night." He paused and shot her a wink. "But I'm having fun."

They rode silently for several minutes as Len took them by houses brightly decorated for the holidays, then turned down a road where there was nothing other than the night sky filled with the moon and a million stars.

Roe leaned her head back and glanced up at the heavens. "My puny moons and stars are nothing compared to this."

His arm stole around her shoulders, giving her extra support as she studied the heavens. "I'll never forget your moons and stars."

Her heart warmed. "That's nice of you to say."

"I mean it."

Cupping his face with her hand, she kissed him. As desire surged, she realized her mistake. She wanted him even more now than she had last night, if that was possible.

With great effort, she pulled her mouth from his. *Focus on something else.*

"You know, every time I see a performance of *A Christmas Carol*, I'm struck by the timeless lessons." She chuckled. "I never leave without resolving to make changes in my personal life."

He toyed with a lock of her hair with his gloved finger. "What kind of changes are we talking about?"

Roe found it difficult to think with him so close, so it took her a few heartbeats to get her thoughts in order. "You know, things like keeping in mind that my actions and attitudes not only affect my life but the lives of those around me. Like you, for instance."

A startled look crossed Boone's face. "Me?"

"Think about it. If I'm negative or down on life, it could bring you down." Under the blanket, Roe reached over and grasped his hand. "I wouldn't want to be responsible for that."

"I understand the point you're making, but it's also important that you're honest with yourself and with me." Boone met her gaze. "If you're feeling down, let me know. Don't shove down your emotions because you think you have to be a Polly Perfect."

Roe chuckled. "Polly Perfect?"

"It was something my mom used to say to my sister." Boone grinned. "I'd forgotten all about that."

"I know you said you stayed with your dad after the split. Did you see a lot of your mom and sister?"

"Not as much as I'd have liked. My life was training, practice and games. We tried to find the time, but it was difficult."

Roe couldn't imagine what it would be like to be so involved in something that it consumed her entire life.

"Sometimes I'd go see them when I had a week off." He took a contemplative drink of his cocoa. "It was awkward. The closeness we once shared wasn't there anymore. My life was as much of a mystery to them as their lives were to me."

"Was there ever anything else you wanted to do?"

He hesitated. "You'll laugh if I tell you, just like my father did. It is pretty funny, I guess."

Roe guessed it hadn't been funny to him. Not at the time. "I won't laugh."

"I wanted to write."

"Books?"

"Told you it was funny."

"What kind of books? Fiction? Nonfiction?" With him so involved in football, she could see his topic being something related to the sport.

"Fiction. Space opera."

"I don't know what that is, but it sounds intriguing."

"Probably the best example that most would recognize is the book *Dune* by Frank Herbert." Boone continued without giving her a chance to respond. "Space opera is a subgenre within sci-fi and fantasy. It focuses on grand, epic narratives in interstellar settings with themes of heroism and large-scale conflicts."

"I'd love to read what you've written."

"I haven't completed anything. Every so often, I'll pull up the manuscript and add another chapter. But there is usually no time. And really, what's the point?"

Something told Roe not to push. "Do you ever regret all the time and effort you put into football?"

"No." In the dim light, his eyes were unreadable, but his voice was firm and didn't waver. "I love the sport. I always have. My teammates are my best friends. Getting drafted out of college was the happiest day of my life."

Roe knew what it was like to work for a goal and to achieve it. That's how she'd felt when she'd learned she'd gotten the job in Minneapolis. It had been as if she'd been rewarded for all her hard work.

"This time in Good Hope has been good for me," Roe confided. Though he didn't ask how or why, she continued. "I'd been so focused on my career, there was little time left for anything else. Oh, I participated on a TeamWomen committee, but it wasn't because I wanted to support their mission, though I did believe in it. My participation was a calculated move, a way for me to build community contacts."

"That was where you met Dakota."

Roe realized he really had been listening to her when she'd spoken of how she'd met Dakota.

"Yes, her friendship turned out to be a wonderful side benefit of joining that committee. The point I was trying to make, very badly, is that I can identify with Scrooge. He neglected his family and personal relationships and focused instead on accumulating wealth." Roe chuckled. "Though working behind the scenes in theater is hardly a road to wealth—not like being a star NFL player."

Boone only nodded.

"My short time here has made me realize I want connection. I'm ready to find a place that I love where I can do what I love but also settle and put down roots. Where I can have friends and relationships outside of my job."

As emotion rose to clog her throat, Roe fought to steady. "When they called me in and told me the children's theater was letting me go, it cut me off at the knees. I understood the money issues, but it taught me that no matter how much I tried to convince myself that the theater world was my family, it wasn't. I was expendable and likely forgettable. I bet, even in this short time away, there are people who are having trouble recalling my name."

Boone had never released her hand, and now he squeezed it. "I assume you have some thoughts on what you want to happen moving forward."

"Though there are no guarantees, I will look for something stable, even if it's not the highest-paying position. It will also need to be located where I would want to live long term. Nothing too hot or too cold. Like Goldilocks, I hope to find something that is 'just right.'"

"It appears you've given this a lot of thought."

"Yes," she said, "and no. The play tonight helped put some of my tangled thoughts in order. I've been struggling with where I should apply. Now, I know why I was hesitating."

"Are you still planning to talk to Fin to see if she has any suggestions for you?"

"I am. It will be easier now because I'm clearer in my own head about what I'm looking for." She thought about refocusing the conversation on Boone, asking if he would give writing a try if returning to the NFL proved impossible.

She decided there was no reason to put negative vibes into the atmosphere.

Unlike her, he had a job that wanted him back.

They rode in contented silence for several minutes, his arm around her shoulders, their fingers entwined beneath the blanket.

Roe wasn't sure when her mood changed from contentment to longing, from feeling relaxed to feeling like every nerve ending in her body was firing.

When she slowly turned her head toward him and found him staring at her mouth, the desire that had been heating in her veins surged.

Leaning close, she brushed his lips with hers. "Merry Christmas."

His hand released hers to slip around her waist, pulling her to him as his mouth closed over hers.

The kiss started out slowly, as if they had all the time in the world. She wasn't sure when exactly warmth became heat, and desire coursed through her veins like a runaway river. All Roe knew was that, like last night, she didn't want him to stop.

She lifted her hands and slid her fingers into his hair, holding his head as they continued to kiss.

When his tongue swept along her lips, leaving fire in its wake, she opened her mouth, and he plunged inside.

Roe gasped as sensation after sensation washed over her, leaving her weak and breathless and filled with overwhelming need. She couldn't find her control. It was as if she were in a car with the foot pedal pushed to the floor.

The exhilarating ride had her pressing her body close, cursing the coats and sweaters that separated them.

She flung off the blanket. She didn't need any more heat. She was burning up. Burning with a need for him that could be quenched only one way.

"We're nearly back, folks," the driver said without looking around.

His words, underscored by amusement, were like a splash of cold water.

Roe pushed back from Boone, her breath coming in little puffs.

How had she let things get so out of control?

She didn't know why she'd thought the question. Roe already knew the answer.

It was how Jason Boone made her feel. All there and gone.

Roe exchanged a rueful smile with Boone as the sleigh slowed to a stop.

What had happened between them in the tent hadn't been a one-off, destined never to happen again. Instead, she knew now that what had happened last night was destined to happen again and again, until they finally said good-bye and returned to their real lives.

CHAPTER EIGHTEEN

After that, Boone and Roe made love nearly every night. He couldn't get enough of her, and it appeared by her enthusiastic response that the feeling was mutual.

Each time Boone wondered if he'd made the attraction out to be more than it was, all he had to do was walk into the same room as Roe.

It wasn't just sex. He genuinely liked and enjoyed her company. They talked about everything except their future, because they both knew they didn't have one—not together.

When he arrived home from the YMCA on Wednesday, her car was already in the garage. He was surprised she'd beat him home. She'd started going to the theater immediately after her shift ended at Muddy Boots, usually arriving home shortly after he did.

With his doctor's approval, Boone had begun swimming before his workouts. Though he wasn't close to being in shape to return to the team, it felt good knowing he was doing all he could.

Entering the house, he paused. His lips quirked upward. She

was singing. Something he'd discovered she did when she was happy.

Something else captured his attention. Boone inhaled deeply, then followed his nose to the kitchen.

"I'm home," he called on the way.

The singing abruptly stopped.

He found Roe removing a loaf of bread from the oven.

Boone widened his eyes. "You bake bread?"

She turned and laughed. "I've been known to pop a loaf or two into an oven."

Her hazel eyes sparkled like autumn leaves catching the sunlight. The lips that curved upward were cherry red. Her dark hair fell to her shoulders in soft waves and was held back from her face by a stretchy band the same color as her lips.

Even dressed simply in jeans and a sweater, she looked incredible.

"Lovely," he murmured.

Roe wasn't looking at him as he breathed the word. As she'd turned to place the bread on a cooling rack, her eyes remained focused on the fragrant loaf filling the air with its fantastic scent.

Stepping back, she placed her hands on her hips and gave a satisfied nod. "It turned out even better than I imagined."

He moved a little closer on the pretext of looking more closely at the loaf. "I haven't had cinnamon bread in forever."

"I haven't either," she admitted. "I ran across this easy recipe online while looking for something else last week. When we were at the market, I picked up the ingredients I needed, and this is the result. We could have a slice tonight for dessert, and it'll be great with morning coffee."

She looked so pleased with herself that he couldn't help but smile.

Boone liked the routine they'd fallen into. Having coffee together in the morning, telling each other about their days over dinner in the evening and making love at night.

The sunlight from the window cast a soft glow on her dark strands. He remembered how soft her hair felt between his fingers and how her lips tasted against his.

Routines were nice, but there was nothing saying that making love had to wait until nightfall.

"I impressed myself," she said, resting her back against the counter. "I'm determined to fully enjoy the holiday."

He was determined to fully enjoy it, and her, as well. But when she turned and began gathering up supplies, he realized he was the only one interested in changing up their routine this evening.

After rinsing the utensils, she put them into the dishwasher before turning to face him. "I know we've been having wine during happy hour, but since the twenty-fifth is only a week away, I wondered what you'd think of trying a Christmas cocktail this evening."

His first thought was that it sounded like a lot of work. With her job at Muddy Boots and volunteering at the theater, she was stretched thin. Not to mention all the work she'd done to bring Christmas to the cabin.

A wreath made out of pinecones, berries and evergreen branches had appeared on the front door a few days earlier. Yesterday, twinkling white lights and garland with red bows were encircling the porch rail when he'd returned from the gym.

"We don't have to." She spoke quickly when he didn't immediately respond. "I mean, I've already put all the ingredients together for tonight, but that doesn't mean you have to drink it. You can still have wine. We have red or white—"

Boone put his arms around her, stilling her chatter. With a gentle finger, he brushed a tendril of that silky hair back from her face. "I like trying new drinks, but I'd also like for us to go out."

"We go out every day."

"I'm talking about a date. You and I have been given this

chance to enjoy Christmas together." His fingers toyed with a lock of her hair, liking her quick intake of breath when his knuckles brushed her cheek. "It's never as much fun doing things alone, especially during the holidays."

"You're right. This year can be different."

"It already feels that way. You've made the cabin feel like a home."

Her gaze shifted to the simmering pot of cinnamon, cloves and orange peels, another recent addition. "I'm enjoying infusing a little Christmas spirit into the place."

"Well, you've succeeded." He smiled. "Now, tell me about tonight's cocktail."

She shot him a teasing smile. "How about I show you the drink, and you guess what's in it?"

Clearly, she was in the mood to play. Well, he liked games. "Sounds like fun."

His comment had her smiling and gesturing to the sofa. "Relax while I get the drinks."

Boone dropped down on the sofa, but waiting for her to serve him didn't feel right. They always worked together. When it was time for happy hour, either she or he poured a glass of wine. Dinner was also a joint effort.

It was usually nothing fancy, just something they could throw together. But they'd gotten good at working side by side, developing a nice rhythm.

Boone enjoyed being part of a team. He pushed himself up from the sofa when she appeared with two rocks glasses on a small tray.

He sat back down. Once he took his drink, Roe set the tray aside and sat beside him, holding her own drink. Her fingers, sporting bright red nails, added a pop of color against the white liquid in the glass.

"What's this green thing?" he asked, pulling out the sprig of green protruding from the top of the white liquid.

"Rosemary."

Boone set it aside on the napkin she'd handed him.

Whether it was the heat from the flames that danced cheerily in the hearth or the softness of the overstuffed leather sofa, as Boone sat in the great room in front of the fire and stared at the rocks glass filled with ice and topped with cranberries, he felt enveloped in the spirit of the holidays.

He studied the glass in his hand. Boone had no idea what went into this drink but knew that sometimes the name gave a clue. "What's it called?"

"Mistletoe Kiss."

"I need a little inspiration to solve this mystery."

For a second, confusion furrowed her brow, but when he held the sprig of rosemary over his head, she chuckled.

Smiling, she leaned forward and pressed her lips against his.

She tasted like cinnamon and sugar, and Boone immediately knew one kiss wouldn't be enough. When she pulled back, he heaved a dramatic sigh. "I believe more inspiration is needed."

She laughed a joyous sound that reminded him of the tinkling of a thousand bells. "Perhaps taking a sip will help."

"I think another kiss would have given me the answer, but we'll do it your way." Boone took a sip and discovered he liked the taste. Really liked it. "Vodka."

"Ding, ding, ding."

Her bright smile and obvious enthusiasm were all he needed to continue with the game.

"Ice."

She rolled her eyes.

"Rosemary stalk."

"Sprig." Roe laughed. "And I gave you that answer."

"Club soda."

She nodded approval. "Very good."

Boone took another long drink. He'd never been that adventurous with alcohol. He liked different wines, both white and red, and he had his favorite craft beers, but he'd never cared about specialty cocktails one way or the other.

He let the alcohol linger on his tongue. There was some subtle ingredient that he was missing, but try as he might, he couldn't identify it. "I'm done. I have no idea what else is in here, but I like how it came together."

"Lemon juice, rosemary syrup and cranberries."

"The cranberries go without saying." He glanced pointedly at the berries floating atop his drink.

She chuckled. "Sometimes we miss the obvious."

Boone knew that to be true. He'd noticed that the place had started to feel like home, but now understood that had less to do with the decorations and food than the woman sitting beside him. "Well, this drink is a winner."

"I'm glad you like it." Her eyes turned distant as if she was looking back. "Last week, I started thinking that Christmas will be here before we know it. In the past, I was usually too busy to do much around the holidays. I'd buy gifts and have them shipped. I'd decorate a small tree, but that was it."

"Many of the guys on the team looked forward to time off around the holidays."

She must have picked up on something in his voice because the gaze she settled on him held a question. "Not you?"

"Not really."

"Didn't you tell me you'd had a girlfriend that you'd been with for several years? Surely, holidays were different when you were together."

"Holidays were a busy time for Ella. Heck, what am I saying? The woman was busy year-round. Ella was driven. I respected that because I was driven, too."

"What did she do that kept her so busy?" Roe sipped her drink, her hazel eyes never leaving his face. "If you don't mind my asking."

"Ella was an on-air sports reporter for ESPN."

Though her gaze remained watchful, Roe's lips quirked up in a slight smile. "You two obviously had a lot in common."

"We knew many of the same people." Boone realized now that those common contacts had been the glue that had held them together long after they should have gone their separate ways. "Our relationship involved seeing each other only when it worked for our schedules. Eventually, I think she decided the logistics were too much of a hassle."

"You think? You don't know?"

"She said she thought we should go our separate ways, and I agreed." Boone continued, not wanting Roe to get the mistaken idea that he still had feelings for Ella. "It wasn't just her who knew it was over between us. I knew it, too. She was simply the first to voice it."

Roe slowly nodded. "Do you think it would have been easier to maintain a relationship if you'd been under the same roof? Or did you live together?"

"No, we didn't." Boone shook his head. "Ella had an apartment but was rarely home. They had her flying all over the country. She loved it. If we'd lived together, I'd have been coming home to an empty place. It's extra lonely at the holidays when you're alone and everyone else is with a partner or family."

"It is," she conceded.

He hesitated for a long moment, then figured if he was thinking it, he might as well say it. "Now, when I leave the gym, I look forward to coming home." Then, realizing how that sounded, he gave a little laugh. "I know technically this isn't our home. But it feels that way."

"It feels like home to me, too." Roe made a sweeping gesture with one hand. "Decorating, baking bread and trying out new cocktails are fun, but not so much if you're doing them for just yourself."

"This year, you have me to experiment on."

"Yes." Her eyes softened, looking like golden orbs in the light. "This year, we have each other."

Once happy hour concluded, he and Roe moved to the kitchen and began to prep for the chicken tacos they'd decided to have for dinner.

While Boone handled browning the boneless chicken breasts cut into half-inch strips, Roe gathered the other ingredients, then set about cubing a medium-ripe avocado.

While she worked, she quizzed him about his day.

She appeared genuinely interested in the types of exercises that he was doing and the machines Trent had him on. When he mentioned how far he'd swum today, she smiled.

"Maybe I'll come with you sometime, and we can race." Her eyes sparkled with good humor.

He couldn't tell if she meant that.

"You're welcome any time. I'll give it my best shot, but if you're any kind of swimmer, you'll reach that wall before me." As the words left Boone's mouth, he frowned and immediately reframed, "I'm getting faster and stronger every day."

"I'm sure you are."

Boone rested his back against the counter. "The swimming is simply conditioning that I do before I meet with Trent. He also wants me to continue to walk."

He couldn't keep the disgust from his voice. *Walk.* As if he were eighty years old. He was an athlete. He was in his prime, or had been before he'd been taken down.

Understanding filled her hazel eyes. "It's difficult for you to hold back. You wish you could hit it harder."

"A kid playing JV football in high school would be in better condition than me."

"Not if they'd had major surgery."

Boone shrugged. He knew he should be grateful that the doctor let him do as much as he did. Thinking that maybe the surgeon was being too strict, Boone had contacted the team doctor and the head trainer. When they'd expressed surprise that the surgeon had loosened the reins as much as he had, Boone had known that pushing for more—at least at this time—would be pointless. That didn't make the restrictions any easier to bear.

The enforced inactivity chafed, so he was glad he and Roe were going out tonight, even if it was simply to tour Victorian homes decorated for Christmas.

The doctor would be pleased that he'd be getting in his *walking*. "What time do you want to leave?"

She didn't need to ask for clarification. While he didn't understand it, they always seemed on the same wavelength.

"The tours start at seven. I thought we could leave here at six fifty."

"That works." It appeared that writing the new scene in his head would have to wait. The manuscript he'd tentatively titled *Nebula's Wrath* had been resurrected. Recently, Boone had begun adding scenes—just for fun, of course.

Though he'd thought the words might come hard after so long away, that hadn't been the case, and the plot was coming together in a way that had him eager to write more.

Each night, when Roe would yawn and stand, ready to head to bed, he had to force himself to stop writing.

Only the knowledge that he would be going to bed with her had him closing his laptop. After making love, she'd curl up against him, and they'd fall into an exhausted slumber.

Sleeping a solid eight hours was another of his doctor's recommendations. Adhering to a regular schedule and getting enough rest at night was apparently crucial to his recovery.

Tonight, a Victorian home tour was on the agenda. He couldn't imagine anything more boring. Boone would much rather stay home and write.

When she'd initially mentioned the event, Roe had told him that Ami and Beck's home was on the tour and that it was a fundraiser for the Giving Tree.

He said he'd go because, while walking through other people's homes decorated for Christmas didn't particularly interest him, spending time with Roe did.

While Roe had made it clear he didn't have to go with her if he didn't want to, he knew it would be more fun for her to go through the homes with a partner.

Boone watched her return to intently chopping tomatoes at the counter and wondered what she'd do if he wrapped his arms around her and kissed her neck.

The knife in her hand was a deterrent to such impulsivity.

Roe looked up suddenly. "How's the chicken coming?"

He glanced down at the skillet and the strips that were now a golden brown. "Almost there."

This cooking gig was more fun than he'd thought it could be. When they worked together, it didn't take much time, and the food they made was better than grabbing takeout every night. *If the guys could see me now,* he thought with a smile. Heck, if his dad could see him now. They'd never believe that Jason Boone had become domesticated.

He was not domesticated, he told himself. He was simply being a good roommate. Besides, he liked coming home after working out and then enjoying "happy hour" with Roe before they began preparing dinner.

"Let me add these to the bowl." Stepping close, she swept the tomatoes into a bowl with the avocado, corn and lime juice. Boone inhaled the tantalizing scent. "Smells terrific."

"The avocado has a nutty scent, and the lime—"

"I was speaking about you." He sniffed again. "Vanilla?"

She smiled. "My roommate used to say I should go for a sultrier scent, but this one suits me."

"It does suit you." Boone found the warm and inviting scent, which reminded him of sweet cream, incredibly sexy. But then, everything about her appealed to him.

"We talked so much about me earlier that I just realized I never asked how things are going at the theater."

"Gladys is amazing. She knows everyone and everything that goes into mounting a production." Roe's expression brightened. "She's been letting me act as stage director, so it's been enjoyable for me."

Boone wished they didn't have to go out this evening. He didn't understand how he, who used to love going out with friends, was content spending evenings in a cabin with one woman.

It wasn't just making love, though he enjoyed that immensely, but making a meal and talking.

This contentment was likely due to his being still sluggish from his surgery. His body needed to relax and recharge, and he was making the best of the enforced rest.

Or maybe it was knowing this time with her wouldn't last forever.

Come February, he would be on his way. Roe would be here for Dakota's wedding, then off to parts unknown.

Very likely, they would never see each other again.

He slanted a glance at her. When she turned and caught him staring, she smiled, and his heart swelled.

One thing Boone knew for certain: He would never forget her.

CHAPTER NINETEEN

While Roe had enjoyed seeing the Victorian homes decorated for Christmas last evening, she and Boone agreed that, after the first house, the homes started blurring together.

Tonight's event at Rakes Farm should be more entertaining. The Snowflake Music Festival was a new event put on by the Women's Events League. The group, commonly known as the Cherries, was responsible for planning most of the holiday events in Good Hope.

The party had been billed as an indoor holiday street dance. Three bands would each play forty-five-minute sets with a fifteen-minute break between them. When Boone originally suggested they go on a date, Roe had been resigned to a dinner at Muddy Boots.

But when Boone had texted and suggested this instead, she'd said yes immediately. Peyton had told her that she'd heard the event was casual but festive. Peyton warned she would likely see more corny Christmas sweaters than anyone should be exposed to in this lifetime.

Roe settled for black leggings and boots and a cherry-red sweater the same shade as her lipstick. From the appreciative look in Boone's eyes when she came down the stairs, the choice had been a good one.

Though he'd gone for simple in jeans and a gray sweater, her heart flip-flopped when he looked up at her and smiled. "You look amazing."

"Thank you." She returned his smile. "You clean up pretty good yourself."

On the drive to Rakes Farm, she mentioned that Gladys would be contacting him.

Boone slanted a sideways glance as he wheeled the truck down the lane leading to Rakes Farm. "Why would she be calling me?"

"Melvin Boggs… You met him," Roe began.

"Yeah, nice guy."

"Well, his heart condition is a little more serious than first thought." Roe didn't really know what was going on with the older man known for a penchant for pranks. "He's in Milwaukee undergoing tests. It sounds as if he'll be staying and having surgery."

"What does that have to do with me?" Boone asked.

"Gladys wants you to take over his sound job at the theater."

Relief flooded Roe when Boone didn't immediately say no.

"Did she want you to ask me?"

"Actually, Gladys plans to contact you herself." Roe smiled. "She believes coming from her the request will carry more weight."

"Well, she's wrong."

As Roe had already begun to fantasize how nice it would be to have Boone at the theater with her, his comment had her heart sinking. "You don't want to do it."

"That's not what I meant at all." Boone pulled into the parking lot and cut the engine. "I meant she's wrong if she thinks her request will carry more weight coming from her. You're the one I have difficulty saying no to."

Hope blossomed, and an eagerness filled Roe's voice. "You'll do it?"

Cupping her cheek, Boone leaned forward and kissed her. "All you needed to do was ask."

The music from the first band of the evening spilled out into the snowy night as Boone opened the door.

"What the—"

"This is incredible." Roe tipped her head back. The snowy archway decorated with snowflakes, icicles and faux snow created a dramatic entrance.

Boone took care of the ten-dollar cover charge once they stepped through the archway, and she tipped the young man who took their coats.

Now, they were ready to enjoy.

A gobo projector cast snowflake patterns onto the dance floor while various snowflake decorations hung from the ceiling at different heights to create a snowfall effect. Tulle and fairy lights had been draped across the barn's beams.

"I didn't expect anything like this." Boone's gaze traveled around the room, lingering on the faux snow around the edges of the dance floor, tables and windowsills.

"We do things up right in Good Hope."

Roe blinked. It was as if Gladys had appeared out of nowhere.

The older woman was dressed in a pale blue and silver caftan, with sparkling jewels around her neck and on her fingers—it was as if the décor had been designed to match her.

Boone offered Gladys a warm smile. "That's what I'm beginning to discover."

"You're enjoying your stay here."

Said as a statement, but Boone must have heard the question because he nodded. "Very much."

Gladys glanced at Roe. "I'm betting some of it has to do with this young lady."

Boone surprised Roe by slinging an arm around her shoulders. "You'd be right again."

The older woman beamed before her gaze turned calculating. "I don't know if you heard that Melvin has been—"

"Roe told me. I'm sorry to hear of his troubles. But if you need my help, I'm happy to step in."

Gladys blinked, clearly startled. "Just like that?"

The warm glance Boone cast at Roe had her grinning like a loon. "Just like that."

"Well, perfect. Roe can give you the rehearsal times. I'll…" Gladys fluttered a hand in the air. "I'll see you both there."

Once the older woman was out of earshot, Roe leaned close to Boone's ear. "You surprised her. That isn't easy to do."

He turned her toward him. "It's a win-win. She gets a sound guy, and I get to spend more time with you."

Roe wanted to kiss him. She wanted to fling her arms around his neck and kiss him.

Never one for public displays of affection, she hesitated. Then a tiny voice inside her head reminded her that in a month, he'd be gone. Maybe sooner.

All she'd have were memories.

Flinging her arms around Boone, Roe kissed him with all the love in her heart.

For the next two hours, Boone and Roe spent every minute on the dance floor. In addition to all the favorite—and expected—dance tunes, they let themselves get swept into participating in a Jingle Bell Rock Dance Circle to the upbeat melodies of "Rockin' Around the Christmas Tree" and "Jingle Bell Rock."

When it was his and Roe's turn to dance in the center, Boone joined her without worrying how lame it would look and had a blast.

Now, the second band was on a break, and he stood beside Roe, his palm resting lightly against the small of her back while she chatted briefly with Peyton.

Boone wasn't sure if Peyton was there with someone, but the way her gaze kept straying to the single men in attendance while she spoke with Roe told him she might have come alone. Either that, or she and her boyfriend were open to new opportunities.

It had been that way with Celine. He'd always felt she kept her eyes peeled in case someone better showed interest.

Peyton's expression suddenly brightened. "I'll catch you later." Then she was gone.

Boone watched her make a beeline for a rugged-looking man with red hair.

"Hey, you."

The feminine voice had Boone shifting his attention. Where Peyton had recently been, the blond woman who'd sat across from him and welcomed him to Muddy Boots now stood, her arm wrapped proprietarily around a dark-haired man in his late twenties.

Boone pulled her name from his memory. "Evie. It's good to see you again." He gestured to Roe. "You've met Roe."

At least, he assumed they'd met, as Evie had seemed to be a regular at Muddy Boots.

"We've met." Evie smiled at Roe, then stroked the sleeve of the man standing beside her. "This is Hunter. He's a big fan."

Boone and Hunter exchanged handshakes.

For several minutes, they talked football before the band began to play, and Evie squealed. "A polka. C'mon, Hunter. This'll be fun."

"Good to meet you both," Hunter said before being tugged along by Evie, a pained look on his face.

Boone recognized—barely—the polka take on a Christmas classic. He turned to Roe.

She lifted her hands, palms out. "If you really want to, I'll do it. But a polka…"

Her face held the same pained expression as Hunter's had only moments earlier.

He laughed. "No polka for me. In fact, I'm ready to go if you are. But if you want to stay, that's cool, too."

"This has been so much fun." She glanced in the direction of the dance floor, where the twins and their friends were getting down and crazy with the polka. "I'm so glad we came, but I'm ready for dessert."

Boone glanced over at the dessert tables lining the walls. They'd stopped there earlier, sampling everything from snowflake sugar cookies to snowball cake pops. "We haven't tried the frosted cupcakes yet, the ones with the edible snowflakes. Does that sound good to you?"

She slipped her arm around his and gazed up at him, her eyes dark with desire. "That's not the kind of dessert I have in mind."

Boone grinned. Once again, they were on the same page.

On Monday, after finishing the lunch shift at Muddy Boots, Roe headed straight for the theater. With Christmas only two days away, this would be the last rehearsal before the cast and crew took a couple of days off for the holiday.

Boone had been at the theater every day this past week, helping out. It was tech week, which meant that over the past seven days, technical elements such as lighting, sound, set changes and special effects were integrated into the performance. Though theater wasn't Boone's passion, he'd thrown himself into the tasks.

Sometimes Roe would catch his eye, and they would share a

smile. The shiver traveling up her spine at the interaction made her feel like she was back in high school again.

Roe had to admit she initially hadn't expected much from the small production, especially when she'd learned the musical's focus was on Gladys Bertholf's life.

As the days and weeks had passed, Roe found herself blown away by the quality of the production. She discovered the musical score was written by a woman Gladys had mentored nearly thirty years earlier—a woman who'd gone on to achieve great success on Broadway.

It wasn't simply the music that was top-notch. The librettist, a term for the book writer responsible for crafting the narrative structure, creating the characters and writing the dialogue that connected the songs and advanced the story, was also a former mentee of Gladys.

Now, living in Connecticut and in his eighties, the man had clearly retained the talent that had brought him fame and fortune for over a quarter of a century before his retirement.

Thanks to the contributions of these two talented industry professionals, *Spotlight* shone brightly. The production was a heartwarming and inspiring musical about the life of a girl who dreamed of being onstage from a young age and in the "spotlight."

The storyline followed Gladys's journey from childhood, starting with her first stage performance as Little Bo Peep in *Babes in Toyland* at age nine and ending with the woman's final performance in this show at the age of a hundred.

The musical, a story of perseverance and passion, highlighted Gladys's lifelong commitment to the theater. The premiere, set for the eve of her one hundredth birthday, was touted as a rich and emotional narrative filled with music, dance and the enduring spirit of a woman who lived her dream to the fullest.

The casting of Ami's daughter, Sarah Rose, as young Gladys

and Fin Rakes as Gladys in her prime, then ending with Gladys portraying herself at the end was inspired.

Roe wasn't surprised that Gladys had retained the final say on all casting decisions. What surprised Roe was the amount of decision-making Gladys had given to her.

Gladys, the official director, was on set every day. Yet, the older woman had sat back and encouraged Roe to take the lead on tasks she normally would handle.

Roe worked hard to preserve Gladys's artistic vision and didn't take for granted the opportunity she'd been given. Though no pay was involved, gaining this additional experience as a stage director would only strengthen her résumé.

It was obvious that this show was important to Gladys. While Gladys had willingly handed over the reins, the older woman scrutinized Roe's every move. There was not a doubt in Roe's mind that if she made a decision Gladys didn't agree with, she'd hear about it.

The actors and crew had been in high spirits all day. With one last run-through scheduled for the twenty-seventh and then the dress rehearsal on the twenty-eighth, the finish line was in sight.

As much as Roe enjoyed life in Good Hope and working on *Spotlight*, she was well aware it would come to an end. New Year's Eve was fast approaching.

Roe couldn't delay speaking with Fin about her theater contacts any longer. Immediately after everyone was dismissed, Fin slipped into the office for a closed-door meeting with Gladys. Roe saw no option but to stay behind and try to catch Fin after her meeting.

Time ticked on. Roe paced and practiced her speech in her head. Everyone else had walked out the stage doors an hour ago, but Roe would wait for as long as necessary. If she didn't seize this opportunity, she might not get another chance until after the production. And she wanted to get another batch of résumés sent out as soon as possible.

No matter how much she wished otherwise, this wonderful life she'd been enjoying wasn't going to last.

Finally, after another fifteen minutes, Fin stepped out of the office with her phone to her ear. Roe stayed in the shadows until the woman pocketed the phone.

"Fin, do you have a minute?"

Fin jolted and whirled. A smile quickly replaced the startled look on her face. "Oh, hi, Roe."

Roe would have preferred to ease into the conversation, but she could see Fin was in a hurry. "I know you're eager to get home, so I'll get to the point. I've heard you have contacts in the entertainment industry in LA and possibly elsewhere, too."

Fin gave a cautious nod, her expression watchful.

"As you might already know, I'm searching for a new job. I've been sending out résumés, but so far, no nibbles. I've been a stage manager and a director and have stellar references, but it's a tough market. Thanks to Gladys allowing me to help out, you've seen my work. I was hoping you might have contacts you'd be willing to share. And would you be okay if I used you as a reference?"

There was more Roe could have said, but she'd run out of breath.

"You've done a stellar job, Roe, you really have. In fact, Gladys and I were just discussing that."

Pleasure rippled through Roe. "Thank you. I love hearing that. I pride myself on giving every production my all."

"I must admit I'm surprised by your request." Fin paused. "Gladys said…" Fin stopped herself. "No matter. Yes, I can get you names. Let me speak with Gladys to see if she has anything to add."

Roe hadn't thought to ask Gladys. Now that Fin had mentioned it, why hadn't she thought of it? Gladys had been around a long time, and the people she'd pulled in to help with this project were icons in the industry. "I'll ask her—"

"Leave that to me." Fin rested a hand on Roe's arm. "I'll speak with her. You'll have what you need by the end of the year. Does that work for you?"

"Ah, yes." Roe couldn't hide her pleasure. "That would be wonderful. Thank you so much."

"Like I said, you've done an excellent job here. Gladys and I… We'll find a place that's perfect for you."

~

"Then Fin said, and I quote, 'We'll find a place that's perfect for you.'" Roe had saved this little tidbit of news until she and Boone were seated in front of a roaring fire, enjoying Lucky Charms green martinis.

Boone glanced down at his martini glass and took a cautious sip. He discovered that while the drink might look strange, he liked its sweet and creamy flavor. So much so that he took a second sip before speaking. "That sounds extremely promising."

He was happy for her—truly, he was—but he had to force enthusiasm into his voice. "You're on your way."

"I don't have a position yet," she reminded him.

"You will." He never doubted that Roe was meant to soar.

Working the sound equipment for the past week had given Boone time to observe her. She'd been out there doing whatever was necessary to improve the production and keep everything moving forward.

While she could be stern at times, she was also fair and usually right on target with her suggestions.

"I can't believe how fast this month has gone." Roe took another sip of her drink.

Soon, it would be time for them to go their separate ways. Boone tried not to think about that day. It was difficult for him to imagine a life without Roe.

He'd never known anyone like her. They just fit.

They didn't talk about the future. What was there to say? His future was still up in the air. While he continued to heal, rehab was slow-going, and there was no guarantee the team would want him back even if he did get back to full speed.

Which left his future as unsettled as hers.

If only they had more time...

"I was thinking today that we haven't even talked about what we're doing for Christmas." She gave a happy laugh.

The simple act of Fin telling her that she would help her out had clearly put Roe in a stellar mood.

"You're right. We haven't." He inclined his head. "What are you thinking?"

She always had an opinion and was never afraid to voice it. That confident honesty was only one of the many things he admired about her.

"I don't know your thoughts on church, but I thought we could attend a Christmas Eve service."

Surprise flickered across Boone's face. "You want to go to church? I didn't realize you were religious."

"Well, I don't know that I'd say I'm religious, but growing up, we went to church every Sunday."

"Did you have a church in Minneapolis?"

"Not a regular one. The first couple of years, I'd at least go at Christmas, but it wasn't as nice not having anyone to go with. Is your family religious?"

"Not at all. At least, not growing up. My parents never went and never took us. I had a couple of teammates who were religious, and they invited me to go to services with their families. I went once or twice. I can't say it was my thing, but I can appreciate the community feel. And I liked joining them for volunteer work."

Roe waved a dismissive hand. "It's okay, then. We don't have to go."

"No, let's go. It's something you've been missing, and I'd be happy to experience it with you."

CHAPTER TWENTY

The Christmas Eve service at First Christian was crowded. Roe felt like she'd hit the jackpot when she spotted two seats at the end of a row near the front. As she and Boone made their way down the aisle, Roe was surprised by how many people they recognized.

Waving and calling back greetings of Merry Christmas boosted her already high spirits into the stratosphere. Roe recalled listening with a mixture of envy and skepticism to Dakota rave about her hometown. She'd taken all the gushing about community and the whole neighbor-helping-neighbor thing with a grain of salt.

Dakota had grown up here, and she had always seen the community as welcoming and caring. In only a month, Roe had discovered that Dakota hadn't been sugarcoating it—her community was just as wonderful as she'd described.

Roe slipped into the pew, and Boone took the seat beside her. It was a tight fit, but pleasurably so. His arm resting on the back of the pew just above her shoulders gave them a little more room. Still, she liked the feel of Boone's muscular thigh pressed tightly against hers.

Unsure how everyone would be dressed, Roe had chosen a red fluffy sweater, a plaid skirt, black tights and knee-high boots. Pants would have provided a little more warmth, but she felt more holiday-ready in a skirt.

"This is such a pretty little church," Roe said in a low tone to Boone. The sanctuary's wooden pews gleamed, as did the stained glass above each tall window. The pretty glass added a nice pop of color to an interior that otherwise would have been too plain.

The church, filled with parishioners in their holiday best, added even more brightness while the boughs of greenery at the end of each pew—complete with pinecones—wafted the pleasant scent of pine through the sanctuary.

"I love the smell of pine," Roe whispered.

Boone only nodded. From how he kept glancing around, she realized she wasn't the only one taking it all in.

Hymnals were stashed on the back of each pew, but a quick glance at the bulletin they'd been given when they'd entered the church revealed to Roe not only the order of the service, but also the words to the two hymns that would be sung.

Easy peasy, Roe thought and felt her shoulders relax.

The service moved smoothly. Singing "Joy to the World" with the rest of the congregation had Roe recalling that night when she and Boone had gathered in the town square and sung carols with strangers.

When the minister moved behind the pulpit for the sermon and began talking about the reason for the season, Roe tuned out, knowing there wasn't much he could say that she hadn't heard before.

Instead, her mind wandered to the woman she hoped would help her find her next position. She'd considered telling Fin she did have some parameters on where she wanted to settle and that she hoped to find a spot where she could see herself living long term.

In the end, she'd left it open. There were so many factors that would go into locations she would seriously consider, it seemed easier just to see what Fin and Gladys came up with and go from there.

"We have choices in our lives."

Pastor Marshall's words caught Roe's ear and had her refocusing on the front of the small church. It seemed funny that he should mention choices when that was exactly what she'd been pondering.

The minister's Scripture reference, followed by something about Christmas representing God's ultimate choice to send His son as a gift to humanity, had her almost tuning out again.

"Not long after I took over this congregation, I was offered the opportunity to become the pastor at a large, well-established church in the city where my family lived."

Roe's attention returned to the minister. She'd always loved presentations that used vignettes as a teaching tool. In her mind, the more detailed, the better.

"It was clear that my choice would shape the course of not only my career, but my life." The pastor paused to make sure he had everyone's attention before continuing.

"You might think it was the same path. After all, I would still serve the Lord—the only difference was where. I'm here to say that wasn't the case at all. Each choice would lead me down wildly different paths and affect all aspects of my life."

Roe thought of the choices she would soon face. She understood what the minister had faced in a very personal way.

Being a director at a wealthy theater in a metropolitan area would be very different from accepting a position at a theater in a smaller town.

"The offer from the large church was incredibly tempting. It represented security, prestige and a clear path to success in my ministerial career." A slight smile lifted Pastor Marshall's lips. "On the other hand, the church where I currently serve faced challenges with no guarantees of success or stability."

Once again, the minister's gaze swept the congregation. He had everyone's rapt attention. "I prayed. I sought guidance from others. The advice I received was mixed, but one piece of advice stood out: 'Sometimes the path God calls us to is not the easiest or most obvious one. It's the path where we can make the most difference.'"

There was more, but Roe had heard enough to get her mental wheels spinning. Like the decision the minister had once faced, Roe stood at a crossroads. The decisions she would make during the next month would set the course for her life.

Roe slanted a sideways glance at Boone, and her heart flip-flopped. They had never talked about a future, not one together.

Everything had been about the here and now.

Did he want a future with her? He'd never given any indication that he did, but then, she'd never told him how much he meant to her.

It seemed far too soon to talk about forever. But if they didn't speak soon, would it be too late?

Large white flakes began drifting down just as they stepped outside. Feeling like a child from the South experiencing her first snowfall, Roe resisted the urge to turn in a circle with arms outstretched and catch a snowflake on her tongue.

A tiny smile played at the corners of Boone's lips as if he could read her thoughts. "Ready to head home?"

Home.

Just the word brought a feeling of contentment.

"Yes." Roe took another deep breath of the cool, fresh air, knowing she would always remember this night. Ending the church service with lit candles to the tune of "Silent Night" was the perfect way to spend Christmas Eve.

Boone took her arm, and they turned toward where his truck was parked. "I wonder if they expected this many people."

"Roe. Boone. Hold up."

They turned to see Marigold hurrying toward them.

Roe stepped to the side so they wouldn't block foot traffic. "Merry Christmas, Marigold."

"Merry Christmas." Marigold's blond curls spilled out from a red hat that matched her cashmere coat. "I have something to ask you two."

"What is it?" Roe offered an encouraging smile. At the moment, she was inclined to say yes to just about anything.

"Are you and Boone available to serve Christmas lunch tomorrow at Muddy Boots?"

Roe blinked. "The café is closed tomorrow."

"Technically, yes. But Muddy Boots serves a free meal to whoever shows up. It's become a holiday tradition. While there is no cost for the meal, if someone wants to donate, there's a jar for a free-will offering to the Giving Tree on the counter."

"This is the first I've heard of this." Roe couldn't stop the smile. "What a fabulous idea."

"So, anyone can come and eat?" Boone asked, speaking for the first time.

"That's right." Marigold brushed a curl out of her face with a gloved hand. "Ami and Beck see it as a way for those in the community to gather with others. Some come because they can't afford to eat otherwise, others because they don't want to be alone on Christmas. And others for the fellowship. It's grown more popular each passing year, and more servers are needed for the buffet line."

"How long is a shift?" Roe asked, already knowing that no matter how long it was, she would agree.

"Two hours," Marigold advised. "Once your shift is done, you're encouraged to stay and eat."

Roe glanced at Boone. "I'd like to do it."

"Me, too." He smiled at Marigold. "What time do you want us there?"

~

"You've certainly embraced this time in Good Hope," Boone commented on the drive home.

The thought of leaving this small community on the Door County peninsula brought an ache to Roe's heart. "I don't understand it, but Good Hope feels like home."

"A home you'll soon have to leave."

Like all the others, Roe thought. Only, she vowed this next move would be her last.

"I don't see that I have much choice." She offered a slight smile. "Not if I want to eat."

"The minister sure hit the topic of choice extra hard."

"You listened to the sermon?" Roe didn't bother to hide her surprise.

Puzzlement filled his eyes. "What else was there to do?"

Ponder your future, she thought but didn't say. Unlike her, he had a place to go once his time here was up. "I listened to most of it. Which part was your favorite?"

"My favorite?"

"Yes, your favorite." Roe smiled. "I liked the example of the big church and the small church."

"I bet most in the audience would have chosen the big church."

"You're probably right."

"No probably about it."

"Like I said, I'm sure that's true, but I liked when he said that sometimes the best path isn't the most obvious one. We must consider all factors and then pick the one that will give us the life we want."

Boone studied her for a couple of seconds and then shook his head. "Did you make that up? I don't recall him saying that."

"I'm paraphrasing." Roe waved an airy hand. "That's probably why you don't immediately recognize the sentiment."

Boone chuckled. "I'm sure he'd just be glad you were listening and got something out of the sermon. I can't imagine going to all that trouble and having no one listen."

"We all want to be heard." Roe had read that somewhere, and it rang true. "I hope Pastor Marshall had someone who listened as he struggled to decide."

Boone's gaze met hers. "If you ever want to talk about your options or bounce ideas off me, I'm a good listener."

"Same goes for you."

He gave a noncommittal nod.

"When I start getting offers," she said, "I may take you up on that. Not many understand my passion for theater. God knows my parents and siblings don't." Roe laughed humorlessly. "They see careers in the arts as frivolous and unstable. In their minds, being let go from this last position only supports that belief."

"Unless you're in the military, I don't know many positions that come with guarantees." His dark eyes met hers. "Being around the theater this week has made me realize it's a unique setting, its own world."

She nodded, wondering where he was going with this but wholeheartedly agreeing with what he'd said so far. "The feeling of camaraderie and community is what attracted me in the beginning. Plus, making a production the best it can be is always an exciting challenge."

"How did you get involved in theater in the first place?" he asked, turning the truck toward home.

"Music was never my forte, and I'm not great at sports." Roe's lips lifted in a halfhearted smile. "I discovered early on that high school productions are always looking for someone who can handle the technical aspects—you know, set design, lighting and sound. I became knowledgeable in the behind-the-scenes stuff. Eventually, I moved into stage management and discovered I loved it and was surprisingly good at it."

"I was only good at one thing—football."

"That's not true. What about your writing? That scene you read to me the other night was great."

"One scene does not a book make."

"True, but you've got a lot more than one scene," she reminded him. "Maybe being a novelist isn't for you, but surely you've given some thought to what you'll do when the time comes to retire from football."

His eyes took on a distant glow. "It's been my life for so long, I can't fathom it being over."

"What do you like about it?"

Boone smiled. "The friendships, the camaraderie and the adrenaline of game day rank at the top."

Roe inclined her head. "Would you miss being in the spotlight?"

"No."

"Not even a little bit?" she teased.

"I know some guys love it, but for everyone who wants to congratulate you on your performance, there are a dozen who want to tell you everything you, your teammates and the coaches did wrong."

"Sounds like there's definitely a downside to fame."

He nodded.

"Are there other downsides to playing?"

"Of course. The practices, the need to maintain peak physical condition, the pressure to perform at an elite level." Boone's expression turned serious. "And, like we talked about before, there isn't time to do much else."

He stopped in front of the garage, and the door slowly opened. Instead of immediately pulling the truck inside, he shifted in his seat toward her.

"You know, for the first time that I can remember, I'm not excited to go back." His expression softened as their eyes met.

Her heart fluttered like there were a thousand hummingbirds in her chest. She cleared her throat. "Ah, why do you think that is?"

Boone cupped her cheek in his large hand and kissed her gently. "Maybe because I'm realizing football isn't the only thing I love."

CHAPTER TWENTY-ONE

Football isn't the only thing I love.

Was he talking about her? Could it be that he loved her as much as she loved him? Or was she reading too much into a simple comment?

It had seemed so when, a second later, he'd leaned close and whispered in her ear, "Just so you know, I can't wait for us to get out of these clothes...and watch episode four."

Roe had laughed then, and the air of watchful waiting shimmering in the air between them had shattered into a thousand pieces.

Once inside, they headed off to their respective rooms to change into something more comfortable. It hadn't taken Roe long to pull on a tee and loose-fitting cotton pants. Instead of shoes, she slipped on her beloved Ugg slippers.

She was adding popcorn to a bowl when Boone strode into the kitchen.

Roe turned and smiled. It really should be a sin for a man to look that handsome in sweats. His hair was mussed, as if she'd just run her hands through it.

Either his fingers or the sweater coming over his head were to blame. She hadn't touched him—not today, not yet.

When they reached the great room, as was his habit, he dropped down beside her on the sofa.

After taking a sip of cola, she picked up the remote. "Ready to dive back in and see what happens next?"

Boone had turned her on to an obscure sci-fi series that she was now as excited as he was to watch.

"Not yet."

Roe looked at him, puzzled. "You changed your mind about episode four? I'm open to watching something else."

She really had wanted to see what happened in the next episode but reminded herself it was Christmas Eve. Perhaps Boone had changed his mind and wanted to watch *Elf* or some other holiday classic.

"The series still works." His warm smile chased away any doubts. "But it's Christmas Eve, and I have a gift I'd like to give you."

Roe's heart gave a little leap. "You got me a present?"

While she'd gotten him something, she hadn't expected him to reciprocate. After all, they hadn't spoken about exchanging gifts.

She couldn't stop the pleasure rising inside her any more than she could keep the smile from her lips.

"Of course." Reaching down beside him, he pulled out a small box.

Roe saw immediately that he'd discovered the leftover Christmas paper she had used to wrap his gift. The fact that he'd wrapped her gift himself made it extra special. "I-I don't know what to say."

"Don't say anything. Not yet. You haven't seen it. You may hate it."

She shook her head. Roe could never hate anything that came from him. Turning her attention to the small square box in her hands, Roe ripped off the paper.

Removing the lid of the white jewelry box, she stared at the sterling silver bracelet engraved with a celestial moon and small, sparkling stones as stars.

Her heart rose to her throat as Roe looked up. "Th-this is so incredibly lovely. And thoughtful."

Relief washed over his face. "I hoped you'd like it."

"I don't just like it." She carefully lifted the delicate bracelet from the box, letting it dangle from her fingers. The light caught the stones and sent out little prisms of color. "I love it."

She rested her hopeful gaze on his. "Will you put it on me?"

His big hands looked even larger as he fumbled with the clasp, but in only moments, the bracelet encircled her wrist.

Smiling, she held up her hand. "Every time I look at it, I'll remember our night in the tent."

Heat flared in his dark eyes. "I'll never forget that night."

She dropped her gaze again to rest on the bracelet. "You couldn't have chosen a more perfect gift."

"Now we can start the episode."

"Not so fast." Roe pointed to the tree. "There's a gift under there with your name on it."

Boone turned. His lips curved when he spotted the brightly wrapped package. "That wasn't there when we left for church."

"I grew up with four brothers who used to unwrap gifts to check them out, then rewrap them and put them back under the tree." She smiled. "I was taking no chances."

Boone rose and crossed the room, returning seconds later with the gift. He shook it. "What's in here?"

"I'm not saying." She leaned back against the sofa. "You're going to have to unwrap it if you want to know."

In three pulls, the paper fell to the floor and the box was open, the tissue paper inside the box shoved to the side, revealing the leather-bound hardcover book.

"It's an autographed copy of *Empire of the Cosmos*." Roe spoke quickly. "I picked it up at Book & Cup. Bea Chapin said it's the first book in a new series by an up-and-coming space opera author. She said since you love *Dune*, you'll love this book. If you don't like it, you can exchange—"

He leaned over and kissed away the rest of what she'd been about to say. "It's perfect. I love it."

What was perfect was sitting with him on the sofa, his arm around her shoulders and a crackling fire filling the room with warmth. Roe tried hard not to think about when all this would be gone, and she'd be left with only memories.

"I contacted a few people I know in Denver." Boone tossed out the information halfway through the episode. "They're going to put out feelers and see if there is anyone in the area looking for a stage director."

Roe paused the show and shifted to face him. "When did you do that?"

"Last week." His dark eyes searched hers. "I hope you don't mind."

"No, no." A lump rose to her throat. "I don't mind. That was nice of you."

She nearly said it would also be nice to be close to him but stopped herself just in time. Boone had never mentioned them continuing their relationship once he was back on the team.

That fact, as well as recalling all the friends she'd left behind over the years who promised to stay in touch but then stopped responding to her texts after a few months, had Roe keeping her mouth shut.

He planted a kiss on the top of her head. "I want you to be happy, Roe."

Her heart swelled, becoming a warm, sweet mass in her chest. "I want that for you, too."

Gazing up at him, at his strong profile, Roe felt the love in her heart rise and spill out. If she couldn't have him forever, she'd savor every last minute of what time they had now.

"Forget the show," she heard herself say. "Let's go to bed."

~

Roe opened her eyes Christmas morning and found Boone's side of the bed empty and cold. Slipping on a soft chenille robe and her slippers, she wandered down the hall, coming to an abrupt halt when she heard voices.

She'd started backing up, then heard the word *Dad* and realized they didn't have unexpected visitors. Boone was talking to his father on speaker. Her lips curved. Despite the chill in the air, her heart warmed. He was such a good son to call his dad on Christmas.

She had already done her duty, extending her wishes in her family's group chat yesterday. That was when she'd learned her parents would be having brunch with friends today, and her brothers and their families would be celebrating Christmas doing, well, family things.

Roe wondered if Boone had called his dad first or if he'd already spoken with his mother.

"You better start pushing those doctors to let you do more," his dad ordered. "The Grizzlies won't wait for you forever. You're not young and fresh anymore. Now that you're injured, they—"

"I didn't call to discuss my rehab with you." Boone's voice held a steely edge. "I've got that under control."

"But—"

"I called to say Merry Christmas, that's all."

Roe heard the strain in Boone's voice.

"Since I've done that, we can catch up another time. Good—"

"Is it that woman? Is she the reason you're not in any hurry to get back to Denver?"

For a second, Roe wondered what woman Boone's father was talking about. Then it hit her that he was talking about *her*.

"This doesn't have anything to do with Roe. It—"

"Be smart, son." Boone's father steamrolled right over his son's protest.

Though Roe had never met Maury Boone, she didn't think she'd like him. Not based on what she was hearing right now, anyway.

"There will be lots more women down the road," Maury was saying. "Your focus needs to be on your career, not—"

That was all Roe heard. Boone must have taken the phone off speaker and walked farther into the kitchen, because while she could hear his murmured response, she could no longer make out the words.

She waited in the hall until everything was silent, then strode into the kitchen.

Boone stood at the stove, already dressed for the day in jeans and a forest green sweater.

He must have heard her footsteps because he turned before she could greet him, a smile on his face and a spatula in one hand. "I hope you like French toast."

Because he looked stressed, she crossed to him and brushed his cheek with her lips. "You know the way to my heart."

The second the words left Roe's lips, she wished she could call them back. Regardless of what his father might think, she would never try to tie Boone to her or interfere in his career in any way.

"You'll have to take a few bites first. Then tell me if I succeeded."

His lighthearted comment and teasing smile eased her worry. Obviously, he hadn't taken his father's warning seriously.

Minutes later, she sat across from him at the table, a plate of French toast smothered in syrup in front of her and a cup of steaming coffee to her right.

"You were up early." She lifted the mug to her lips but didn't take a sip, studying him over the rim.

"Since I won't be going to the gym today, I did what exercises I could." He forked off a large bite of French toast. "Then I called my parents. Because, Christmas."

"I texted my parents and brothers yesterday."

"Good job."

Roe nodded, thinking how nice it was to have him around to spend Christmas with. She'd spent many holidays alone, especially in the past five years.

"I'm glad I let you stay."

He didn't pretend to misunderstand. "I'm glad, too."

After pushing down the ache in her chest that wanted to rise up and choke her, Roe told herself to let it go. What she'd said was enough. There was no need to get mushy and embarrass them both.

But there had been so many times in the past, so many friends she'd had to leave behind, so many times she hadn't let those who'd made a mark on her life know how much they'd meant to her.

"You've made this time in Good Hope special."

"That sounds an awful lot like good-bye." Boone eyed her thoughtfully over his next forkful of French toast. "Are you going somewhere?"

Roe struggled for the right words but found it difficult to think when he settled those warm brown eyes on her.

"E-eventually," she finally managed to stammer. "We both will."

"True enough." Boone chewed the bite he'd finally put in his mouth. "But not now. Today, we're together, and we have a job to get to."

CHAPTER TWENTY-TWO

The atmosphere at Muddy Boots reminded Boone of a party. The small café was filled with laughter, conversation and good food.

When he and Roe arrived, they were directed to the back room to wash their hands and grab aprons.

"How does this work?" Boone asked Ami, who appeared to be coordinating the activity.

"Merry Christmas, Boone and Roe." Ami's smile widened to include both of them. "Thank you so much for volunteering. Roe, I have you on potatoes, and Boone, you're on ham duty." As if sensing their continued confusion, Ami pointed. "It's like a buffet line, except the volunteers do all the dispensing. The line starts there, and as the diners move to each station, the volunteer puts that particular selection on their plate."

Boone watched the process for several seconds. "So, the volunteer next to me asks if they want turkey, and when they step to me, I ask if they want a slice of ham. What if they want both?"

"They can have a slice of each, but only one." Ami looked almost apologetic. "We have to limit the portions to ensure we have enough for everyone."

Roe, who'd been studying the line, lifted her gaze to Ami. "It's all free?"

"It is," Ami confirmed. "It's our way of giving back to the community that has given so much to our family."

Roe nodded as she glanced around the dining area. "The tables have been moved around and pushed together."

"We did that to allow more people to be seated at once, and because many who come would otherwise be eating alone. This allows them to see that they aren't alone and that we are all family in Good Hope."

"I love that."

"It's the way it is here." Hearing her name, Ami turned. Lifting a hand, she called out, "I'll be right there."

When her attention returned to him and Roe, Boone knew it was time to get to work.

"C'mon, Roe." Boone slung an arm around her shoulders. "Let's get to it."

As the end of their shift neared, Roe found herself glad she'd left her pretty heels at home. Standing in place for two hours was worse than running from table to table, taking orders.

Though she preferred taking orders and tending to the needs of those in her section, she loved this, too. She had interacted with many people and had seen some familiar faces and others she'd never seen before.

Even though working a buffet line could have seemed boring or mechanical, Roe focused on making the guests feel welcome. She loved being part of a team. All the volunteers enthusiastically embraced their duties, including Gladys, who stood by the dessert table, encouraging diners to grab a piece of pie or a slice of cake.

Since many didn't get their dessert until they were through

with the main part of their meal, Gladys and her friends Katherine and Ruby had ample time to chat and mingle.

Several times during the shift, Roe caught Gladys's eyes on her and Boone, whom, it seemed, everyone wanted to speak with.

During a slow time, when Clay Chapin stood talking with Boone about football, Roe left the line to grab another large spoon after hers ended up on the floor.

"I'll be right back," she mouthed to Boone, who only smiled.

By the time she returned, Clay was already seated with his wife and kids, chatting up several older people Roe didn't recognize.

"You and Clay seemed to be having quite the discussion," Roe said, dipping the new serving spoon into the whipped potatoes.

Boone smiled. "Clay loves football. He's a huge Grizzlies fan."

"I bet you get that a lot."

Boone cocked his head.

"Football fans wanting your autograph or to talk about past games."

"Like I said before, more often, people ask why the coach called a certain play rather than another." Boone chuckled. "Or, my personal favorite, asking why we lost when we should have won and giving their thoughts on what we could have done differently."

Though Boone kept his tone light, Roe heard the irritation.

"Is that what Clay was doing?"

Surprise flickered across Boone's face. He shook his head. "Naw, he just wanted to speak with me about some other stuff."

"Well, volunteers, your time is up," Ami said. "Thank you so much for stepping up to help. We couldn't have done this without you." Her warm smile made Roe feel like she had done something special. "I would encourage you to grab something to eat and perhaps share a table with someone you don't know. In Good Hope, we say that strangers are simply friends we haven't met yet."

When they stopped in the back room to drop off their aprons, Boone turned to her. "Do you want to stay and eat?"

"Sure." She smiled. "I'd love to meet some new friends."

Instead of strangers, they ended up sitting next to Gladys, Katherine and Ruby, whose shifts at the dessert table had ended at the same time.

For a brief moment, Roe considered asking Gladys about references and recommendations and then reminded herself that today was Christmas. She could speak with Gladys on the twenty-seventh.

"Mr. Boone, did Roe tell you how marvelously she's doing as our stage director?"

Using Boone's name when Gladys was gazing at him was unnecessary. It wasn't as if there could be any misunderstanding about who the question was meant for.

Boone smiled.

Roe wasn't sure if it was because of the Mr. that Gladys had placed before his name or the ridiculousness of the question.

He stabbed the piece of ham he'd just cut. "Did you forget I was there all week, handling the sound duties?"

A sly smile lifted Gladys's red lips. "I didn't forget. I just wondered if you noticed Roe's efforts."

"Of course I noticed." Boone's expression remained serious.

"How do you like living together?" Ruby's blue eyes danced as she settled her gaze on Roe.

"We, ah, the cabin is lovely." Roe kept it simple. "There's so much room."

"I don't believe that's what Ruby asked you." Katherine, whom Roe had learned was a former accountant, glanced from Roe to Boone, then back to Roe.

"She tolerates me," Boone said with a grin.

"I love living there with you. You know that." The words popped out of Roe's mouth before she'd given them any thought.

Perhaps if they'd sounded teasing, the way his response had, instead of heartfelt and honest, it might not have caused such a reaction.

Gladys's smile broadened. She and her friends exchanged glances.

"And we love hearing that," Ruby began before a look from Gladys silenced her.

"Ruby meant to say that we love knowing you've been happy during your time in Good Hope."

Gladys's clarification lifted the tension off Roe's shoulders. She certainly didn't want to give them the wrong impression—or rather, she didn't want everyone to know just how much she would miss Boone.

"It's been wonderful." Roe chose her words more carefully this time. "I can't believe that the performance and party are almost here. I will miss the crew, as well as you and Fin. You've been so great to work with."

"I imagine not everyplace you've worked feels the same." Though Katherine didn't frame it as a question, Roe heard it.

"You're right on that score." Roe tapped a finger against her lips, recalling her challenges. "Dealing with creative differences and unprofessional behavior wasn't always easy or as quick a fix as I'd have liked, but I enjoyed being in a position to facilitate change."

Gladys nodded, her eyes sharp and assessing. "I'd love to know what you did."

"Regular meetings, team-building activities and a clear delineation of roles and responsibilities. On *Spotlight*, for the most part, everyone has worked together for the betterment of the show." Roe resisted the urge to sigh. "I can only hope that wherever I end up is somewhere just as wonderful."

She might have said more, would have said more, in fact, was ready to ask Gladys if she had any recommendations, but then Boone spoke.

"Tell me, what do you ladies have planned for the rest of the day?"

The discussion took off like a racehorse exiting the starting gate. Roe couldn't have reined it in even if she had tried.

Besides, Boone had been right to change the subject. Today was Christmas. Enjoying time with family and friends should be the focus, not her search for the perfect position.

The next morning, by the time Roe rose to prepare for the day, Boone had already left for the gym. She smiled, thinking of the past two days. She couldn't recall having a nicer Christmas. Some of it, she knew, was being in Good Hope and doing work she loved.

A lot of it was Boone. It was as if she'd been living in gray scale, and the world was now steeped in full, vibrant color.

She started at the knock on the door. Roe had to admit that the first day of driving up and finding someone unexpected at the house had made her more careful. When she was home, which was how she now thought of the cabin, she kept the doors locked.

By the time the second knock sounded, Roe had pulled up the Ring app on her phone. The postal carrier stood on the other side of the door, shifting from one foot to the other.

Roe pulled it open. "Hi, what can I do for you?"

"Good morning." The woman, with a broad face and red cheeks, glanced down at the package in her hands. "I have a package for Rosalie Carson."

"I'm Rosalie Carson."

"I have Krew and Cassie Slattery at this address." The mail carrier's gaze never wavered.

"They own the home. I'm staying here through February fourteenth. Jason Boone is also here."

"This package requires a signature." The mail carrier held out a form on top of the box.

Once Roe scribbled her name, the package was hers. "Thanks."

Closing the door, Roe gave the box a little shake. The gift had traveled all the way from Germany. In the past few years, her parents had simply sent money.

She'd already noticed the funds in her bank account, and she'd thanked them in a private text on Christmas Eve. They hadn't mentioned mailing a gift.

Roe set the package on the kitchen table and, after pouring herself a cup of coffee, sat down to open it.

As a child, she'd loved to guess what was inside a present just before she opened it. Most of the time, her guesses were spot-on.

Today, she didn't have a clue. Roe couldn't summon up even a single possibility.

Well, she would find out once she got it open.

In less than a minute, she stared at the diary she had kept when she was thirteen. The family had moved that year, for what had felt like the zillionth time. Friends she'd left behind hadn't stayed in touch, and she'd been having trouble making new ones.

That was the year she'd first tried theater—even there, she'd struggled to fit in.

Roe cringed, recalling only a few of the harsh words she'd written in this red leather-bound journal about her father and his choice of careers.

Many years ago, she and her mother had searched high and low for the journal but had never found it. Roe had prayed it had gotten tossed in the garbage. In her mind, that would be better than someone reading it and snickering.

Her mother had enclosed a letter with the diary.

Roe unfolded the sheet of vellum with fingers that trembled. *Please, please, don't have read it,* she prayed.

Dearest Roe,

I found this journal at the bottom of a box of old tax documents and receipts. I'm embarrassed to admit that this box has come with us for numerous moves without ever being opened.

Most of what was inside could be shredded, but when I came to this journal, I knew exactly what it was and who it belonged to.

I remember how frantically we searched for it and then had to conclude it was lost.

I didn't look inside. I didn't need to know that this diary was yours and that these were your thoughts and feelings.

All the moves were difficult for you. I know that, and I'm sorry for it. Please know I'm so proud of you and the woman you've become.

Right now, you're once again in transition. I hope this next move is precisely what you've been searching for.

All my love,

Mom

A lump rose in Roe's throat as she emailed her mother, letting her know the diary had arrived safely and how much she appreciated getting it.

Though Roe would have loved nothing more than to sit in front of a roaring fire with a cup of steaming coffee and read through this record of her thirteenth year, she had to get to the playhouse.

Today, they would run through the show, looking for areas needing last-second tweaks.

Tomorrow would be the dress rehearsal.

A shiver of excitement traveled up Roe's spine. Seeing everything come together was her favorite part.

The soft ding indicating an email had arrived had Roe picking up her phone, expecting it to be her mother's response.

But the email wasn't from her mom. It was from Wonder Theatre in San Antonio. They were among the first places she'd contacted when her position in the Twin Cities had been eliminated. The parent of one of the child actors she'd worked with in

Minneapolis had once lived in San Antonio and still had connections there.

When she'd discovered Wonder would have a position open for a theater director beginning March first, Roe had sent in her résumé. The parent had also promised to contact her friend on the board and put in a good word for her.

She'd had a Zoom interview with the board shortly before leaving Minnesota. Roe thought it had gone well, but when she'd heard nothing, she'd assumed they'd hired someone else.

With the money they were offering and the opportunities for continuous learning and development, this position would appeal to anyone in the industry.

Roe quickly read the letter.

It proposed a Zoom meeting with her on January third to discuss terms. Once they came to an agreement, the job would be hers.

Roe waited for the rush of excitement, but it didn't come.

She was in shock, she told herself. The joy would come once she had time to digest that this fabulous job was being offered to her on a silver platter.

Later.

Right now, she had a performance to direct.

CHAPTER TWENTY-THREE

During the rehearsal, Roe kept her focus on the business at hand. Sarah Rose had her lines nailed. With her dark hair and spunky personality, the girl not only looked like a young Gladys, but she acted the part.

The voice coach had done a stellar job helping to hone her singing skills, and the child's desire to give the best performance possible was evident.

Fin Rakes, well, Fin had star quality. Gladys had mentioned that she'd seen that in Delphinium since she was a teen. A career in LA, then returning to Good Hope to marry her high school sweetheart, have three sons and handle PR for Good Hope had kept Fin busy in the last ten years.

Shortly after Roe had started, Gladys had told her she was close to luring Fin over to the dark side, which Roe took to mean Fin would be onstage more in the future.

As for Gladys, Roe never tired of watching the older woman onstage. She danced, sang and commanded the stage each time she stepped onto it.

In Roe's mind, *Spotlight* was a celebration of aging, showing that age was just a number and that passion and talent can endure throughout one's life.

How lucky Gladys was to have been able to pursue her passion while being surrounded by people she cared about and who cared about her.

Near the end of the performance, Clay and his sister, Greer, came in and sat at the back of the auditorium. Though today's performance wasn't open to the public, the high school principal and the former mayor weren't just anyone.

Once the cast and crew were dismissed, Roe saw Clay motion to Boone and then walk out with him a few minutes later.

Roe hadn't had a chance to say more than two words to Boone today and was disappointed when she saw him leave. She consoled herself that she would spend the entire night with him.

Roe was nearly to the door when Gladys, who'd been in a deep conversation with Fin only moments before, suddenly appeared in front of her like a spirit rising from the mist.

"I was going to say good-bye, but you were speaking with Fin," Roe said, "and I didn't want to interrupt."

"We were talking about you."

The serious look on the older woman's face had a knot forming in the pit of Roe's stomach. "Is something wrong? If there is something in the show you want to change, we can make it happen, even though it's late. If you let me know what it is, I can get with anyone else it might impact—"

Gladys's hand on her arm stopped Roe's rambling. "This doesn't have to do with the show."

Fin walked up, chic and gorgeous in tailored pants and a cashmere sweater. "There're are a few crew members still around. Let's take this discussion somewhere private."

Fin glanced at Gladys for confirmation and received a nod of agreement.

"Excellent idea." Gladys turned. "We can meet in my office."

Roe's head whirled. She couldn't think of what to say. Had she done something to offend the two women? She thought back to today's performance and her constructive comments.

"Is it about what I said to Jimmy about the lights?" Roe tried to come up with something else but failed. She turned to Gladys. "I know you wanted the full spotlight on you, but it was too harsh and—"

"This doesn't have anything to do with Jimmy. I happen to agree with you. That change was necessary." As if sensing Roe's unease, Gladys placed a bony hand on Roe's bicep and steered her toward the office. "This change is also necessary."

They were going to fire her right before the dress rehearsal.

Roe couldn't imagine why, and she had only heard of it happening once at this late stage.

Most of the time, if the stage director was going to be dismissed, the powers that be waited until after opening night— unless, of course, the person was totally botching everything up.

That hadn't been the case with this production. Fin and Gladys had often told her how well she was doing, complimenting her on how she interacted with both the cast and crew.

When they reached the office and shut the door behind them, Roe told herself she wouldn't beg. This production's success was due in no small part to her efforts.

No, she thought as she sat in the chair Gladys indicated, she would thank them for the opportunity and, when the time came, walk out with her head held high.

Fin sat in a chair to Roe's right while Gladys took what Roe thought of as the seat of power behind the desk.

Roe stared into Gladys's unblinking blue eyes for several exceedingly long heartbeats. The paleness of her eyes had initially thrown her off, but over the past weeks, she'd seen warmth and approval so often in those depths that Roe had been able to relax.

Until now.

She wondered if Gladys expected her to start the conversation. Not happening. If they wanted to let her go, she wouldn't make it easy on them.

"Gladys and I have something we want to discuss with you." Fin's words pulled Roe's gaze from Gladys to her.

"That's what you said," Roe said when the silence once again lengthened. It felt as if days rather than hours had gone by, but Roe knew it just felt that way.

"I'm not sure if you're aware, but I'm the sole owner of the Good Hope Community Theater." Gladys, her deep voice still strong and capable of reaching the back row of any theater, tossed out the information.

It explained a lot, Roe thought. She'd wondered how they had such uninhibited access to the facilities. "I didn't know that."

"Not surprising. Typically, community theaters are nonprofit organizations that are run by a board of directors or a group of volunteers dedicated to promoting the arts. That's how this theater was run for many years. It broke my heart to see it floundering from incompetence and lack of attention." Gladys waved a dismissive hand. "No matter. I had the vision and the resources to make it what it is today."

Despite the seriousness of the discussion, Roe smiled as admiration surged. "You've done well."

Gladys accepted the compliment with a regal nod. "I have."

The older woman's eyes took on a distant glow before she returned her gaze to Roe. "This upcoming birthday has made me face facts. I'm not getting any younger, and it's important to me that I leave the theater in good hands."

Roe moved uneasily in the straight-backed chair that was

becoming more uncomfortable by the minute. She didn't know how to respond or even why Gladys was telling her all this. She just wished the woman would get to the point.

Gladys turned to Fin, and the two women exchanged looks. "I'm signing over ownership of the playhouse to Delphinium. I could wait until after I'm gone, but why? This way, she can benefit from my tutelage while I'm still around."

The concern that shot through Roe had her leaning forward, her gaze riveted on Gladys's face. "Are you ill?"

Gladys's full-throated, husky laugh seemed to rise from her belly. "Oh, no. I'm fine. I'm just getting older, and I've always liked having my ducks in a row."

Roe nodded. That made perfect sense.

"You may be wondering why Delphinium? I'm sure many will be asking that question." Gladys's fondness for Fin was evident in the smile she bestowed on her. "From when this one was a little girl, I saw her talent and passion for acting. I always hoped she would be the one to take the reins when I deemed it was time."

Gladys shifted her gaze to Roe. "I see the same passion in you, Roe. Only for managing people. That's why we'd like to offer you a permanent position as stage director."

Dakota's phone call on Roe's way home from the theater couldn't have come at a more opportune time. She needed to talk out her options. With her friend knowing both Gladys and Fin personally and being from Good Hope, who better to bounce ideas off of?

The wedding update came first, followed by talk about respective Christmas celebrations.

"I wish Nolan and I could have sung carols in the square with you. And serving dinner to one and all at Muddy Boots on Christmas Day was one of my favorite things to do." A wistfulness filled Dakota's voice. "No place does the holidays quite like Good Hope."

"Speaking of Good Hope, there's something I want to ask you."

Knowing that Dakota's time was precious, Roe leaped in and laid it all out for her friend. The job offer from the large children's theater in Texas and Gladys's unexpected offer for Roe to manage productions in Good Hope.

"Wow. I don't know what to say." Dakota gave a little laugh. "When it rains, it pours."

"Feast or famine," Roe agreed.

"They both sound like fabulous opportunities." Dakota paused. "Are there any other possibilities in the works that you're waiting on?"

Roe thought of Boone mentioning that he'd reached out to some friends in Denver but knew she couldn't count on that leading to an offer. So many people she knew had reached out to friends in far-off cities, and nothing had come of those efforts.

"No. I was going to get some contact names from Fin and reach out to them, but it seems unnecessary now."

"I assume you've done a pro-con list?"

"I haven't," Roe admitted. "Only because I haven't had the chance. I just received the Texas offer this morning and the Good Hope one this afternoon."

"I think making a list might be a good place to start."

Roe nodded and then realized they weren't on FaceTime, so she responded, "I agree."

"Dakota…" Roe began and then stopped, wondering why she hadn't ended the call yet. But she hesitated, not ready to say good-bye.

But why? Then it struck her. Considering Dakota's love for Good Hope, Roe had expected Dakota would push her to accept Gladys's offer.

She made that point to Dakota, who responded, "These kinds

of decisions are never easy." Sympathy filled her voice. "I know what one I think you should choose, but I'm not you. Only you know what it is you're looking for in life."

~

Roe couldn't wait to speak with Boone when she got home, but the house was empty when she arrived. The last time she'd seen him, he'd been walking out of the theater with Clay.

For a second, she couldn't figure out where he could be, then she realized. Like all of the cast and crew, he'd spent most of the day at the theater, which meant he hadn't gotten his workout in yet.

Boone never missed going to the gym. He was convinced that the sooner he was up to full speed and could rejoin his team, the better. It was as if he feared they'd forget all about him if he was gone too long.

Roe didn't know how that worked, but she could see it was a valid concern.

Selfishly, she wished he would stay in Good Hope through Dakota's wedding. He'd have to move out of the house when Dakota and the bridesmaids arrived, but surely there was a place in town he could stay temporarily. The truth was, she wished he never had to leave.

Roe couldn't imagine her life without him in it.

Not meant to be, she told herself.

She'd been down this wishing road before each time she'd had to leave close friends behind. Then she'd gotten smart and quit letting others get close so it wouldn't hurt so much when she had to go.

Somehow, Boone had slipped through her defenses. He'd scaled the wall she'd long ago erected around her heart.

With Boone, it didn't matter whether she accepted the position in Texas or Good Hope—either way, she would be without him.

Heaving a heavy sigh, Roe poured herself a glass of wine and opened her laptop. Pulling up a blank page, she began listing each job offer's pros and cons.

The person she'd spoken with in San Antonio had given her until January third to give them her answer, with a starting date of March first. That would allow her to attend Dakota's wedding before moving to Texas.

Adding that as a pro under the Texas column, Roe began to make her list.

One hour and another glass of wine later, the list appeared complete. Roe was staring at the computer screen when she heard footsteps, and Boone called, "Roe?"

"In the kitchen." Saving her work, she pushed to her feet and moved to greet him.

His expression brightened when he saw her.

Unable to keep from touching him, she wrapped her arms around him, smiling when he tugged her close and held her tight for several heartbeats.

Planting a kiss on top of her head, he stepped back.

"I wasn't sure where you were, but that slightly damp hair tells me my suspicions were correct." She smiled brightly. "Did you have a good workout?"

"Trent pushed me hard."

Though his matter-of-fact tone should have reassured her, Roe pulled her brows together as concern flooded her. "Within the doctor's parameters, right?"

"Right." He glanced around the kitchen, his gaze lingering on the open laptop. "Looks like you were working while I was at the gym."

"I have a tough decision to make," she said, taking his hand. "I was hoping you could help me decide."

"Sure. What do you need assistance with, m'lady?"

Roe rolled her eyes, then motioned for him to sit. "It's serious stuff."

Concern filled his dark eyes, and suddenly, he was all business. Reaching across the table, he grasped her hand. "What is it?"

"I have two viable job offers, and I'm not sure which to choose." Taking a deep breath, Roe laid it all out for him, then gave him a hopeful smile. "I'd love to hear your thoughts."

CHAPTER TWENTY-FOUR

Boone had taken any number of hard hits on the field over the years. Each time, ignoring the pain and the cameras trained on him, he'd schooled his features and gotten up as if his ribs weren't throbbing or the hip that he'd injured years ago felt perfectly fine.

Relying on those acting skills now, Boone kept a slight smile on his lips as he listened to Roe read through the pros and cons on her list.

The pros for Good Hope were that she knew all the staff and liked those she'd be working with, as well as loving the community. She said more than once she could see herself putting down roots here.

He understood. Like her, he could see living in this community after his playing days were over.

That's what he'd told Clay this afternoon when the man had offered him a position at the high school coaching football.

If he had accepted the position, if he had even seriously considered it, Boone already knew what his dad's reaction would be.

Maury Boone would laugh his ass off.

Boone could almost hear him jeer. A small-town football coach? What was next, a space opera novelist? How far the mighty had fallen.

It wasn't just his father's reaction that had kept Boone from taking the offer seriously. He wasn't ready to give up his position on the Grizzlies or stop playing the sport he loved.

Yet, a tightness filled his chest at the thought of being without Roe. In the weeks they'd been together, he'd fallen for her.

While he was happy she had these opportunities, he'd secretly hoped she would find a position in Denver, or at least close to Denver so that they could be together. He'd thought that when he'd mentioned reaching out to people in Denver, she'd understood what he was saying.

Though they'd gone into this relationship with the understanding of it being a holiday fling, it had morphed into more along the way.

"Sounds like you've taken everything into consideration." Boone could have cheered when his voice came out casual and offhand, just as he'd intended.

He knew she needed a job, but he wished she would turn down both and hold out for something in Denver, even though his own future there was uncertain. He knew that was totally irrational.

Boone was suddenly seized with the overwhelming desire to pack up and return to Denver.

But he knew he couldn't leave. Not now.

He was the sound guy for *Spotlight*. At this late date, no one could take his place.

Boone would do his duty and then start the New Year back in Denver.

Without the woman he loved.

Roe glanced at Boone. When they'd made plans last week to go to the Flying Crane tonight, she'd been excited to check out the waterfront bar and support the Giving Tree.

"You're quiet tonight," she said when it suddenly struck her that she'd been the only one talking since they'd gotten into the truck.

Boone slanted a quick sideways glance at her. "I was just listening to your tale of the lost diary. I can't believe you went to all those lengths to find it and came up empty."

"Like I said, I have no idea how it ended up in the bottom of that box under all those papers." Roe chuckled and shook her head. "And I really can't believe that, after all these years, my mother decided to look through that box."

"Have you had a chance to read any of the entries?"

Roe had been ready to change the topic, but she answered because he appeared truly interested. "A few. I was a really sad kid at thirteen."

"That can be a tough age."

She nodded, recalling the pages she'd read. "We'd just moved again, so I was starting over."

Roe recalled that was the year she'd become involved in theater, but she hadn't gotten to those pages yet. She'd had to set the diary aside as the loneliness of those early pages had leaped off the pages and tugged at her heart.

"Now, you'll be moving again."

Something about the way he said the words made her wonder if he was finding it as hard as she was to see their time together in Good Hope come to an end.

When he'd mentioned returning to Denver after Gladys's birthday party, she'd wanted to ask him to stay longer. But she was the one who had to find a new life, not him, and she wouldn't make him feel guilty about getting back to what he loved.

He'd never said anything about them keeping in touch once

this time was over. It wouldn't matter if he had. How many times had friends promised to keep in touch? And they had, but as time passed, their interactions had become fewer and fewer.

But Boone wasn't just a friend. He was…more.

"Right?"

She blinked, realizing he was waiting for a response to his observation about her moving again. "Unless I decide to stay here. I'd still have to leave the cabin, but I could stay in Good Hope."

"Have you made your decision, then?"

She shook her head. "I'm still considering."

He only nodded, and they rode the rest of the way to the bar in silence.

A heaviness settled on Roe's shoulders, but she shrugged it off. She would not let thoughts of the future without Boone take the joy from their evening together.

She put a smile on her face as they left the car and climbed the steps to the bar. Hadn't she read somewhere that the simple act of smiling could raise your spirits?

When he squeezed her hand as they reached the door, she realized a smile was no match for a breaking heart.

With sunlight shining through the windows of the Good Hope Living Center, Gladys sat with her friends in the lobby of the place they'd called home for the last handful of years.

They arranged their chairs in front of the massive stone fireplace while they relaxed after breakfast. Soon, Gladys would head to the theater for tonight's performance of *Spotlight*, followed by her NYE birthday bash.

As much as she was looking forward to the performance and the bash, Gladys wanted to savor these last few minutes alone with her two best friends. Over the years, she'd come to realize the importance of friends.

Family, well, her husband was gone, and her son had retired to Florida. Her grandchildren were busy with their own lives. However, to her surprise, she'd received a text from her son, Frank, this morning. He'd told her he and his family were all making the trek to Wisconsin to attend her performance and party.

Albert August, her dear friend, now living with his children out of state, had messaged that he wouldn't miss it!!! His use of exclamation points in the text had made her smile.

It would be wonderful to see them all again and to have them with her on this auspicious occasion.

Family and friends, all together to celebrate her.

Gladys's gaze lingered on the two women seated beside her. Over the years, Ruby and Katherine were the one constant. Their matchmaking efforts were a blast, and seeing the couples the three of them had brought together lead happy lives was another blessing.

She found herself wondering if Roe and Boone would…

Gladys abruptly straightened and fixed her gaze on Ruby. "Did you ever get the relationship cards to Boone and Roe?"

The deck, filled with questions designed to help couples deepen their connection by sharing personal thoughts, feelings and experiences, had been around for years and passed from one couple to another.

"I have them right here with me in my pocketbook." A stricken look crossed Ruby's face. "I know I said I would give them to Roe, but with the holidays, everything has been so busy that I forgot. I could give them to her tonight before the performance and—"

"It's too late," Katherine said before Ruby could finish. She took a sip of her mimosa before continuing. "It also isn't necessary. When I stopped by the theater last week, I saw the spark."

Ruby's gaze dropped to the cards she'd just pulled from her purse. A tiny smile lifted her lips as she looked up. "Do you realize we've never answered any of these questions ourselves?"

Gladys's hearty laugh had a theatrical quality. "Why would we?"

Katherine nodded in agreement. "We're not dating each other."

Ruby's chin jutted upward. "They're relationship cards. We're friends. We should each at least answer one."

Katherine opened her mouth, and Gladys saw she was ready to reject Ruby's suggestion. But none of them was getting any younger, and if not now, then when?

"Ruby brings up an excellent point. You don't extoll the virtues of a particular drink without first tasting it. We should each answer at least one." Gladys's tone brooked no argument. "If we draw one more appropriate for a couple, we'll draw another."

Ruby's lips lifted in a sly smile even as she feigned disappointment. "So, you're saying we won't answer the ones that talk about sex?"

"Absolutely not," Katherine responded before Gladys could answer.

"Gladys should go first," Ruby said immediately. "She's the birthday girl."

Gladys wasn't about to argue with getting top billing.

When Ruby held out the cards, Gladys reached midway into the deck and slipped one out.

"'When you're ninety years old, what will matter most to you in the world?'" Gladys rolled her eyes. "It figures I'd get a boring one."

Ruby pointed to the card. "Boring or not, you still have to answer."

"Well, since my ninetieth birthday was ten years ago, I will answer how I would now." Gladys glanced at her two friends. After getting their nods, she milked the moment, tapping a long nail against her red lips as she pretended to think. The truth was, the answer came easily. "What is most important to me is family and friends. I have loved my life in the theater, and it has given me such satisfaction. But at this point in my life, when I count my blessings, it is my family and the two of you who mean the most."

"Same here." Sniffling, Ruby dabbed at her eyes.

Katherine, never one to show much emotion, surprised Gladys by reaching over and squeezing her hand. "Your friendship meant the world to me."

"I'm still here," Gladys reminded her, keeping her tone light. "Who's next?"

"I'll go." Katherine took the top card and silently read it, her expression giving nothing away.

"Did you get one of the fun ones?" Ruby asked, her voice shaking with eagerness.

"You mean one of the—" Katherine stopped before saying more. She held up the card, her short, serviceable nails perfectly manicured. "'If you found out today was your last day on earth, what would you do?'"

Ruby made a face. "Talk about the opposite of fun."

Bringing a finger to her lips, Katherine's gaze turned thoughtful. "Last day on earth?"

"Party like there is no tomorrow?" Ruby suggested, then added, "Because there isn't."

Ruby's laughter at her joke had Katherine's lips curving.

"Actually…" Katherine put down the card. "I would do nothing different than I'm doing now. Enjoying a mimosa with friends…" Katherine lifted her glass in a toasting gesture. "Then attending a performance of my favorite actress of all time and celebrating her birthday."

An unaccustomed lump formed in Gladys's throat, but thanks to her theater training, her voice was clear and steady when she spoke. "I couldn't think of a better way either."

After a nod, Ruby reached for a card.

"My turn." Ruby heaved a dramatic sigh. "Finally."

Her eyes lit up when she pulled out a card and read, "'Is there a part of foreplay that—'"

She had only gotten halfway through the question when Gladys nipped the card out of her hand.

"Pick another," Gladys ordered.

"Aww, you're no fun," Ruby said, but she was already reaching into the deck. "'How have your dreams changed over time?'"

Ruby's smile disappeared, and her expression grew serious as she carefully considered the question. "I don't think they have. I wanted to marry a wonderful man and build a life with him. I did. I wanted to have a child, and I did. Now, I have a wonderful son, three amazing grandsons and a daughter-in-law who I love as my own. I've been blessed with wonderful friends, so I've never felt alone. I never had lofty career goals, just family and friends, so I'd say my dreams haven't changed, and best of all, they've all come true."

Gladys studied her two friends. "Having you both with me on my birthday is the best gift I could have asked for. You two are—"

"Pick one more." Ruby shoved the deck into her face.

Startled, Gladys jerked back. "What?"

"You're the birthday girl." Ruby's voice took on the tone often used by carnival barkers. "You get to pick another."

"You're just hoping she'll get one like the one you wanted to answer," Katherine remarked.

"If you insist, but then I need to get ready for my performance." With a theatrical flourish, Gladys chose a card.

She read the question and laughed aloud.

"What does it say?" Ruby asked with undisguised eagerness. "What does it say?"

"'If you could be any animal, what would you be and why?'" Gladys read.

Before she could answer, Ruby waved her hand wildly. "Oh, oh, I know."

"This is Gladys's question to answer," Katherine reminded her.

"No, let her answer." Gladys smiled at Ruby. "What kind of animal do you think I'd want to be?"

"A crow," Ruby said triumphantly, as if getting the final word correct in a spelling bee.

Gladys couldn't help it. Her eyes widened. She'd imagined a peacock or perhaps a graceful gazelle. But a crow?

"Why a crow?" Katherine asked, apparently as perplexed as Gladys.

"The grandboys love crows and were telling me all about them," Ruby said, referring to Jeremy and Fin's three sons. "Crows are extremely intelligent."

When Ruby paused, Gladys tipped her head in silent agreement. That characteristic certainly fit.

"They have amazing communication skills." Ruby glanced at Gladys.

"So far, you're batting a thousand." Gladys smiled. Who'd have thought she had so much in common with a crow?

"And they're very loud," Ruby added, setting the card down.

Gladys winged up one of her dark eyebrows.

"That's a positive thing," Ruby hastened to reassure her. "Your caw—I mean, your voice can make it to the back of any theater."

"One other thing about crows that I think we all have in common." Reaching out, Gladys grasped her friends' hands. "Crows are very social and loyal. Just like us, they have lifelong friends. So, they're not simply smart—they're very lucky."

CHAPTER TWENTY-FIVE

Spotlight played to a packed house.

Boone knew that because he could see the entire theater from the sound booth. Besides his one quick scan of the audience, he focused on making sure the audience clearly heard all dialogue and effects and that all sound elements were seamlessly integrated with the lighting and special effects.

While the dress rehearsal had gone smoothly and without incident, electricity sizzled in the air tonight. Perhaps it was because the theater seats were filled with Gladys's family and friends, all here to pay tribute to an amazing woman who'd been a part of their lives for so long.

But even if the audience hadn't been friendly and inclined to like whatever was presented, *Spotlight* was simply a fantastic production.

When the curtain closed, Boone wanted to stand up with the audience and add his applause and cheers. But he stayed put until Roe poked her head into the sound booth.

Her cheeks were flushed pink, and happiness danced in her hazel eyes. "Come with me. We don't have seats, but we can stand in the back. Gladys should be making her speech any second."

"Thanks to your efforts, the production was top-notch, Roe." He reached out and took her hands in his. "Congratulations."

"It was a joint effort," she said, although he could tell his words had pleased her. "Everyone stepped up, and it was amazing."

The New Year's Eve production and after-party—or as most referred to it, Gladys's Birthday Bash—was a semiformal affair, with most men in suits and the women in pretty dresses.

Boone had removed his suit jacket while working in the booth, but he slipped it on when he strolled with Roe to stand at the back of the theater to wait for Gladys to appear onstage.

Still dressed in the purple and silver caftan she'd worn during her last scene, complete with a huge peacock feather in her hair, Gladys strode to the center of the stage, holding a flute of champagne.

For nearly a minute, thunderous applause erupted, stopping only when Gladys motioned for quiet.

"Good evening, everyone. First and foremost, I want to thank each of you for being here to celebrate this special day with me. Turning one hundred is a milestone I never imagined reaching, and I am overwhelmed to be surrounded by so much love and friendship."

Gladys's gaze scanned the audience as if she wanted to let each person know she was aware of their presence and appreciated them showing up.

"As I look back on my life, I am filled with countless memories of joy, laughter and even a few tears. Please know I never meant to make any of you cry."

Laughter rippled through the audience like a rolling wave.

"From my childhood days picking thimbleberries and running barefoot in the countryside, to the many adventures I've had with friends and family, I've considered every moment a gift."

Boone wondered if Roe was familiar with thimbleberries. He

pushed the question from his mind and refocused on Gladys's speech.

"I am grateful for my family, who surprised me by making the trip to Good Hope to celebrate with me today. To my children, grandchildren and great-grandchildren, you are my legacy, and I love you more than words can say."

Once again, Gladys's keen-eyed gaze swept the audience.

"All of you here today are my friends. You were invited to this momentous occasion because you have been a special part of my life. Two such friends have been my rock for more years than I can count. Ruby Rakes and Katherine Spencer, you have brought joy into my world. Life wouldn't have been nearly as fun without you in it."

From where he stood, Boone had a good view of both women. He watched them smile broadly through their tears.

"Life has taught me many lessons, but perhaps the most important one is to cherish each moment and never take anything for granted."

Nods could be seen throughout the audience.

"To the younger generation here today…" Gladys paused, and it seemed to Boone that her gaze settled on the Brody boys, or maybe on Brynn Chapin, who was seated next to them. "I encourage you to follow your dreams, be kind and always remember the importance of love and family."

A smattering of applause broke out, but Gladys wasn't finished. "Thank you for all being part of my journey. Earlier today, my dear friend Ruby compared me to a crow."

Gladys waited for the laughter to subside before continuing. "She explained that crows are very social and loyal. Just like us, they have lifelong friends. So, they're not simply smart, they're very lucky. All of us in this room are lucky. We have each other, and we will create more beautiful memories together tonight."

Gladys held her flute of champagne high. "Cheers to life, love and many more happy days ahead!"

~

Roe walked into the theater lobby and saw that during the performance, it had been transformed into a Travel Through the Decades party atmosphere. Beginning in the Roaring Twenties and continuing to the present, signs had been created for each decade, highlighting key events in Gladys's life.

A photo booth with props and backgrounds from each decade appeared to be a hit with the younger guests, while the most popular drink from each decade drew the over-twenty-one crowd.

Gladys, Roe observed, was in her element, laughing and talking with family and friends.

Boone had told her he'd be the designated driver tonight, and he'd chosen a Gin Rickey for his one drink before switching to soda. Roe had never heard of it, but the bartender told them it contained cognac, orange liqueur and lemon juice.

Roe went with a Harvey Wallbanger from the 1950s. She liked vodka, and she drank orange juice every morning. She wasn't sure about the Galliano, but she loved the taste of licorice and found the three ingredients came together in a pleasing combination.

Drinks in hand, they'd gone only a few feet before they ran into Ami and Beck.

"Fabulous job." Ami hugged her, then smiled at Boone. "The sound was fantastic."

Boone placed a hand on Roe's shoulder. "Roe kept us all on track."

"My sister told me about the job offer." When Roe opened her mouth, Ami rushed on. "I know you haven't given Gladys and Fin your answer, but if you do end up choosing Good Hope, I host a monthly book club. If you like to read—"

"I love to read," Roe said.

"Well, if you stay, I'd love to have you come and check us out."

Ami smiled. "It's a great way to get acquainted. We read all kinds of popular fiction, from romance to space opera."

Roe slanted a sideways glance at Boone, but his expression remained placid. She didn't mention his writing. He talked to her about his book, and she loved the plot, but as far as she knew, he hadn't spoken of his efforts to anyone else.

"Thank you for thinking of me." Roe hesitated. "I'd love to participate, but even if I stay, it will likely be a while before I visit your group. Dakota's wedding is in February, and after that, I would need to find a place to live."

"We have an empty apartment above the bakery," Beck advised. "It's a one-bedroom and on the small side—"

"It's super cute," Ami added, then laughed. "I told myself I wouldn't push, and here I am pushing. We can discuss housing options after the holiday once you decide to stay."

Ami flashed her a cheeky smile.

Roe only laughed.

Once Ami and Beck strolled off, Roe turned to Boone, who was now speaking with Gladys's son, Frank.

It didn't take Roe long to conclude that the older gentleman was a football fan with strong opinions.

Though she knew Boone didn't mind talking the sport with fans, when Frank mentioned a call the Grizzlies head coach had made in a game earlier in the season that Frank thought was "beyond stupid," Roe knew it was time to intervene.

She'd met Frank earlier and offered him a warm smile as she slipped her arm around Boone's. When Frank paused to breathe after explaining another instance where, in his opinion, the coach had made the wrong call, Roe jumped into the momentary silence.

"I hope you don't mind if I steal this guy away." Roe gestured to the photo booth. "I'd like to grab some photos with him. For the first time tonight, there isn't a line."

Frank, a genial fellow despite his strong opinions, waved a hand. "Not at all. Boone and I can catch up later."

"Thanks for the save," Boone said in a low tone.

"You're welcome."

"Where are we going?" Boone asked as she kept walking.

"To the photo booth." Roe smiled. "I was thinking we should go for a 1920s look. What do you think?"

Boone had to admit that the fedora and fake mustache he put on added to the fun. Roe had gone with long strands of faux pearls draped around her neck and an elegant fan in her hand. The background of a speakeasy bar completed the picture.

They received a photo strip of four images. Boone took two strips of paper from the table, stuffing one into his pocket with the address of a digital gallery where they could view the rest of their images online.

By the time they left the booth, there was a line again.

"Do you want to dance?" he asked Roe.

As there wasn't room in the theater lobby for dancing, once the performance had ended, the crew had gone to work transforming the stage. It had been turned into a dance floor with pedestals sporting gold lanterns wrapped in garlands of roses, baby's breath and ivy. Rose petals were scattered around the pedestals, which formed a perimeter to ensure no one got close enough to the edge to fall into the orchestra pit.

The band members, who'd played during the show, remained in the pit, covering all eras with tunes designed to bring both young and old to the dance floor.

When the era shifted from early-2000s pop and hip-hop music to the 1930s big band era, Boone smiled as Roe stepped into his arms. He liked feeling her soft curves against his body and smelling the clean, fresh fragrance of her shampoo.

236 | CINDY KIRK

"This is nice," she said, twining her fingers through his hair.

"You like my hair longer?" Boone hadn't bothered with a haircut since leaving Denver.

"Yes." She gave a little laugh. "I do like it longer. The feel of its silky softness against my cheek is…nice. But I was referring to all of this."

Leaning back in his arms, she glanced around the stage, at the string lights hung overhead that created a soft, magical glow and at the projector casting images of couples dancing during the various eras on the walls.

"It's got a good vibe," he conceded. "The stage crew did a bang-up job."

"It's not just the setting," She brushed her lips just under his jawline. "It's being with you."

Boone tightened his grip on her, trying to ignore the ache in his heart. How much longer would she be his?

At that moment, he wanted nothing more than to head home and show her how much she meant to him.

Bending his head, he put his lips close to her ear. "Come home with me?"

He felt her lips curve against his cheek even before she spoke. "You read my mind."

Roe woke up the following day to find Boone fast asleep beside her. Their lovemaking last night had been fast and furious, as if they'd both wanted to wring out every last ounce of pleasure before they called it a night.

Or maybe, Roe thought, before it all ended.

Cuddled beside Boone's warm body, Roe let her mind drift over the past twenty-four hours—the offer from Wonder in Texas, then another offer from Gladys and Fin.

Move in the direction of your dreams.

Those seven words, printed on a strip of paper nestled inside a tiny envelope that, according to Gladys, was "meant for her," circled in her head.

The two viable offers she'd received had brought her to this crossroads. Wonder was a large children's theater. The salary and benefits put their offer in a class by itself. In Good Hope, she would direct both children and adult productions. The variety would be a definite plus, though the salary wasn't close to what Wonder had offered.

The question was, which would get her closer to her dreams —dreams that included putting down roots, building friendships and having a well-rounded life?

What Gladys had said in her speech about creating beautiful memories had stuck with her. Roe couldn't do that if she kept moving every couple of years. While the Good Hope theater position might not pay as well, this was a community where she could put down roots.

It was a place where she could attend a book club with friends, sit at a waterfront bar and listen to music and eventually buy a house and plant a garden.

Perhaps even marry a man she couldn't wait to come home to at night, a man who made her feel cherished and special.

Her heart lurched as she glanced at the man sleeping peacefully beside her. Boone was the one she loved, the one who made her feel cherished, the one she couldn't wait to come home to at night.

This time, it wouldn't be her moving on, but him. He would return to Denver soon, and she would likely never see him again.

Tears slipped down Roe's cheeks. Brushing them away with her fingers, she pulled the covers up and lay down beside Boone. She held him close, desperately wishing she never had to let go.

~

Boone loaded his suitcase into the truck and turned back to Roe. He offered her a slight smile.

It took everything in Roe to smile back. She held up a to-go cup and a bakery sack. "I just put in fresh coffee for you, and these pastries are from Blooms."

When he had gone to the gym for one last workout before leaving town, Roe had driven to the bakery, wanting to do something special for him on his last day in Good Hope.

"Thank you." He took the sack and cup from her fingers, his gaze never leaving her face. "This isn't good-bye. Or, at least, not forever."

How many times had she said those words just before her family had gotten into a car or on a plane and left a place that had been their home?

There were too many to count. Each time, it had been forever.

"I don't want to leave you, Roe." He set the cup and sack down, then pulled her into his arms. "I don't want to go."

Then don't. The words had nearly left Roe's mouth before she pulled them back. His contract and obligations to the team made it complicated. He had to return to Denver.

"This won't be the last time we're together. We'll find a way. I'll find a way for us to be together." He kissed the top of her head. "I promise."

He drove away under a sky the color of dull putty. That was okay with Roe. The gray fit her mood.

Roe wanted to believe he'd be back, but she feared this would be the last time she saw him.

Standing on the porch, she waved, watching until his taillights disappeared from view before going back into a house that had once felt like a home.

CHAPTER TWENTY-SIX

"It's good to have you back." Krew steepled his fingers and studied Boone, his gray eyes sharp and assessing.

Boone shifted in his seat. Having Krew ask to see him wasn't the same as being called to the front office, but Boone still had to fight to project an aura of calm. "It's good to be back."

"Is it?" Krew arched a dark brow. When Boone didn't immediately respond, Krew continued. "You don't seem fully here. Are you still in pain? Or is it something else?"

"The pain is gone," Boone confirmed.

The coach leaned forward, his gaze never leaving Boone's face. "Look, you're at a crossroads. Physically, you're ready, but this game is more than physical. You've got to be mentally ready."

Boone nodded.

"It's not fair to your teammates or the Grizzlies franchise to have players on the squad who aren't leaving it all out on the field."

When Boone had walked into the weight room after being cleared by the doctors and heard the good-natured jeers and cheers from his teammates, he hadn't been able to help but grin.

Being on the field again, evading a defender, catching a long pass and scoring had been familiar.

In many ways, being back with the team had felt like coming home.

On the other hand, it felt as if something was missing.

Not *something*, Boone thought. *Someone*. In only a handful of weeks, Roe had become an integral part of his life.

Now she was back in Good Hope, and he was here.

"I would give you more time off if I could, but we don't have that luxury." Krew met Boone's gaze. "So, it's decision time. Are you ready to be a Grizzlies player again or not?"

Six long weeks had passed since Boone had left Good Hope. He and Roe had talked and texted, but it wasn't the same as having him here. He'd hoped to return for Dakota's wedding, but that hadn't happened.

Dakota's parents hadn't spared any expense on her Valentine's Day wedding. But it wasn't the amazing flowers or gorgeous dresses that Roe would recall when she thought of the ceremony. It was the love in Nolan's eyes when he saw Dakota walking toward him on her father's arm.

It was the joy on Dakota's face when her new husband whirled her around the ballroom of the Bayshore Hotel. The fantastic food and open bar were wonderful, but the love wafting in the air made this reception special.

With great effort, Roe managed to keep her sadness under wraps. Thankfully, none of the bridal party knew how special Boone had been to her or what his leaving had cost her emotionally.

Roe had been determined that all the pre-wedding festivities, culminating in the wedding and reception, would be joyful. Dakota deserved nothing less.

Sitting alone at one of the round linen-clad tables, it seemed to Roe that everyone was here with someone, while she was once again alone.

When sadness once again threatened to overtake her, she told herself to get a grip. If she was going to make this long-distance relationship work, she had to accept that Boone's schedule would be flaky, and he wouldn't be able to attend every event.

So, Roe kept her happy face on, waiting for the moment when she could leave. Instead of heading to the cabin with the other bridesmaids and Dakota's parents and brothers, Roe had told Dakota she would spend the night in the apartment over Blooms Bake Shop.

Ami had told her to sleep there a couple of nights and let her know if the apartment was what she was looking for.

Dakota had been okay with her staying at the apartment. She and Nolan had a suite at the Bayshore. In the morning, they would head to Chicago to catch a plane to Fiji.

Roe was edging toward the door when she ran into Dakota's father. She couldn't believe this handsome man was old enough to be Dakota's dad. Because of his team responsibilities, Krew had barely arrived in Good Hope before last night's rehearsal.

Dakota had mentioned earlier today that her dad would return to Denver in the morning.

Krew's smile came quickly when he saw Roe. "Leaving so soon?"

"It's a fabulous party." Roe's gaze slid to the dance floor, where Dakota danced with her head against Nolan's chest.

She remembered Gladys's party and how good it had felt to be in Boone's arms. Roe shoved aside the memory and focused on the man before her.

"Thank you again for letting me stay in your amazing cabin. It's a gorgeous home."

"It is pretty nice," Krew agreed, "but impractical—at least for my family. I had hoped we could all gather here regularly, but with everyone's schedule, I can already see it won't work."

"You could rent it out."

Krew shook his head, then an odd look filled his eyes. "I sold it."

Roe blinked. "You did?"

She wasn't sure why the news hit her so hard. Although she'd driven away from a number of houses during her lifetime and had missed a few, this place held a special place in her heart.

This was where she and Boone had met. Where they'd fallen in love...

Krew's phone pinged.

"I'll let you take that and—"

He lifted a hand. "Hold on a sec, if you don't mind."

Glancing down at the screen, a slight smile tipped his lips. "There's someone in the lobby for you."

"For me?" Why would someone from the hotel staff be contacting Krew?

"In the lobby," Krew repeated.

"Ah, okay, thanks." Roe hurried out of the ballroom and down the hall, her heels clicking on the marble floor.

Reaching the lobby, she glanced around. When she saw who was waiting, her heart stopped. She wanted to run to him, to fling her arms around him and never let go.

Instead, she remained where she stood, unable to move. Her legs felt mired in concrete. Thankfully, her voice still worked.

"Boone," she called out.

His head jerked around. She knew the instant he saw her, because his entire face lit up, and he covered the distance between them in several long strides.

His arms were around her, and her world, which had been thrown off its axis when he'd left Good Hope, righted itself.

He kissed her, and she kissed him back with all the love in her heart.

Joy bubbled up and spilled over. "You were able to come after all."

"I'm back." His gaze met hers. "I told you I'd find a way."

"How long can you stay?"

"I'm not going back to Denver."

"What?"

"I'll explain it all." Taking her hand, Boone tugged her to a nearby settee and pulled her down next to him.

Even when she sat beside him, he didn't release his hold on her hand. That was fine with Roe. She didn't want to let him go. Not again. Not ever.

"I've missed you so much." Despite her efforts to steady it, her voice shook with emotion, and her lips trembled.

Lifting his free hand, he brushed back a tendril of hair with the side of his hand. "Not as much as I've missed you."

Roe's breath came out on a shudder. If this was a dream, she didn't want to wake up.

"I retired," Boone explained. "It was time to say good-bye to the NFL and hello to the rest of my life."

"I don't understand." From the look on Boone's face, he considered it a positive, but she wasn't sure.

"The details aren't important. What is important is I'm now free to live wherever, and do whatever, I want."

Roe breathed slowly in and out. Was he saying what she thought—hoped—he was? The air between them, which had crackled with electricity, took on an air of watchful waiting.

"I want to live here in Good Hope with you, Roe. I accepted Clay's offer to be the high school football coach, and I'm going to finish writing my book. When that one's done, I'm going to write another."

"Those are big decisions."

"Yes. And no." Boone smiled. "On the way back to Denver, I found that scrap of paper from the Christmas party."

"The fortune cookie one?"

He smiled. "That's the one."

Her mind had gone blank after he'd said he wanted to live in Good Hope. With her. "Remind me what yours said."

"'True love is not something that comes every day. Follow your heart—it knows the right answer.'"

Roe cocked her head.

"Don't you see? It was all meant to be. Me coming to recuperate in Good Hope, the cabin being double-booked and us getting to know each other." His gaze searched hers. "I realized I was ready to turn the page and start a new chapter in my life. I'll coach, and I'll have time to write my book. Best of all, I'll be able to build a life with the woman I love."

Though Roe's heart had begun to sing, she was still afraid to hope. "You really are staying."

For the first time, he appeared unsure. "Only if you want me to."

"Yes, oh, yes." Roe flung her arms around his neck and held on tight. "I'm never letting you go."

Standing off to the side, the three women studied the couple.

"You know he bought Krew's cabin for them." Gladys tossed the words out there as if it was common knowledge, pleased when Ruby and Katherine glanced at each other and then back at her, clearly startled.

"I didn't even know it was for sale," Ruby sputtered.

"Who'd you hear that from?" Katherine demanded.

Gladys's lips curved as she thought of Ruby's crow analogy. "Let's just say a little birdie told me."

Thank you for joining Roe and Boone on their journey. If this is your first time visiting Good Hope, I hope it won't be your last!

Celebrate in Good Hope is the final book in the heartwarming Good Hope series, which began with *Christmas in Good Hope (another wonderful Christmas love story).* Order your copy now or keeping reading for a sneak peek.

SNEAK PEEK OF CHRISTMAS IN GOOD HOPE

Chapter One

It may have been only the first of December but historic Hill House, in the small village of Good Hope, Wisconsin, was already gussied up for Christmas. In spite of the festive evergreen wreaths with red ribbons at each window and pinecone garlands around the white porch rail, the home reminded Amaryllis Bloom of an aging film star trying to conceal wrinkles beneath a thick coat of grease paint.

If anyone understood a desperate need to hide flaws beneath a polished veneer, it was Ami. God knew she'd tried. But she finally had to accept that guilt wouldn't go away just because she prayed and that past errors, no matter how much she regretted them, couldn't be undone.

Old memories dipped her sunny mood briefly into overcast. But the clouds cleared when Ami entered the 1870's home. She perked up, eager to see what decorations the historical society had in store for visitors this year.

It certainly wasn't off to a rockin' start, not if the gold bows and garland draped on the massive staircase to her right was any indication.

The greenery was a nice touch, although a bit boring.

Things improved slightly when Ami reached the parlor. Her gaze was immediately drawn to the corner where a seven-foot Frasier Fir stood. Though normally a fan of bright holiday colors, the dark green foliage decorated in an understated color scheme of silver, gold and bronze took Ami's breath away. Instead of a traditional star, fresh holly and large gold temple bells adorned the top.

The elegant scheme extended to a mantle arrangement. There, peacock feathers and mirrored ornaments coupled with curly willow branches added accent color, complementing the tree.

After admiring several less obvious touches the volunteers had added to the room, including shimmering oversized Mercury glass ornaments in a basket by the fireplace, Ami heeded the five minute warning and took a seat.

The monthly meeting of the Women's Events League began precisely at one. As red tart cherries were the main crop on the Door County peninsula, the group had been dubbed, The Cherries. These prominent women planned all holiday events in the village of Good Hope.

As the treasurer launched into the financial report, Ami glanced around the semi-circle. While some of the women were near her age, many were old enough to be her grandmother. Or, in the case of the current treasurer, her great-grandmother.

Ninety-six-year-old former community theater star, Gladys Bertholf, went for flare as she reported on the organization's current financials. Cadaver-thin with a shock of dark black hair boasting a swath of silver, Gladys gestured broadly as she reported, the sleeves of her purple caftan dress fluttering around birdlike arms.

The older woman's voice carried easily throughout the richly decorated room. Unfortunately, there was only so much even a former actress could do with pitch, tone and movement to make a P&L statement interesting.

While a trifle eccentric, the woman was amazing. Not only was she a whiz with figures and a master of public speaking, as of last month Gladys was now the oldest member of The Cherries.

Her elevation had occurred when Cassie Thorpe had passed away at one-hundred-and-three. It had been Cassie's passing that had opened a spot for a new member.

Ami had been the chosen one. She'd been thrilled to be asked. But sitting here now and feeling completely underwhelmed, made her wonder if this was freshman year in college all over again. She'd gone through Rush, only to realize several months later that sorority life wasn't for her.

Give this a chance, she told herself sternly and refocused on Gladys.

Ever since her mother died three years ago, Ami had been even more determined to receive a coveted invitation to join the group. Some of this desire sprang from the fact that membership had been something her mother had pursued, but never achieved. But mostly it was because Ami, like her mother, believed strongly in their mission.

From a merchant's perspective, she recognized the monetary value of celebrations. The events planned by The Cherries brought much needed tourist dollars to their small township. But for Ami, the increased revenue was an ancillary benefit. It was the warm sense of community and camaraderie, the way holidays brought people together, that made the planning worthwhile.

As far back as Ami could remember she'd been a holiday planner. The oldest of four girls, Ami recalled with much fondness the cookie baking marathons, the ice skating races on Rakes Pond and all the neighborhood Fourth of July parades she'd helped her mother organize.

Sarah Bloom had loved everything about holidays and had

gone out of her way to make them special for her family and neighbors. Her mother would have been an asset to The Cherries, but a stay-at-home-mom and wife of a high school teacher hadn't been on their radar.

Ami found it reassuring that once she got past the sixty-day probationary period, she would be a member for life.

So, she had to sit through a few boring meetings to get to the fun stuff. What else was there for an almost thirty-year-old single woman to do on a snowy Monday afternoon? An image of a roaring fire, a book and a glass of wine flashed before her. She shoved it aside and caught the tail end of the report.

As Gladys returned to her seat beside Ami, the current president, Eliza Shaw, took the podium. With her tall, slender figure and natural elegance, she looked more like a New York model than the owner of a General Store in upper Wisconsin.

As usual, Eliza was dressed more for style than the weather. While Ami wore tweed pants and a bulky cable-knit sweater with her beloved UGGs, Eliza had chosen black pants that hugged her slender legs like a second skin, a tunic of cherry red and shiny heeled boots.

When Eliza's gaze scanned the group of women, it passed over Ami as if she wasn't there. It pained Ami to remember that at one time she and Eliza had run in the same circle of friends. But that had been a lifetime ago.

"We'll start with our biggest problem first. Beckett Cross." Eliza's voice snapped like a freshly washed sheet hung to dry in a brisk wind. "Mr. Cross absolutely refuses to allow his home to be part of the tour."

A murmur of disbelief rose like a crescendo through the group. Eliza quieted them with a hand.

"He actually said no?" Gladys's rich voice filled the momentary silence as she slapped a hand sparkling with jewels to her breast.

"Oh, he did more than that." Katie Ruth Crewes, who'd gone

to school with Ami, spoke without waiting to be called upon. "Mr. Grumpy Pants threw Eliza out of his café. I was headed to lunch and witnessed it firsthand."

Katie Ruth grinned. The pretty blonde retained the perky bounce she'd had in high school. Now, instead of leading cheers, Katie Ruth was the front desk manager at the BayShore Hotel.

In her spare time she served as editor-in-chief of The Open Door, a daily electronic newsletter. Targeted primarily to peninsula residents, it included local news and events as well as a popular gossip feature.

"That man is impossible," someone muttered in an overly loud voice.

"I believe that is something all of us agree upon...with perhaps one exception." Eliza shifted her gaze to Ami. "Do you realize that your friend will likely—out of sheer pigheadedness-- disrupt one of our most cherished traditions?"

Though cherished tradition might be stretching credulity, there was no denying that the 'Victorian Holiday Traditions' Annual Tour of Homes was much loved by residents and tourists alike.

Traipsing through prominent and primarily historic homes festively decorated for Christmas definitely drew the crowds. Since the event began, the historic Spencer-Shaw house—the one Beck purchased last summer--had always been the first on the tour. Not to mention the most popular.

Ami frowned. While Beck could be a bit gruff at times, he wasn't an unreasonable man. "Did you mention to him that touring the Spencer-Shaw home is a tradition in Good Hope?"

"He doesn't give a fig about traditions." Eliza flung a frustrated hand in the air. "He pops up here from God knows where, and not only buys the café but snatches my cousin's home out from under our noses. None of the family had a clue Katherine was even considering selling it."

Perhaps if any of you bothered to visit her, she'd have told you.

Ami kept the uncharitable thought to herself. She and the spry octogenarian met weekly for tea and the sale had been as much of a surprise to her as it had been to Katherine's family. Never once had her elderly friend mentioned selling her home and moving to Arizona. Not until it was a done deal. But then Kate had always been an intensely private person and a little eccentric.

"We must stay focused." Gladys raised a clenched fist, much like a general rallying troops. "We can't give up."

"Since Eliza wasn't able to persuade Mr. Cross to open his home, perhaps Ami should try," Katie Ruth suggested. "She might have better luck."

The cushioned seat beneath Ami turned rock hard and she shifted uncomfortably. All eyes were now on her. "I'm sure Eliza laid out the facts quite clearly. I don't know what I could do. Mr. Cross has made his decision."

Though she wanted to help, Ami's contact with Beck was minimal. Sure, she saw him every morning, but theirs was a superficial relationship, kept alive by a mutual predilection for pastries and strong coffee. She had no more insight into what made him tick—and regardless of what Eliza believed—no more influence on him than any other woman in the room.

"I don't believe what I'm hearing." Eliza's gaze narrowed. "Are you refusing to help?"

The direct question—and the venomous undertone--caught Ami off-guard. "No. No. Of course not. I was merely saying—"

Eliza leaned forward, resting her arms on the podium, her gaze riveted on Ami. "Though some in the group expressed concerns about bringing you in as a member, the majority was convinced you strongly supported our mission in this community."

Ami had no doubt one of those who'd expressed concerns had been Eliza. She knew why the woman hated her, understood and accepted the animosity. But Ami wouldn't allow her—or anyone —to impugn her loyalty to Good Hope.

For years, Ami had worked tirelessly to increase participation by the merchants in the holiday celebrations planned by The Cherries. As owner of Blooms Bake Shop, located in the heart of the Good Hope business district, Ami knew the extra revenue these celebrations generated.

This was especially true in December when the entire village was transformed into a winter wonderland for the "Twelve Nights" celebration.

"I have always supported the group's efforts. I believe strongly in the mission." Ami spoke slowly and distinctly so there could be no misunderstanding. "But Mr. Cross isn't from here. He--"

"—refuses to be a team player," Eliza interrupted, pulling all eyes back to her. Her dark hair, cut in a stylish bob, swung like a shiny black curtain as she whirled to directly face Ami. "You will make him see the error of his ways and secure his cooperation."

When Ami opened her mouth to reiterate—again--that she had no control over the man, Eliza lifted a hand, palm out. "Don't bother to deny your connection. We're all aware of your tete-a-tetes when the café is closed."

Heat rose up Ami's neck at the openly speculative looks directed her way. "His café is next to my shop. We—"

"It's settled." Eliza's tone brooked no argument. "Your first official assignment as a Cherrie is to convince Beckett Cross to open his home to the tour."

Irritated by the autocratic tone, Ami took a few seconds to rein in her temper. She drew in a breath, let it out slowly. Some-how, she managed a smile. "I'll give it a try."

"Trying isn't good enough. Take whatever measures neces-sary to achieve the goal." Eliza lifted a shoulder in a careless shrug. "Otherwise…"

"Otherwise what?" Ami asked bluntly, her patience gone.

"Just make sure he agrees." Though Eliza smiled, her eyes remained cool. "That will be in everyone's best interest, including yours."

Ami thought about Eliza's threat on the short stroll to her apartment over the bakery. Considered it again as she polished off a late lunch of corn chowder. It was obvious that if she didn't get Beck to agree, the vote to grant her full membership in The Cherries might not go her way.

Who needs them anyway? But then Ami remembered her mother's unfulfilled dreams. She'd give the next sixty days her all. If they booted her out, well, she'd have done her best.

At peace with the plan, Ami slipped downstairs to the shop she considered her second home. A scent of yeasty earthiness with a dash of cinnamon teased her nostrils. She paused in the doorway to survey her kingdom and experienced a rush of pride.

The interior was still very much a work-in-progress. Yet, every day, with each acquisition, it became more her own. Ami adored the antique chandelier and the exposed brick walls she'd painted a soft turquoise.

She let her gaze linger on the bright yellow shelving holding vintage tea tins, each brimming with an assortment of growing herbs.

As most of the business was carry-out, seating in the shop was limited to two tables and a counter with stools by the window. Wanting to build on the boho-chic vibe, Ami had sanded down the tables to bare wood then painted one a bright watermelon pink and the other, an eye-popping cobalt blue. Brightly-colored, mismatched chairs added to the vibrancy of the room.

When the bakery was closed, Ami liked to sit at one of the tables and enjoy a scone with a cup of tea. She always took her time picking from the eclectic mix of china cups dangling from the mug tree on the counter. With the shop now on winter hours and only open Friday through Monday from ten to four, Ami had plenty of time of time to sit and savor.

When she first purchased the bakery several years earlier, she'd felt like a slacker working such short hours during the winter. After a couple of summers working ten hour days, seven days a week, she'd come to see this as a much needed opportunity to relax and recharge.

Until Ami expanded the bakery hours in February, her only employee was Hadley Newhouse. With curly blonde hair and expressive blue eyes, the young woman from North Dakota—or so she said--reminded Ami of her sister, Marigold.

Perhaps because of that resemblance Ami had liked Hadley the instant she'd strolled into the shop last spring with the 'Help Wanted' sign from the front window in her hand. Once she tasted Hadley's Scandinavian breads and pastries, she'd hired her despite a dearth of references.

Ami was a big believer in second chances. Over the past six months, Hadley had proven herself to be hardworking and honest. A friendship between the two women had blossomed, fueled by a mutual passion for baking.

Although her sisters were all proficient in the kitchen, from the time Ami had been a small child she'd shown an aptitude for what her father called the 'womanly arts.' Pies and cookies were now her specialty.

"How was the meeting?" Hadley asked when Ami entered the shop.

Ami rolled her eyes.

"That good, huh?"

"I'm not sure *good* is the right word," Ami said with a wry smile.

"Now, I definitely want details." Hadley glanced at the "It's Cupcake Time" clock on the wall and grimaced. The small hand pointing to the carrot cupcake with cream cheese frosting showed her shift had ended.

Hadley removed her apron and sighed heavily. "Darn second job. I need to scoot. Promise you'll tell me tomorrow?"

"I'll give you all the gory details." Ami shivered for effect then paused. "Is it cold in here?"

"I can't believe you just noticed." Hadley laughed. "I can practically see my breath. Old Ralph hasn't kicked on since you left."

Old Ralph was the ancient furnace she'd hoped would last at least another year. By then she planned to have enough money saved to get a new one. With parts impossible to find, replacement was the only option. "I asked for a bid, just in case Ralph croaked. I wanted to know how much a new furnace would set me back."

Hadley inclined her head. "What did you find out?"

When Ami told her the quote, the other woman whistled.

"That's a chunk of change. Do you have it?"

Her directness was only one of the many things Ami liked about Hadley.

"I have some of the money. I suppose I could charge the rest." A knot formed in the pit of Ami's stomach. "The problem is I use that credit card for business expenses. Right now I'm able to pay off what I charge each month. Carrying a balance would mean paying high interest."

Hadley tapped a finger against her lips. "I may have a solution."

"You're a rich heiress and I can be your philanthropy?" Ami joked.

A startled look crossed Hadley's face then she laughed. "Yeah, right. I'm wealthy. That's why I work two jobs."

Ami snapped her fingers. "Bummer. Okay, what's your idea?"

"Muddy Boots is looking for a cook." Hadley cast a speculative glance in Ami's direction, then pulled a tube of lipstick from her bag and expertly applied it to her wide mouth. "Janey got a call and left right after lunch today for Milwaukee. Something to do with her mother. Supposedly she won't be back until the first of January."

"I'm sorry to hear that." Ami knew Janey Eversoll's mother had been struggling since her stroke last month.

"It'd be a perfect way for you to earn some extra cash over the holiday," Hadley said, returning to her earlier point.

Ami hadn't considered taking a second job, but it might be the answer. If Beck would allow her to work in the café on the days the bakery was closed, it could be a win-win for both of them. Assuming he'd hire her, of course.

"I am a good cook," Ami murmured.

"You're an excellent cook." Hadley added another coat of mascara to her already thickly-coated lashes. "Not to mention you have an "in" with the boss. You and Mr. Cross have quite the thing going in the mornings."

"It's called being neighborly." Ami ruined the righteous tone by flushing like a guilty teenager.

That made her angry. At herself. At the gossipmongers. She had no reason to feel guilty. It wasn't as if her banter with Beck had ever had any *sexual* connotations.

Simply thinking of *sexual* and *Beckett Cross* in the same sentence caused her cheeks to burn. Out of simple embarrassment, she told herself, nothing more.

Thankfully, Hadley's gaze was on her purse as she rummaged through the contents. Emitting a sound of triumph, she pulled out her cell phone.

"Now that I've found my baby--" Hadley gave the phone a loving stroke before her gaze pinned Ami "—let's talk what being neighborly means to Amaryllis Bloom. I mean, some neighbors have sex. And Beckett Cross *is* uber hot."

"I'm not sleeping with Beck," Ami protested.

"Even if you are, it's not my business." Though Hadley's hands rose in a gesture of surrender, a smile played at the corners of her lips. "Though if you'd want to share what he's like in bed, I'm willing to listen."

"I don't even like the man," Ami retorted, then immediately felt a flash of guilt. Okay, so that wasn't entirely accurate. Still, all the talk linking her and Beck--a man she barely knew--flustered her.

"Methinks the lady doth protest too much," Hadley teased.

"I thought you needed to get to your other job."

Hadley glanced at the clock. The small hand was now on the chocolate cupcake. She yelped. "One more thing, real quick. When you interview with Mr. Sexy, don't sell yourself cheap. He'll be desperate. That means he's likely to agree to any demands."

"But I don't have any experience. I've never cooked for anyone but family and friends."

"That won't be a problem. You'll simply pretend you're cooking for your sexy next-door neighbor." Hadley slung the bag the size of Texas over her shoulder and winked. "The one you're not sleeping with."

Ami laughed and shook her head.

Hadley had barely disappeared down the block--headed to her other job as a server at The Flying Crane—when large white flakes appeared outside the picture window.

Ami shivered. The heat still hadn't kicked on. If she didn't take care of this furnace fiasco soon, her pipes would freeze and then she'd have an even bigger expense.

With a resigned sigh, she pulled out her phone. By the time she hung up, she had an installation date for Wednesday and her credit card had sustained a massive hit.

She wished she could speak with Beck about the job right this minute. But he was likely occupied with the supper rush and her dad would be here any minute to pick her up.

Tonight they were attending an all-you-can-eat-fish-fry at the high school. One of her father's fellow teachers had been recently diagnosed with cancer--the same type that had taken her mother's life--and the staff had organized a fundraiser to help with medical expenses.

It was these types of events that brought a swell of pride to Ami's heart and made her love Good Hope all the more. Friends helping friends was a way of life in this corner of the world.

Later, after she'd eaten her fill of white fish and fries, she would stop by Beck's home.

Once there, she'd tackle the tour issue with him first. Hopefully, it would be a simple matter of putting things in perspective for him. Of pointing out that when he moved here, he hadn't just gained a beautiful house and a business; he now had an extended family that would always be here for him.

Ami would lay it out in such a way that Beck couldn't help but see that with such blessings came certain responsibilities. It certainly didn't hurt that they were headed into a wonderful time of the year, when peace and joy filled every heart.

She could see it now. Beck would catch the spirit and agree to open his house for the tour. Once that deal was struck, he'd generously offer Ami a job with the hours and pay she requested.

Hey, if a girl was going to dream, she might as well dream big.

With a light heart, Ami hummed a tune as she went upstairs to grab her coat. She had a feeling this was going to be the best Christmas ever.

Bring Good Hope home for the holidays. Grab your copy of this feel-good Christmas romance today

If you love to **binge entire series,** the twenty-two uplifting novels in this series will give you hours of reading pleasure…and all are available in Kindle Unlimited!

*"I love it when authors do long series on the same characters! But then, when it is over, **I always wish for more!**"*

Your wish is being fulfilled. Look for **Connections: Callum & Brynn,** coming early 2025 in **Good Hope-The Next Generation** series.

To keep updated via email when I have something of interest, a new release, or a special sale, click here to sign up for my newsletter.

Those who sign up for my newsletter will receive a complimentary ebook of LOVE ME SWEET, a story I know you'll enjoy!

ALSO BY CINDY KIRK

GraceTown Series

Enchanting stories that are a perfect mixture of romance, friendship, and magical moments set in a community known for unexplainable happenings.

Good Hope Series

The Good Hope series is a must-read for those who love stories that uplift and bring a smile to your face.

Hazel Green Series

These heartwarming stories, set in the tight-knit community of Hazel Green, are sure to move you, uplift you, inspire and delight you. Enjoy uplifting romances that will keep you turning the page!

Holly Pointe Series

Readers say "If you are looking for a festive, romantic read this Christmas, these are the books for you."

Jackson Hole Series

Heartwarming and uplifting stories set in beautiful Jackson Hole, Wyoming.

Silver Creek Series

Engaging and heartfelt romances centered around two powerful families whose fortunes were forged in the Colorado silver mines.

Sweet River Montana Series

A community serving up a slice of small-town Montana life, where helping hands abound and people fall in love in the context of home and family.

Made in United States
North Haven, CT
14 December 2024